"I care not if you forget or remember thoughts of lust. Just do not come to my bed with only those thoughts on your mind."

Adrienna shook her head, seeking to find a tiny grain of self-control. She straightened her spine and lifted her chin. "Lust, sex—what difference would it make when the end result would be the same?"

He didn't answer, but his rumbling laugh teased her ears and settled lightly upon her heart.

"Should I ever decide to come to your bed, what would you like me to have on my mind?"

Hugh moved closer and narrowed his eyes. In a deep husky voice, he whispered, "Desire. A burning need to set your soul afire."

* * *

Commanded to His Bed
Harlequin® Historical #845—April 2007

Commanded to his Bed

DENISE LYNN

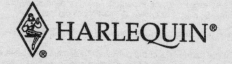

HARLEQUIN®

TORONTO • NEW YORK • LONDON
AMSTERDAM • PARIS • SYDNEY • HAMBURG
STOCKHOLM • ATHENS • TOKYO • MILAN • MADRID
PRAGUE • WARSAW • BUDAPEST • AUCKLAND

ISBN-13: 978-0-373-29445-9
ISBN-10: 0-373-29445-X

COMMANDED TO HIS BED

Prologue

Death seeped into the small chamber. Inch by inch it swirled across the floor toward the pallet on the raised dais in the center of the room. Like a plume of smoke from burning incense, it wafted to and fro with the breeze. Steadily and surely, it enveloped the room, bringing along a bitter cold draft. One that chilled Hugh of Ryebourne, favored slave of Sidatha, to the bone.

"Leave your anger and hatred with me, my son. Let me carry it away. Let your desire for revenge die an easy death. Forgive. Forget."

Hugh knelt beside his master's deathbed, clutching the papers that gave him and three of his fellow slaves their freedom in his fisted hand. "I cannot. They took too much from me."

Torn from all he knew on his wedding night. Denied

the pleasures of his bride's body. Tortured and starved. They stole his freedom. His heritage. His future. They brutally crushed what was vital within him. His innocence. His dreams. All because of a vain girl's lie.

"Son."

He flinched when Sidatha placed his withered, frail hand over Hugh's heart. "Remember all you have learned."

Unashamed of the tears that escaped, Hugh nodded and took Sidatha's cold hand in his own. "I will, Father."

"You will still be welcome here when I am gone."

That was far from true. Sidatha's new son-by-marriage Zirtha detested Hugh. If he wished to live, he had to leave before the palace power changed hands. But he'd not burden Sidatha with that knowledge. "I know, but I must go back to my home." If not for Zirtha and one other openly vicious man it would be easy to remain here, to live the life he'd grown accustomed to, but Hugh also longed for England. If he was to have a future, he had to regain the past that was stolen from him. There were debts owed to him—payments he wished to collect.

"Were you not given more in return? Does all I have done amount to nothing?"

Hugh looked down at the man he'd once hated bitterly. It had taken many beatings to learn respect. And many hard lessons to finally learn love. "You know that is not true. There is not enough gratitude in the world for what you have done for me."

"I can say nothing to sway you from this path?"

Hugh gritted his teeth against the wish to lay his pride and pain aside, then he shook his head. "No."

Sidatha's chest rose and fell on a heavy sigh. "Promise this old man one thing."

"Anything."

"In this quest for your truth, bring no harm to the innocent." Sidatha's words were broken.

Hugh knew there was little time left. Sidatha's wife Halona waited for him to leave her husband's side. There was no time for debate. "I swear, Father. I swear I will follow your wisdom."

A smile curved Sidatha's lips. "Then go, with my blessing."

Hugh leaned down and placed his lips on Sidatha's forehead. "And you, my master, my teacher, my father, may your journey be easy."

He rose and hastily wiped the tears from his eyes before leaving the chamber. He watched Halona enter, before he walked out of the palace and to his waiting party.

Lost in their silent thoughts, the four men left the gates and walls of civilization behind. For Hugh the taste of freedom was bittersweet.

Somehow in the hard days and nights ahead, he and his companions would need to find strength and sustenance to complete this long, arduous journey. Sustenance would be found from what the earth provided.

Revenge would be the fuel to build his strength.

Chapter One

Queen Eleanor's Court at Poitiers—May 1171

In the three months she'd been at Queen Eleanor'
court, men had called her many things—the least un
pleasant, and familiar, had something to do with ice an
frost. She'd heard that complaint more times than not

Yet now, each article of clothing seemed to evaporat
like the morning mists. Her gown fell from her body
leaving the evening air free to whisper across her quiv
ering flesh. With nothing more than a smoldering stare
he undressed her slowly, one agonizing layer at a time

Adrienna of Hallison trembled with anticipation, fea
and a longing so intense she was certain she'd die. Sh
wanted more than just his gaze. She wanted his breath
on her neck, his lips against hers. Her breasts strained
against the bodice of her gown, seeking his caress, ach
ing for the touch of his hands.

Beneath the tight layers of linen and silk that concealed her body, her skin tingled. Fire and ice coursed through her veins. She prayed she'd not reveal her desire by blushing. To her utter dismay, heat filled her cheeks. She studied the richly laden table before her, hoping to hide her flaming face from him.

Men were the same everywhere. Fortified keep or lush palace mattered not. They had fought for the right to thaw her composure. All had failed.

Their false, near-fawning attention held little interest. At times, when it wasn't downright tiresome, it bordered on the ridiculous.

If they could perceive her thoughts at this moment they would be shocked. No man had ever caused her blood to rush in this manner. Never had anyone conjured this unbidden state of desire from her. They would be appalled by the heat coursing through her body at the mere stare of a stranger. A dark and dangerous stranger dressed in the deepest shade of blue she'd ever seen. The near-black attire made him even more noticeable than the brightly adorned peacocks that filled Eleanor's court.

Yet, those peacocks had been correct. Her body, as well as her heart, had been frozen for what seemed a lifetime.

Until now.

The stranger's stare bore through her, forcing her attention back to him. His eyes stripped away her clothing and laid her body bare.

With a quick ragged breath she yearned for his touch. Would his fingers be rough against her soft flesh? Would his hands carry the same flame that burned from his eyes?

Adrienna tore her gaze away and stared at the ornate tapestries hanging on the walls. His unwanted attention would do naught but give lie to her carefully built reputation. He would peel away the cloak she'd so carefully wrapped around herself in an attempt to shield her heart from pain.

Nay. No matter how extreme the temptation, she'd not let any man, especially this unknown one, break through. She'd cared about one man and he'd deserted her, leaving her alone and a maiden still in her father's keep.

Never again would she be drawn into any man's promises or lies. No. This time she would do the choosing. Her life, her future, would be laid out by her own hand alone.

"Adrienna."

Torn from her thoughts, Adrienna leaned toward her dinner partner.

Elise of Fairway nodded toward the stranger. "Who do you think he is? I've not seen him here before."

With feigned indifference, Adrienna glanced about the crowded hall. "Who? There are so many strangers here this night."

Her friend lowered her voice to a whisper. "The one staring at you as if he'd like to dine on your body for his supper."

There was little she could hide from Elise. They'd been friends since the moment they'd both arrived at the queen's court. Two not-quite-young widows with little to offer except the power inherent in land and men. They shared a common bond—both had been sent to court to find a husband.

Not just any husband, but someone who could advance their fathers' ambitions. A goal neither of them cherished.

When faced with the options her father dangled before her, Adrienna chose marriage. It had been an easy choice. Her sire had offered to find her a position with the court, or to remove her from his keep and allow her to fend for herself. Marriage, or certain death.

Adrienna was not ready to die. But neither was she ready to become some man's chattel.

"Oh, him. Hopefully he finds someone else to play the gallant with this night." She studied those seated at the high table. "Ah, no worry. Sarah has spied him."

Elise's unladylike chortle drew the attention of several nearby diners. She covered her lapse in manners with a cough, managing to hide her mirth. "The poor man. Shall we pray for him?"

Adrienna did her best not to imitate her friend's reaction. "What and spoil Sarah's fun?"

"Lady Adrienna?"

Startled by the queen's page standing at her elbow, Adrienna hastily swallowed. She wiped the amusement from her voice. "Yes?"

The youth looked down his nose at her. "Queen Eleanor requests your presence." His voice cracked, giving lie to his manly attitude.

Elise asked, "Would you care to guess who is with her?"

The question required little thought. Adrienna knew the answer before she looked toward the queen, and the stranger beside her. He caught Adrienna's perusal and nodded in a knowing, near-intimate manner. *Dear God, could he read her thoughts? Did he know of her desire?* Her stomach fluttered. Her pulse raced. She silently cursed her body's reaction, the queen and the stranger all in one thought.

The page held out his arm and announced, "Milady, I am here to escort you."

She rose and placed a hand on his arm. Before leaving, she looked down at her friend. "My pardon, Elise, I will return anon."

Elise pointedly looked across the hall and back to Adrienna. "Do not make any wagers on that. I would hazard to say you will be occupied elsewhere for the rest of this evening."

Adrienna ignored the sudden racing of her heart. She gritted her teeth and shot her friend a look that sent the other girl into a fit of laughter.

"Milady?" The page's voice held a note of impatience. She nodded at the young man. "Let us go."

While holding her head erect, she forced her legs to carry her across the floor. It proved a hard task to clear the distance between her table and the queen's dais at the end of the hall. Her knees shook. She could barely draw in a steady breath. *What was it about this man that caused her to react in such a manner?*

Lord, this stranger was a sight to behold. When the troubadours composed their tales of mighty heroes, surely they'd sung of him. Had she ever seen anyone as tall? Was there any other man present who appeared as strong? The breadth of his shoulders bespoke of someone accustomed to the grueling tasks of war. Surely he would wield a broadsword as if it were a feather. She doubted if he needed more than one mighty swing to cleave an enemy in two.

Gem-studded blue eyes from his sun-darkened face pierced her with a knowing gaze. She felt as if she could hide nothing from him.

Her footsteps faltered under his hypnotic stare. A laughing countenance flashed through her memory. Did she know this man? Had she seen him before? She shook her head slightly. No, it was just a passing thought easily pushed aside. The memory lingering in her mind was of a boy. Not the confident, self-assured man she now faced.

As she knelt in obeisance, Adrienna was startled by a firm touch on her arm. With a large, callused hand, the stranger helped her rise.

"Lady Adrienna, may I present the Earl of Wynnedom." Queen Eleanor smiled and then nodded toward the earl. "He has graciously requested your company for the meal."

Hugh, Earl of Wynnedom, looked down at his wife in amazement. Lord, how she'd grown. The pale hair of childhood had darkened to a burnished gold. The slight figure had blossomed into a lushness that beckoned a man's touch.

Like a beautiful and rare lotus flower blooming amongst roses, she stood out from most of the women at court. His wife had not grown into a pale, frail beauty of legend. Instead, she'd developed into a woman whose very appearance bespoke of untold nights of passion.

When last he'd laid eyes upon her, she'd been nothing more than a girl. A child sitting atop their marriage bed dressed in wedding finery and playing with a cloth doll. A sight that twelve years ago had amused and confused him.

Quickly, the image of the child fell from his mind. Just as quickly, the anger and thirst for revenge rushed forward to fill him. *Do not be led by pride and revenge alone.* Words learned long ago echoed in his ears. With great effort, he quelled his thirst—for now. Eventually, he would let her experience the soul rending taste of heartache, lies and deceit.

"Lady Adrienna, will you join me?" The look she turned on him made him want to laugh. He'd been correct. She knew him not. He held back a smile. This would prove all too easy.

When she hesitated, Hugh prompted, "You've no husband or lover awaiting your return?"

The queen interceded. "No. Lady Adrienna is a widow."

He bit back another smile. Not only did Adrienna not know him, it was obvious that King Henry had not informed the queen what was afoot. Good. He mentally thanked the king for his silence. Then he wondered how much it would cost him.

Adrienna shook her head at the queen's statement. "You can hardly call me a widow when there was nothing worth calling a marriage."

And whose fault was that? He swallowed his question before it left the recesses of his mind. Instead, he offered her his arm. "Ah, milady, you whet my curiosity. Such a contradictory turn of events must be explained. Perhaps your regaling of the incident will keep us amused during our meal."

Hugh led her to one of the private tables tucked away in a shadowed alcove. These small chambers permitted more private conversation. Subdued light from the well-placed wall sconces added a measure of intimacy.

Adrienna hesitated briefly before following him into the recessed room. She said nothing, but made certain the curtains were left open. While they ate and conversed in the shadows, they would still be able to see the high table directly before them.

He didn't mind. After all it was not as if he intended to bed her during dinner—that could wait for a time. Her shoulder brushed against his thigh as she took her seat on the short bench. The brief contact felt like a flame against his flesh. The unbidden image of her kneeling naked before him flashed through his mind. Hugh frowned. Thinking with his loins would gain him little.

After filling her goblet with wine, he coaxed, "So, Lady Adrienna, you were saying?"

"'Tis nothing entertaining, milord. I was married young and my husband disappeared on our marriage night."

Disappeared? What an interesting description to use for what took place that night.

She lifted the goblet and took a sip of wine. When she licked away a red droplet from her lower lip, Hugh's gaze was riveted to the tip of her tongue. He wasn't certain which desire was stronger—to have been the one to remove the last trace of wine, or to have been the wine.

He cleared his throat. "What happened to the man?"

"Man?" Her brittle laughter gave lie to her humor. Earlier, Hugh had watched her converse with her friend. The easy smiles and laughter then were nothing like the one that seemed forced from her lips now.

After regaining her composure, she explained. "He was but a boy and I know only that somehow he died."

Her statement was like a knife in his chest. How many times had he wished for death in the beginning? How many nights had he cried himself to sleep thinking of death and her? "Died?"

"That is what I was told."

Adrienna popped a cherry into her mouth. Hugh swallowed hard against the blood rushing to his groin. Every courtesan in Sidatha's palace had been his for the taking. When he was younger, he'd refused few. But he'd long ago mastered control over his urges. So why did he now react like a randy youth? He changed the direction his thoughts were taking. "This must have happened long ago. Why did you not seek to remarry?"

She furrowed her brow. The sparkling green eyes dulled. "Yes, he disappeared long ago, but even though years went by with no word of him, I could not in all good faith petition for an annulment."

How noble of her. "Many women would not have had the fortitude to carry on alone for such a long time."

Adrienna shrugged. "It was not my choice. My father did not wish to lose the lands he gained with my marriage."

So instead he destroyed what he'd taken from me and left the land to rot and the people to die. "Why did he wait so long to seek another husband for you? What changed to bring you here now?"

A brief flash of anger crossed her face so quickly that Hugh wasn't certain if he'd seen an emotion, or if it'd simply been a play of light. "My father had petitioned for another marriage, but for some reason I am not privy to, King Henry kept putting him off until recently."

"You sound bitter."

She glanced down at the table. A faint blush tinted her cheeks with the delectable color of a ripe peach. "To my shame, I am bitter." The eyes she lifted to him glistened like dew-covered grass in the moonlight. "I beg your pardon, milord. I wish not to spoil your dinner."

"It was an observation, milady, not an accusation."

Adrienna nodded. "Very gallant of you, but I've no wish to burden you with my personal difficulties."

Hugh looked out at the hall. Everywhere he glanced, men and women sat head-to-head in conversations he imagined were of a more personal nature than the one he shared with his wife.

He leaned closer and caught the scent of roses and lavender—the true English lady. What would she smell like wrapped in nothing but the pure scents of musk, woman and lust?

He inched closer still until he could feel her heat caress his face. "Is that not what all of this is about?"

She frowned. "I follow not your meaning."

Hugh nodded toward the high table. "This court, this

gathering, are they not designed for the sole purpose of becoming more personally acquainted?"

"Milord, surely you do not think anyone here is truly sharing any personal information that holds even a grain of truth?"

"What about you, Lady Adrienna? Is this story about a disappearing husband naught but a cleverly contrived tale?"

She froze, her body as unmoving as a statue chiseled from ivory. "And pray tell, what would be my purpose in telling so bold a tale?"

"Pity? Sympathy, perhaps? I am sure there are many here who would welcome the chance to console you in your time of loss."

"Many have tried."

"And how many have succeeded?"

Her knuckles whitened as she gripped her knife tighter. He'd gone too far. He knew she resented his question. Hugh sat straighter on the bench to give her anger room to grow. It was, after all, what he wanted— was it not?

"I require neither pity, nor sympathy from anyone. My current status is not an imaginary one. My husband disappeared on our wedding night. For nearly twelve years I knew naught of what befell him. Only recently did anyone bring news of his death." She paused to take a long sip of wine. The goblet wobbled as she set it down. "For all of those years I have remained alone. No home. No children. No husband. Only by my father's grace have I not withered away in an abbey."

Her now blazing glare scorched him. She forced a smile to her lips. "Is that enough personal information to satisfy your curiosity, milord?"

No. It was not enough. Not nearly enough, but what a fine temper she had. It would serve her well in the days to come. "You are yet relatively young. Young enough to still bear children. You possess a well-made form and have untold beauty—"

"A well-made form? Perhaps a little too much form. Untold beauty? Milord, you need save your pretty words for a troubadour's tale. They are wasted on me."

Hugh studied her, pointedly. Her blush of embarrassment at his prolonged stare amused, and amazed, him. How could she think his words false? He gazed out at the women in the hall. After a few moments, he drew his attention back to her.

"Lady Adrienna, I know not what ideals of beauty fill your mind. The women in the troubadours' ballads exist only in the thoughts of uncertain men. Let me assure you that the tales are false." Certain she would not believe him, Hugh drew his questioning back to the original topic. "Why have you remained unmarried when it sounds as if that lofty goal is your true desire?"

Adrienna stabbed at a piece of meat as if she were puncturing someone's flesh. "King Henry refused to grant me any marriage until I've spent time at his wife's court."

"How long have you been here?"

"Nearly three months."

Hugh hid his smile. He'd last spoken to Henry four

months ago. His debt to the king was building. "And you have found none to replace your first husband?"

Again her harsh, too-loud laugh ran across his ear. "Replace him? You make it sound as if I wish to find someone like Hugh."

"Do you not?"

"Milord, I would not know where to begin looking. I spent only part of one day in my husband's company. If by some miracle he were to walk into this hall, I would not know him."

Of course she wouldn't recognize him. The boy who'd been her husband for a few brief hours died long ago. It took Hugh a few long moments to contain his grief for the boy who'd not had the chance to be a husband. "So, it had not been a long betrothal?"

She shook her head. "I did not say that. We'd been betrothed by proxy as children, but did not meet until the morning of our marriage."

For some insane reason he longed to ask her if she'd found anything of worth in the boy she'd married, but he quickly gained control of his overblown pride and changed the subject. "So, which of these fine gentlemen have you found to your liking?"

"None."

His eyebrows rose in surprise. A slow smile curved his lips. "Milady, surely there is one who would fulfill your requirements as a husband."

Adrienna sighed deeply. "These *men* as you call them are nothing more than overdressed pompous peacocks."

He agreed, but asked, "Would not the advantage of

having a safe keep, stocked larder and servants to command help you overlook such a small flaw?"

The sound that burst from her lips was not soft, nor was it very ladylike. It was a blunt, honest response that he found refreshing in this court of artifice and lies.

"*Small* flaw? Surely, milord, a pride-filled countenance is not precisely a small flaw."

"Your peers do not seem to agree with you."

After glancing out at the hall, she shrugged. "An evening spent in the company of a peacock is better than an evening spent alone. It does not mean every woman here wishes to be chained to this evening's dinner partner for life."

Chained? Like a slave to his master? Instead of telling her what true bondage was, Hugh nodded as if he had just learned something new. "Ah, then in reality they are but playing with their partner's emotions."

"That is not what I said."

He opened his eyes wide in mock confusion. "Then what did you say, Lady Adrienna?"

She pursed her lips and furrowed her brows. "A woman cannot enjoy an evening's company with a man without pledging her entire life first?"

The rancor of her tone surprised him. He leaned closer and lowered his voice, "And why, milady, must they talk in breathless whispers?" He knew he'd partially made his point when a tiny tremor rippled across her shoulders.

He wasn't finished and it wasn't as if anyone would stop him. There were none to pay any attention to what he did to, or with, his dinner partner. They were all too involved with their own activities.

Hugh grasped her hand and brought it to his lips.

She tried to pull away from his hold, but he ignored her feeble attempt.

He caught and held her surprised gaze before placing a kiss on her palm.

Adrienna gasped softly, but she did not seek to remove her trembling hand from his.

He trailed the line running to her wrist with the tip of his tongue.

She stiffened under his touch, but no words to cease his attentions were issued.

Hugh thumbed the edge of her sleeve a fraction higher on her arm. He followed the fabric with his mouth. Her pulse flurried to life beneath his lips.

How far would she permit him to go before anger overwhelmed her shock?

Hugh moved slightly and brought his thigh tightly against hers.

Her heavy gown hampered her attempt to move away from his touch.

He released her hand and leaned closer to again breathe against her neck. He could feel her heat. He could smell desire waft past the scent of her perfume.

The shivers running the length of her body set his own desires to build. What had begun as a contest, a test of wills, quickly turned into a game of passion.

No more than a hair's width existed between his lips

and her skin. "And why, milady, must they lean close enough to touch their companion?"

Her heartbeat throbbed. The flesh jumped rapidly. She gasped softly.

"They are in public. They do nothing wrong." Her voice shook. She swallowed hard. "This is a court of chivalry and they know they are safe here."

Hugh rested a hand on her thigh. Her leg quivered beneath his touch, but he knew her own clothing trapped her. She'd not be able to escape his caress without drawing attention to herself. "And you, Lady Adrienna, do you feel safe?"

Visibly shaking, she leaned away from him. It appeared as if all the blood had drained from her face, she was so pale.

"Why are you doing this, milord?"

Hugh smiled. It was time to end the charade. He lifted his hand and ran a finger down the side of her face. When she sought to lean farther away, he grasped the back of her head and drew her back to him. She would not escape him this time. Whether she liked it or not, she was his.

She stared at him. Her eyes wide. Her lips parted. Lord, he wanted to take those lips beneath his own. To lay her on this very floor and devour every inch of her.

With learned control, Hugh reined his wild desire. He wanted her and he would have her. But not by force and not out of fear. He wanted her complete submission. If all were to work according to his plan he could not frighten her away.

He relaxed his grasp, stroked the back of her neck and deepened his smile. "Because, wifeling, you are mine and this is something I have ached to do for twelve long years."

Chapter Two

Wifeling.

Like a stone being cast upon the water, the odd, childish endearment rippled up from the depths of her memory. Adrienna's breath halted. Her hot, passion-filled blood froze in her veins. All the other people in the crowded hall vanished. The sun and the moon ceased their journey across the heavens.

Wifeling.

Once the term had angered her. It bespoke of her youthful age at a time when she'd wanted to be considered an adult. A woman worth being called "wife."

Wifeling.

She closed her eyes against the rush of memories assaulting her. Memories and feelings long dead and buried. A myriad of curses and questions sprang to her mind. Curses she would not speak in public. Questions she did not want answered.

Had her father's informant been wrong? Was this an

impostor? Or was he her dead husband? The man looming so close nearly thrummed with life. The heat emanating from his body, the fire created by the touch of his hand on her thigh could never have come from a corpse.

Adrienna searched his eyes. She detected nothing behind the sapphire depths. No anger, no mirth, no hint of emotion glimmered forth.

That very lack frightened her.

This man proclaiming to be Hugh bore no resemblance to the awkward, gangly boy she'd married. This man was a strong oak, unyielding in the face of a storm. She glanced at the well-formed muscles of his arms and remembered how he'd so easily moved. His obvious grace made her believe he'd been born with his over-large frame.

His quick repartee and his smooth seduction of her senses belied the very idea that he could be Hugh. The flash of a lanky boy spilling wine on her wedding finery raced through her mind.

She frowned. Uncertainty chased away her questions before they could completely form.

The man beside her picked up a goblet, took a sip of the dark wine and offered the vessel to her. "This time I will not spill one drop on your gown."

Adrienna swallowed a groan. Not only had her Hugh grown into this warrior seated beside her, but he'd also learned how to read her thoughts.

Certain the wine would provide a measure of calm in this suddenly tumultuous moment, she accepted the offered goblet. Adrienna finished off the contents before placing it back on the table and proclaiming, "Hugh is dead."

His teeth gleamed white and even behind his smile. He laughed at her. A soft, satiny tone that prickled against her scalp. "You have been sadly misinformed." Tightening his fingers around the back of her head again, he drew her toward him. "I do not feel dead."

His breath, hot against her cheek, stole her ability to reason.

"What do you think, Adrienna?" He grazed her chin with his lips before whispering against her mouth, "Does this feel like the touch of a dead man?"

Her head spun. While her mind begged her to back away from his touch, her body leaned closer to him.

Gently and ever so slowly, he ran his tongue across her lower lip. A bolt of lightning sped through her body, leaving behind nothing more than trembling need.

His hand, still resting on her thigh, moved higher. She could feel the heat of his caress through her heavy gown. Insistently he kneaded and stroked her flesh, inching ever so steadily upward.

She gasped for air to fill her straining lungs. The urge to part her legs, to permit him a more intimate touch, nearly won over her still protesting mind.

"Adrienna, I can feel your desire. You want me as badly as I want you."

She stiffened. His assessment broke the spell he had woven so deftly around her. Alarmed at the sensations his touch caused, and angered by his self-assurance,

Adrienna slapped his face before reason could take hold of her actions.

Silence descended upon the high table. All eyes turned to them. What she'd done filled her with shame. The imprint of her palm on his face horrified her. The unyielding heat of embarrassment fired her cheeks.

Hugh released her. Very softly, he stated, "No. I am definitely not dead."

He turned to the staring diners, lifted his empty goblet and said, "I would say the lady likes not my overbold compliments." He gestured toward her. "I do apologize for my crude behavior."

A tense, nervous twitter erupted from a few of the guests. Others appeared disappointed that their entertainment had been short-lived. Soon, all turned back to the activities that had been so rudely interrupted.

"Milady?" One of the queen's squires appeared at the arched doorway. "Is there anything you require?"

Hugh pressed his leg against hers. She choked back a cry for help. It was doubtful the young lad would be capable of removing the man next to her and she didn't want to bring more attention to herself than she already had.

She took a deep breath. "Nay. Thank you. All is well."

After the squire moved on, she turned back to her dinner companion—her long dead husband. "Where in hell have you been? Why did you leave? What were you thinking?"

He stopped her flow of questions by placing a finger over her lips. "Ladies do not curse, Adrienna. One would think you'd be aware of that."

She was aware of many things. Mostly, she was aware of the warmth of his finger against her sensitive lips. And she was very aware of the throbbing low in her belly. This man was dangerous. He set her afire with a look. His mere touch made ashes of her will.

She worried that he already knew these things.

"Do not speak to me of cursing, milord."

When she sought to move away from him, he captured her chin between his fingers. "I will speak to you of whatever I wish, wifeling."

Fear rushed to the fore, driving away any thought of desire. "Do not call me that."

He stared at her for a moment. His brows furrowed as if in thought. After glancing out at the hall, he turned his attention back to her. "We need to talk, milady."

"Yes, we do, milord."

Another thought-stealing smile crossed his lips. "In my chamber or yours?"

She wanted to somehow reach in and slap her fluttering heart. Instead she gritted her teeth tightly before answering. "Neither."

Hugh only shrugged. "Nay? Then perhaps a stroll in the gardens will suffice."

"Fine. I will meet you there on the morrow." By morning she would find a way to guard against his assault on her senses.

"No. You will join me there now." His words and tone brooked no opposition.

He dared to give her orders? Before she could correct this assumption, he rose and started to pull her up with him.

Adrienna shook out of his hold. "I said on the morrow."

He lifted one eyebrow, then leaned down and whispered, "If you do not come of your own accord, I will pick you up and carry you from this hall. The choice is yours, Adrienna."

Determined to call his bluff, she settled more firmly on her seat and gripped the edge of the bench with her hands. "You would not commit such a scene in public."

He moved behind her, leaned over and placed his mouth against her ear. "I would dare much more than that where you are concerned." He easily pried her fingers from the bench and grasped her wrists. "Choose."

Adrienna swallowed the bitter taste of defeat before rising. "Someday you will pay for this."

"I already have, milady."

Moonlight softly lit the garden path. Strategically placed torches provided light in the darker areas of the queen's foliaged maze.

Bemused, Hugh watched the woman striding in front of him. This would be no lover's stroll in a romantic garden. Her footsteps more resembled those of someone eager to be as far away from him as possible.

At first he had hoped that by remaining silent and permitting her to stomp off some of her anger and confusion she would become less outraged. That had been what seemed like miles ago. He was not in the mood to walk all night.

"Adrienna, it will be hard to converse if I must shout at your back."

She stopped and turned to look at him. While the planes of her face had lost the hard edge of anger, her lips were still pursed with ire.

"Talk. No one is stopping you."

Yes, she was still in a fine rage. He gestured toward a stone bench. "Come, sit with me."

"No. I will stand here, thank you."

His lips twitched. "I will not bite you."

Her eyes narrowed. "It is not your bite I wish to avoid."

Hugh fought hard to hold back a shout of triumph. His wifeling did not like the fact that his touch unnerved her. Good. It would only make the game more interesting.

"What do you want, Hugh?"

"You." He wasn't going to lie.

"I no longer want you."

"Who are you seeking to fool, Adrienna? Me or yourself?"

She ignored his question. "Why are you here now? Where have you been? And what is this *Earl of Wynnedom* business? I married Hugh of Ryebourne."

He eased down onto a high-backed bench and stretched out his legs. Taking his time to get comfortable, he watched her. She swayed from one foot to the other, her arms clasped tightly around her stomach.

He'd answer her easy question first. "Hugh of Ryebourne died the night we wed. As far as the world is concerned, he never existed."

Her gaze darted everywhere but to him. In the shadowed moonlight he could not clearly see her eyes. What did she hide? What did she fear?

"How do you account for the title?"

Hugh shrugged. "Titles are easily bought, easily given. I thought Wynnedom had a nice sound to it. Do you not agree?"

"Would it matter if I agreed or not?"

"No. In all honesty, it would not."

What would it take to make her trust him? What would it take to break that trust? He had all the time in the world to find the answers to those questions.

He patted the empty spot next to him. "Would it not be easier to converse if we had less distance between us?"

Adrienna shook her head, silently holding her ground.

"This is not exactly the most private place for a personal discussion, milady."

She glanced around before stating the obvious. "There is no one else here. We have all the privacy we require."

This did not suit his purpose. He wanted to see every nuance of her expressions while they talked. To watch her eyes as they sparkled or dulled. To see her lips tighten or tremble. To hear her breathe. To feel her heat.

While words were a necessary form of communication, they were easily twisted into lies. Emotions and expressions of deceit were much harder to master. He didn't think Adrienna was capable of hiding what she felt or thought, but he needed to know for certain.

Hugh grasped for a way to draw her nearer. "If you join me here, I vow not to touch you."

She ignored his offer and repeated. "Why are you here?"

"Why wouldn't I be here? My wife is here."

She stared up at the star-filled sky a moment before stating, "I am not your wife."

"Ah, wifeling, the king tells me no annulment was ever issued. You are my wife."

"Stop calling me that." Her voice held anger. "I will petition the queen first thing in the morning."

"Petition her all you like. She did not sign our betrothal documents and can do nothing to help you."

"Fine." Her voice rose. "Then I will petition King Henry and the church."

"You will do no such thing."

He loved the way her back stiffened with anger. The way her lips parted as she drew in deep breaths with which to fuel her rage. Her volatile emotions simmered so close to the surface. Just as her passion had.

She lifted her chin. "Who will stop me? You?"

"Who else? If you even think of petitioning the king or the church, I assure you that I will perform my husbandly duties instantly. It will be rather hard to claim a lack of consummation while lying naked in my bed."

She dropped her arms to her sides, curled her fingers into fists and took a step forward. "You would not force me."

Hugh draped his arms along the back of the bench. "I would not have to force you."

"Why you arrogant—toad." Her shriek frightened a rabbit from beneath a nearby bush.

"Arrogant? No. Merely honest." He crossed his ankles. How long before she flew at him with her nails bared? "Come, Adrienna, do not seek to hide your desire for me."

"Desire? For you?"

The slight tremor behind her show of bravado coaxed him to go even further. "Yes, for me. You nearly swooned back in the hall with little more than a touch."

Anger brought her a few steps closer. "Does your arrogance know no bounds?"

"It is just the knowledge that like all women, your needs are basic."

Her eyes grew large. She opened her mouth. When no sound issued forth, Hugh pushed a little more. "A few soft words, a steady touch and your senses flee. A lingering kiss and you spread your legs."

She flew at him. He was ready for her. Before she could rake her nails across his face, he grabbed her wrists and pulled her down on his lap. He wrapped his arms tightly around her struggling body. "Yes. This is much better."

Instantly, she ceased her movements and glared at him. "You did that on purpose."

"Of course." He brushed a stray lock of hair from her face. "Twelve years ago you were quick to anger. I counted on that remaining the same."

Her back stiffened. "I hate you." She sounded like a petulant child.

"I do not doubt that for an instant." Little did she know that eventually her hatred would grow to unimaginable heights. "Adrienna, I only wish to talk."

His soft statement seemed to calm her. She ceased her struggling. "Where have you been? Why did you leave?"

Hugh loosened his hold on her. What would he tell

her? He'd practiced this conversation in his mind countless times. Yet now that she was in his arms and the time for explanations had come, he found himself unwilling to tell her the truth. And he knew not why. If he were suddenly developing a conscience, he'd have to quell it immediately.

"Well?" She crossed her arms and pierced him with a look of impatience.

"I did not leave."

One eyebrow winged higher. "Your absence all these years was just my imagination?"

Moonlight framed her face in a soft glow. Rage had left her cheeks tinged a pale red. Her eyes still glittered with anger.

"Milord?" She pushed at his shoulder. "Answer me."

He wanted to brush away the last traces of rage. To watch the shimmer of anger fade as the spark of passion grew. He wanted to greet the morning sun naked while buried so deeply within her that—

The mere image of her naked beneath him snapped him out of desire's haze.

"Hugh."

His name on her lips only increased his level of insanity. He slid her off his lap to sit beside him, giving him a small measure of control. To prevent the possibility of escape, he held her against his side. The heat of her thigh, pressed so tightly against his, smoldered with warmth.

"No, Adrienna, my absence was not your imagination. But I did not leave of my own free will."

She tipped her head and looked up at him for a moment. A frown marred the smoothness of her forehead. "I do not understand."

Hugh leaned back against the bench and closed his eyes. He had always known this moment would arrive. So why now did the memories tear at his soul? A familiar voice whispered from inside his soul. *Trust the strength within you. Let the truth of your knowledge guide you.*

"Do you remember that night, Adrienna? How you screamed at me to go away? How I bolted from your hysteria like a frightened rabbit?"

Flames burned her cheeks. "Of course I remember." She placed a hand on his arm. "Hugh, we were both little more than children. Children forced to become adults in mere hours. That was no reason to leave. To so thoroughly abandon me." Her eyes widened. She bit her lower lip. She obviously had not meant to blurt out the last.

He covered her hand with his own. Absently stroking her wrist with his thumb, he continued, "I went to the stable looking for a place to hide my shame, for somewhere to sleep." Thoughts of that night slammed against his temples.

In an attempt to escape the pain, he rose and paced in front of her. "Three men found me there and forcibly removed me."

Adrienna rushed to him and grabbed his arm. "Oh, Hugh, I am so sorry. Why did you not yell for help? Why did you not call out for my father?"

He looked at her, but could not see her through the fog of a boy's terror. "I did."

"Did he not hear you?"

"Oh, yes, he heard me. It was your sire who stuffed the rag in my mouth to silence my pleas."

She backed away. Disbelief etched on her near-white face. "You lie. My father would have saved and protected you. Why are you saying these things?"

"Lie? Your father sought to have me killed."

"Now you prove your words are false. Had my father wished you dead you would not be standing here now. You make no sense, milord, he had no reason to seek your death."

"If he were trying to rid his daughter of an unwanted husband he would."

"Unwanted?" She shook her head. "What are you saying? That I asked him to kill you? For what reason?"

Hugh silently cursed his inability to read her expression. Were her raised eyebrows a sign of confusion or surprise? "You were the only person who knew my circumstance. You and you alone knew my lack of worth, yet you swore it didn't matter."

She lowered her head and briefly turned away for a heartbeat before looking back up at him. "It did not matter."

"You told him that my sire had lost his wealth, his position and the good graces of the king, did you not?"

"Yes, but—"

He cut off her explanation with a sharp curse. "You knew that I had only some worthless land to offer and you vowed that it did not matter. You convinced me to go through with the marriage."

She held out her hands, as if begging him to understand. "Yes, I told him. He was my father and he loved me. I was a child and I knew he would see to it that we would lack for nothing."

"Oh, yes and he did a fine job by seeking to end my life, did he not? Tell me, Adrienna, have you lacked for anything all these years?"

He reached out for her, but when she backed farther away, he dropped his arm to his side. "Have you ever gone hungry, or been so cold that your flesh froze? Have you ever been afraid of dying? Or sought the relief of death?"

Instead of answering, she turned and ran down the path toward the palace.

She left him alone in the dark. Alone with his memories. Alone with a terror he thought he'd conquered long ago.

He'd gone these many months certain his terrors had been left far behind. Now, they returned with a force that threatened to knock him to his knees.

Nearly falling back down onto the bench, Hugh rested his throbbing head in his hands. What was wrong with him? Why could he not find balance? Or at least enough strength to remain in control? Had he forgotten how?

After slipping heavily to the ground, he lifted his face to the moon and stars. He inhaled deeply, exhaled slowly, seeking calm.

Hugh closed his eyes and cleared all other thoughts from his mind. As he concentrated on the clear nothingness of peace, his breathing slowed.

The tinkling of bells jingled in his mind's ear. The scent of sage and myrrh wafted through his senses. Both brought the calm and strength he sought. Bringing his difficulties with the present situation to the fore, he realized that the balance he sought was being offset by the wild, untamable desire he felt for Adrienna.

While he had every intention of seducing her, he'd not expected his own passions to be seduced. He needed to slow down his assault on her. In doing so, he would be better able to follow the path he had set.

A woman's terrified screams tore him from his silent search. He jumped to his feet. In the reputed safety of this garden, the horrified screams were out of place. Yet again the frantic sound rushed through the darkness. *Adrienna.* Hugh ran toward the cry.

He rounded a corner and stopped dead in his tracks. His breath whooshed silently from his body. A man, armed with a knife, held Adrienna's wrist.

Her screams once again ripped through the night. She kicked and pummeled her assailant but Hugh knew her attempts would be futile. Her strength would be no match against the behemoth who had her within his grasp.

The man's face was hidden beneath a black-and-green hood. Riveted to the colors, Hugh swallowed against the lump in his throat. What was a guard from Sidatha's palace doing here? It could not be a coincidence. His captors had not followed him here on a whim. Nor would this man be here alone. There would be others.

He tasted fear. But this was a new fear. Not for himself, but for the woman in danger, and it left a sour taste in his mouth. Adrienna did not know it, but she was in less danger from the knife.

If her attacker completed his task, she would find herself being used in ways she could not begin to imagine. Death would be easier to bear.

While Hugh wanted revenge, he wished her no physical harm. Nor did he desire to see her spirit so thoroughly broken.

He rushed forward, knowing he would lose his advantage the instant he was spotted. He grabbed the man's shoulder, swung him about and rammed the heel of his hand up into the surprised man's nose. Without pause, Hugh tightly curled the fingers of one hand and jammed his knuckles into the man's throat.

After dropping the now lifeless body to the ground, he pulled a trembling Adrienna into his arms. "Hush. It is over."

She clung to his shoulders and buried her face in his chest. "He…he came out of nowhere. I did not even hear him."

Her heart beat so hard he felt it pound against his own. Rubbing her back and threading his fingers into her hair, he tried to soothe her fear. "Shh, Adrienna, he cannot hurt you now. Be still."

When her trembling finally stopped, she looked up at him and then down at the man. "Should we not summon the guard before he awakens?"

Hugh frowned. "Awakens?" If that man woke up it would only be by the hand of God. "He isn't going to awaken in this world, Adrienna."

She eased out of his hold, walked over to the still form and nudged him with her foot. The look she turned back to Hugh did not bode well. "You killed him?"

He reached for her. "There was no other option."

And there hadn't been. Had the man escaped, he'd only have returned with more men.

She retreated and stared at his hands. "You killed him with your hands?"

"It is all I have. I am not in the habit of carrying weapons into Queen Eleanor's hall."

"But you only hit him twice."

"He was dead with the first blow."

She gasped. Why was she acting so strange? Had she never witnessed a fight or a battle? Had she never seen a man die before?

He took a step toward her and stopped when she lifted her hands as if to ward him off. "No. Stay away." She looked back down at the man, before returning an overbright gaze to him. "What are you?"

Hugh shrugged in confusion. He spread his arms wide. "I am a man. I sought only to protect you."

"No." She shook her head. "No. I have watched men brawl before. You did not fight this man. You killed him."

"Yes." Now he realized what he had done. He had not used his fists. He had not wrestled this man down in a manner she was used to seeing. "Adrienna, you do not understand."

Again she asked, "What are you?"

It was useless to reason with her at this moment. She would not hear his explanation and describing things she'd never heard of before would only make matters worse.

Anger at himself and at the assailant who had caused this situation boiled over. He could not contain the heated rage that fired his blood. Before she could realize what he was about, Hugh pulled her forcefully against his chest.

He glared down at her, ignoring the way she tried to shrink from him. "I am a man who belongs nowhere. I am a trained killer of men—a trained lover of women."

Horror filled her green eyes. She beat against his chest. "Let me go. Don't touch me. Let me go."

The frantic rise of her voice tore at him. This fear, her fear of him, sickened him. He moved her to arm's length, then with one hand he lifted her chin and held her firmly before him. "I am everything your father made me."

Tears pooled in her eyes. "Please." Her lips trembled. "You are hurting me. Let me go."

Instantly relaxing his hold, he allowed her to pull free. As she turned to leave, he said, "Adrienna, I am your husband."

She didn't look back. She didn't acknowledge his statement. And he didn't seek to stop her.

Instead, he silently watched her run toward the palace. Away from him.

Chapter Three

"Oh, my sweet Adrienna, I so love the way the sun gleams from your tresses."

"Richard, cease." She brushed his hand away from her hair. Normally, Sir Richard of Langsford possessed the ability to amuse her. Today his bantering set her teeth on edge.

He slapped a hand against his chest, declaring, "You wound me, my love."

One glance at his sparkling eyes gave lie to his absurd statement. The only way she'd be able to wound him would be with a sharp weapon. Even though she considered him a friend, she wished to be left alone today. He meant nothing of what he said, and had only joined her here by the duck pond to annoy and cajole her.

The humor left his gaze. He frowned and asked, "What is wrong, fair lady?"

"Nothing. All is well." He'd dropped his teasing tone, yet she'd no wish to discuss anything with him.

"Then what causes this brooding of yours? Until the last three days you have never been so serious, so withdrawn."

Adrienna rested her chin on her propped-up knees and stared at the glasslike surface of the pond. Nary a breeze ruffled the water. Not a cloud marred the blue of the sky. It was a fine late spring day, meant for gaiety. Yet, a storm raged inside her. The intensity of the winds buffeted her mind with a fierceness that refused to relent. She could find no escape from the tempest.

"If you do not like my sullen mood, you are free to leave." At any other time she'd regret saying that to Richard, but not on this day.

"Lady Adrienna." His words huffed out on an exasperated sigh.

"Sir Richard." She matched his tone and rolled her eyes.

"I am not leaving until you tell me what has wrought such a change."

"If you keep pestering me, *I* will leave." Even had she wanted to confide in him, what could she say? That her dead husband was here? That he had appeared from nowhere? That she hadn't even recognized him? Or that for three straight nights she'd dreamed of no one else but Hugh?

Nay. Just to say those words aloud would only add credence to her thoughts.

Richard sat up beside her. "I will tease you no more." He paused for a moment, as if considering his next words. "Instead, let us talk about the man who follows you."

Adrienna held back a groan. She'd been correct. At

first she thought it was simply her imagination playing tricks on her, but no. It was no phantom dogging her footsteps. Her shadow was a flesh-and-blood man. Every time she turned around, she spied Hugh. Each morning, when she stepped out of her chamber, she'd found flowers on the floor in front of the door.

Flowers. Of all things a man could give her, he'd chosen wildflowers. The same type of flora she'd woven into her hair on their wedding day.

Yet not once, since that night in the garden, had he sought to approach her. She pulled a dianthus from her hair and rolled the stem between her fingers. Its sweet, clovelike scent perfumed the air. The lingering aroma made her wonder if a man who would lay flowers at her feet could truly have meant to kill her attacker in such a cold-blooded fashion.

She forced her attention away from her disconcerting thoughts and pleaded, "No, Richard, let us talk about something else."

"Did you hear about the body the guards found in the maze?" He'd offered another topic she'd no desire to discuss.

Determinedly clasping her arms about her legs, she fought to hold the memory at bay. "Yes, I heard about it. Who has not? Can you think of any subject that might lend a measure of lightness to my day?"

A trace of lines marred his brow for a heartbeat before clearing. "Marry me, Adrienna. Let me remove you from this court. Let me take you to my home and make all your days light and happy."

She'd not have been more surprised had a blizzard blanketed the area with snow. "Where does this come from, Richard? What prompts this sudden talk of marriage?"

"It is not sudden. I have thought about it for a time now."

She stared into his guileless eyes. A gaze so different from Hugh's. Richard's sincerity shone from his pleading look. She'd been able to detect nothing in Hugh's shuttered gaze.

Richard grasped one of her hands. "Please, Adrienna, give me your hand in marriage."

His touch left her cold. He was a friend and nothing more. She could not imagine ever having an intimate relationship with him.

Gently pulling her hand away, she shook her head. "No, we would never suit. I cannot marry you."

"You are wrong." He rose up on his knees, his expression and tone intent. "We go on together quite well. There is no one else I can think of who would suit me as well as you."

"Why? Because we can discuss poetry and philosophy? Because our voices harmonize well together? Because you tell a good story and I laugh?"

"No one else finds my stories entertaining. No one else will sit up until the wee hours of the morning discussing the value of honor or loyalty."

This conversation was all wrong. "Richard, those are not reasons to marry."

"It proves we have much in common."

"And what, pray tell, does that have to do with committing ourselves to a lifetime together?"

"We are not strangers. We know each other well. That alone is beneficial to start a life together."

True, in the few months they'd been acquainted, she'd come to know Richard well. What did she know about Hugh? Nothing. She only knew that the man had the ability to make her feel things she'd only longed for. Things she'd dreamed about repeatedly. Emotions and mind-numbing trills that ran the length of her body, leaving her knees weak. Emotions and feelings that she'd been denied far too long.

She stared at Richard. While there was no humor, no teasing look on his face, or in his eyes, something was not quite right. "Richard, do you yearn for me at night? Do you dream of no one but me? Do you wish for no one else in your bed? For a lifetime?"

He looked away and stared off into the distance. "You have listened to too many tales, Adrienna. Too many stories of grand passions and proclamations of undying love. There is more to marriage than passion."

After returning his attention to her, he continued, "You know I have been married before. I do not lie when I say that passion dies. There needs to be more than heated kisses."

Maybe for him, but not for her. She'd already spent a lifetime without passion. And once before she died, she wanted someone to proclaim his undying love for her. She placed a palm against his cheek, then softly asked, "Why are you truly doing this? What prompts such words from your lips?"

"I only wish to see you happy, Adrienna. Is that too much to hope for?"

When he placed a kiss upon her palm, the memory of Hugh doing so tripped across her heart. "I am happy, my friend." Surely he would forgive her the lie. "Do not worry yourself so."

"I do not believe you, but I will not give up. In the end you will see that I am the perfect choice." The harsh certainty of his tone surprised her.

"Richard, please. Do not seek to ruin what we do share."

He released her hand, leaned forward and placed a chaste kiss upon her cheek. "You will see."

What was wrong with her? She felt nothing at his touch. God forgive her, but she wanted the passion, the lust. She wanted to revel in a man's caress and his kiss. She longed to know the feel of his skin against hers, to bear the weight of his body atop her own.

More than passion, she wanted love. She wanted to stand beneath the stars and hear him promise to love her for all time.

With unspoken relief, she watched Richard stand and walk away. He turned around once, but she refused to call him back. When he was finally gone from her sight, she gazed unseeingly at the pond.

"Did he offer marriage, Adrienna?"

A flush heated her cheeks. It amazed her how he picked just the right moment to make himself known.

She turned to look up at Hugh and nodded. "Yes, he did."

"And?"

His eyes glinted. A wry smile crossed his mouth. Not wanting to give away her sudden nervousness at his presence, she matched his bravado. "We have arranged a brief ceremony."

Hugh dropped down beside her. To her chagrin, he did not take the bait. His smile only widened. "Do I wait until after the bedding to announce your perfidy? Or would you rather I spare you a night in his arms?"

Before this conversation headed in a direction she wished not to go, she asked, "What would you have me do, milord?"

"I can only tell you what I am going to do. I am going to court you. I am going to seduce you. Like a heady wine running through your veins I will set every inch of you aflame with lust. A lust only I can satisfy. Then we are going home."

She'd never before met anyone as bold—or insulting—as he. His candor confused her. Angered her. Embarrassed her.

And somehow intrigued her.

Unable to think of a suitable response she blinked several times before spluttering, "I beg your pardon?"

He plucked a flower from her hair and held it out to her. "I will woo you with attention and flowers. I will be but a step behind you at all times. I will ensure all your needs and wants are supplied instantly."

Already he had begun his professed courtship. He

was always a step behind her, and every time she saw him, fear and excitement slinked down her spine. Every morning, when she opened her chamber door, she felt an odd rush of longing at the sight of the flowers lying on the floor.

But a longing for what? She wasn't certain. Home? Simple pleasures? Love? Would Hugh be able to fulfill her need for that, too?

After placing the flower in her lap, he continued, "Then, when you have learned to trust me, to depend on me, to turn to me, I will ravish you."

Heat pooled low in her belly.

"I will caress your flesh with my hands. My lips will know every inch of your body."

The deep, steady timbre of his voice promised more lust than she'd ever dared dream about. Only his words caressed her and already her blood had heated, and her pulse quickened.

"I will touch your soul with my own. I will take you to heights of ecstasy you never knew existed."

He tucked a strand of hair behind her ear, letting his fingertips linger against the sensitive flesh.

Adrienna clenched her hands. It did nothing to stop the trembling that worked its way up her arms, down her legs. He but played a game with her. Never once did he speak of love, or of honoring the vows they'd made so many years ago.

Just like nearly every other man in this court he sought only to tempt her into his bed. Had he been anyone else, she'd leave him sitting here alone.

But he wasn't anyone else. Vivid images of what he'd done to that man in the maze held her temper in check. While his touch, his voice, could set her afire, a small part of her mind knew this man was dangerous. The same hands that turned her to molten fire, had killed a man with but one odd punch.

He slipped his fingers through her hair and pulled her toward him. "Adrienna, I can smell your fear. I can nearly taste your worry." He leaned forward. "Be still. Be not afraid."

Before she could focus on anything but his husky whisper, he touched her lips with his own. His kiss, so gentle, so warm, chased away some of her fear. The exotic scents surrounding him intoxicated her senses faster than mead.

He tipped her head back, while coaxing her lips to part. She started in surprise when his tongue met hers, but soon returned his tentative, then insistent, caress.

The ground beneath her spun away. She clung to his shoulders for support. Adrienna hoped her heart would not burst with its hard and rapid pounding. When he slanted his mouth more firmly over hers, she cared little if the entire world burst. The only thing that mattered was the feel of his lips on hers, his hand in her hair, the strength of his shoulders beneath her grasping fingers and the throbbing ache between her thighs.

She leaned against him, closing the small space that separated them. She slipped one hand behind his head and wove her fingers through his hair. It rippled through her touch like silk.

Too soon he broke their kiss. Bereft of his touch, she tried to pull him back. He rested his forehead against hers and stared into her eyes. "I would never bring harm to one who so eagerly returns my kisses."

Acknowledgment of her wanton behavior brought flames of embarrassment to her cheeks. "I apologize, milord. Since I have no intention of participating in your intended game, I should not have permitted desire to carry away my good sense."

Hugh tightened his hold when she tried to pull away. His breath was hot against her face. "Your participation is not in question. I will pursue you and you will submit."

When she parted her lips to argue, he closed them with his own. Again, Adrienna found herself lost to the magic of his kiss. Again, she did not care.

He broke the kiss and continued, "Furthermore, your apology is not needed, nor welcome."

"I—" Once more he stopped her words with a kiss more forceful than the others. She moaned as the blood running through her veins turned to liquid fire.

When he finally pulled back from the heat, she noticed that his breathing was nearly as ragged as her own. "There is no shame in lusting for your husband."

In an effort to catch her breath and regain her composure, Adrienna smoothed her hair into place and shook the skirt of her gown. All meaningless gestures meant only to gain a modicum of calm.

Certain she had her swinging emotions in control, she refuted his last statement. "Lust in any form is wrong. It is blasphemous and a sin to permit lust to rule your life."

The gleam in his eyes brightened. "If God did not mean us to be lustful, then why were our bodies formed to compliment each other? Why cannot a man or a woman form a perfect union alone?"

He leaned back on his elbows, silently waiting for her answer. The distance between them provided her the chance to catch her breath and to calm her ragged emotions.

Purposely avoiding his question, she asked, "And what will you do if I choose not to cooperate in this intended quest of yours?"

"Your cooperation has little to do with my quest. Eventually you will comply simply because you will be unable to ignore my attention."

It was all she could do not to let her jaw drop to the ground. He certainly had the ability to shock her. "This is nothing but a game to you."

"If you wish to see it that way, it is fine by me."

"How else can I interpret your plan?"

"Is life not a game, Adrienna? Are you not here at court to see and be seen by one you would consider suitable as a husband? Will you not flirt and smile and simper while he struts and preens and boasts? Is that not a game?"

"Flirting and strutting, as you call it, are a great deal different from what you suggest."

"Are they? How so? Because of the plain words? Another man might mask his intentions with fancy phrases. But are the end results not the same? I simply have the sense to speak plainly."

"Plainly? You tell me that you intend to seduce me and call it plain speaking? I call your intentions despicable."

"Tell me you do not wish to ride the tides of passion and I will call you a liar."

She opened her mouth, then closed it. Had she not just wished for a union filled with passion and desire?

"Why did you not accept your lover's proposal?"

"Richard is *not* my lover."

"It matters not." He brushed aside her denial as meaningless. "Regardless of what he is, why did you not rush into his arms, eager for the salvation he could provide?"

She stared at him. Hugh had the uncanny ability to know her thoughts. Would she be able to lie to him? He returned her steady look and she knew that somehow he'd see through a lie. After lowering her gaze to her lap, she finally admitted, "We are nothing more than friends."

"Marrying a friend would not be a bad thing."

"I am free to marry no one."

"Would you like to be?"

She looked at him in confusion. "Be what? Free to marry?" Was this a trick? Did he seek to build up her hopes and dash them?

Hugh sat up and reached out to stroke her cheek. "Would you like to be free to marry anyone of your choosing?"

Without thinking, she leaned into the warm touch. And then just as quickly, leaned away. "What are you asking me, milord?"

He ran a fingertip across her lower lip. She quivered

at the thrill his stroke caused. "I am willing to make you a bargain."

"A bargain?"

"One month, Adrienna." He replaced his fingertip with his tongue.

His odd, gentle touch turned her mind to gruel. Unable to form coherent words, she simply stared into his eyes.

"A month to coax you into my bed."

His breath was hot against her tingling lip. She fought to clear the spiderwebs from her mind. "A month? Your bed?"

He leaned back giving her thoughts room to gather. "Yes. If I cannot seduce you in a month, I will give you your annulment."

An annulment. A joyous rush of satisfaction raced through her. *An annulment.* Immediately a stab of grief and despair pierced her chest. She could no more explain the conflicting emotions any more than she could explain why the sky was blue.

If she turned down his offer, she would be accepting him as her husband here and now. Did she want that? Was she ready to set everything aside and act like the dutiful wife to a man who so obviously did not love her?

A man's dead body came into view behind her eyes. She did not know this Hugh. She knew not what he'd become, or how he'd reached this point of his existence. He'd said things that made little sense. He'd laid false-hoods at her father's feet and implicated her in them.

But his mere touch gave her more pleasure than she'd ever known before. His kisses promised her more passion than she could imagine. While passion and desire were things she longed for, she wanted more from the man she would call husband.

A month. Surely she could decide in that amount of time if she wished to truly become his wife. Or if she wished to find someone else.

Another thought caught her attention. "What about Queen Eleanor?"

Hugh looked surprised at the question. "What about her?"

"If she discovers our arrangement—"

"Obviously we can't let that happen. Otherwise, the deal is off."

"Hugh, she can be very vindictive."

"Considering that I serve King Henry, I am certain she would be. So, we simply say nothing to anyone."

Since she could think of no other plan, his suggestion for secrecy would have to suffice. "If I agree to this arrangement, you promise to tell no one of our marriage?"

An odd smile lit his face. "It would spoil the fun if I did."

Why did his answers always seem to set her pulse pounding? What did her body know that she did not?

"And you will not at any time force our true relationship on me?"

"What are you planning, Adrienna? Are there others you wish to court at the same time?" He shook his head before promising, "Do not worry, I will not use our marriage as a means of scaring off any suitors you have."

"Then I accept your offer." She stuck out her hand to seal their bargain.

Hugh grasped it and pulled her tightly against his chest. He lowered his head, whispering, "Oh, rest assured, my love, you will accept more than just my offer."

Chapter Four

Lord Hugh of Wynnedom, earl in King Henry's court, renown for his prowess with a sword, dagger and his hands, stared down into one of the many fertile valleys surrounding Poitiers.

And fought the terror snaking into his veins.

His will had been tested by whips and chains, and had emerged unbroken. He had learned to be victorious against swords, jagged-edged daggers and spears, armed with nothing but his wits.

The thought of death had plagued him little. Yet, the sight of the stark white tents gleaming against the lush green of the valley made the blood coursing through him pause.

Something teased his mind. Something half-seen and foreboding. Not a memory of things that had already happened, but a misty vision of what might occur. An ethereal wisp of danger beckoned him to be wary.

Bound by honor to his king, he could not turn his

steed about and leave this valley. Bound by honor to himself, he set his horse on the winding path that would take him forward, to face his past.

The creak of a saddle and the fall of hooves behind signaled that he would not face this test alone. A shadow overtook him. The outline of a colossus hulk of a being engulfed the silhouette of him and his horse. After his companion rode up alongside him, Hugh stated, "You are late."

William of Bronwyn, former dungeon mate, shrugged. "It could not be helped. Your lady took her time returning to the palace. I came as soon as she gained entrance."

His friend did him a great service by watching over Adrienna when he was unable to do so himself. Whether she knew it or not, she was in danger. Not for one moment did he believe the attack in the queen's garden had been an accident. Nor a simple matter of being in the wrong place at the wrong time. He'd learned long ago that all things happened for a reason. And sooner or later he'd discover that reason.

No one was better suited to the task of guarding Adrienna than this formidable giant. As tall as an oak and built like a bear, William required no weapons against a foe. Yet for all his size, the man moved with the grace of a dancer and, when need be, more quietly than a breeze. "I thank you, William. I—"

"Nay. Milord, 'tis I who owe you more than just a favor now and then." William's dark glare swept across the assemblage below. "Were it not for you, I would still be a captive. I owe you my life. For this existence and the next."

"That is not true and well you know it." With a light tug on his reins, Hugh brought their progress to a halt and studied his companion. He had noted the strained tone of William's voice and now saw the tightness around the man's mouth. While he had no great desire to traverse this path alone, he would not subject William to memories that might very well tear the man's soul asunder.

Hugh's lot in captivity had not been as deplorable as William's. It was not fair to ask the man to do this. It was only Hugh's own fear that had prompted him to include his friend in this matter. A shameful cowardice that he now despised.

"William, there is no reason for you to continue." He nodded toward the far side of the encampment. "The king and his men are here. Henry will not permit anything to go wrong this day."

William sucked in a long, heavy breath before straightening his back and turning haunted eyes toward Hugh. "I have demons to quell, too. I cannot do so by hiding safely away, now can I?"

As hard as he tried, Hugh could find little argument in that logic. Barely touching his heels to his horse's flanks, Hugh silently resumed his journey.

Before the memories and the ghosts had a chance to do little more than seep into either man's courage, they entered the camp. After leaving their horses with one of the king's squires, Hugh searched the throng of men for his sire.

Henry stared hard at him for a moment before a smile broke the seriousness of his expression. Hugh walked into the king's outstretched arms, accepting the hearty welcome with a relief he had not expected to feel.

He took strength from the king's jovial attitude and from the twenty or so armed men that made up Henry's entourage.

"Well, what say you, Wynnedom? Shall we conclude these negotiations and then go pester my wife?"

Hugh couldn't help but smile at Henry's attempted humor. The king was as anxious to be gone from this valley as he. But they were both well aware that pestering Queen Eleanor could be more risky than bargaining with the man inside the tent.

While Hugh would rather take his chances angering the queen, there were lives at stake. Captives who had been held so long that they'd been forgotten. Men who had been turned into slaves. Men Hugh had sworn not to forget. Men he had promised to free.

The only way he could keep that promise was to bargain with the devil. Since his father-by-marriage had seen to it that nothing was left of Hugh's lands, he had no choice but to seek aid from King Henry.

And now that the time for bargaining had finally arrived, Hugh found his courage flagging. He took a deep breath, then fell in step alongside the king. "The sooner we are gone from here the better." Hugh glanced at William and nearly tripped with surprise.

The man's face had paled. He looked as if he would faint at any moment. With trepidation he followed William's wide-eyed stare. Hugh sucked in a quick breath.

As vigilant as ever, King Henry paused. "Not who you expected?"

Unable to do little more than swallow, Hugh managed to shake his head before finally finding his voice. "Nay. No, not at all."

Where was Zirtha? Why was Aryseeth standing before the main tent as if it was his own? It took every ounce of willpower Hugh possessed not to let the frightened boy inside him cower beneath the amused stare of the slave-master.

His mind played tricks with him. Back and forth the images leapt. One moment he was a man walking beside King Henry toward a trade negotiation. With the next he was a terrified youth prone before the man who would lace his trembling flesh open with each stroke of the whip.

"Hugh? Lord Wynnedom?"

A hand grasped his arm. A hard touch that brought him a measure of clarity. He mentally shook the images from his mind before turning his attention to the king. "A moment, milord. Only a moment."

A moment was all he needed to gain control of his raging memories. A mere heartbeat that would permit him time to steel his will, to strengthen his resolve and find the courage to take yet another step closer to what had once been his reality.

Hugh calmed himself and eased his heavy breathing. He turned to William. "Stay. I do not require your presence."

William said nothing. He either had enough sense not

to argue, or was so far gone in his own terrors that he did not comprehend.

Hugh turned back to the king and waved one hand toward the tent that would serve as their chamber for this discussion. "After you, milord."

He spared a glance back at William and was grateful that the man stayed with the rest of the king's men.

Aryseeth had brought William to death's door more times than Hugh could remember. Often in ways that Hugh could not even imagine. Never would he have asked William to join him had he known this heartless, soulless demon would be presiding over these talks.

While the scribes for King Henry and Aryseeth made the formal introductions, Hugh studied the man who had ever been his enemy.

The man had always seemed overlarge, a vision of strength and power. A man none would cross for fear of death—or worse.

Even though Aryseeth's body was concealed beneath white robes, Hugh could envision the flesh that bulged over the iron muscles in the man's arms. He still held himself with the air of someone who was certain of his every move. Head high, back straight, Aryseeth met King Henry's gaze directly. As an equal.

Yet, something *was* different. Now, at this moment, in this place, Aryseeth was but a man, like any other. He had no power here outside of negotiations. He could not wield his torturous instruments of pain or bring harm to anyone here. Hugh pitied the men still under his control.

A shard of ice pierced his mind. He instinctively

sought the source of that cold and found Aryseeth's body servant glaring at him. A small, beady-eyed man who acted as a spy for his master.

The minion stepped away from Aryseeth and approached Hugh. "Lower your eyes, scum. Do not dare to look upon your betters."

Hugh looked down in time to see a flash of sun glint off a blade the man pulled from his robes. Before Hugh could react, Aryseeth knocked the dagger from his servant's hand.

Then, grasping the front of his robe, Aryseeth doubled his fist and rapidly landed three heavy blows on the smaller man's face.

He then let the dead man fall unceremoniously to the ground. With a casual shrug of one shoulder, as if he'd done nothing more than squash an insect, Aryseeth wiped the blood from his meaty knuckles. All the while piercing Hugh with a malevolent gaze, as if daring him to remember how easily men died.

Aryseeth turned back to the king and briefly bowed his head. "I beg your forgiveness for this interruption. Pray, let us continue."

King Henry stared in horror. He'd been in many battles, so killing was nothing new to him. Yet this cold-blooded slaughter of the servant appeared to unnerve him.

Immediately, Hugh revised his earlier thought. Aryseeth's position afforded him little sway in Henry's court, but he still retained complete control over those who served him.

Hugh stared down at the lifeless form of the body of

the servant before sending a silent prayer of thanks for his own freedom.

King Henry cleared his throat, "Lord Wynnedom, you are acquainted with our…guest?"

Hugh nodded. "In a fashion, yes." *Well acquainted.*

The king nodded. "Good. Then we can dispense with further introductions."

Henry was doing nothing more than making conversation to quell whatever distaste the vile killing had caused. He knew most of what Hugh's captivity had entailed. The explanations hadn't been a matter of choice, but of necessity. Hugh wanted not only the release of the remaining captives, he also wanted permission to rebuild his keep.

Henry wanted not only the release of the men, he wanted spices. More than Hugh could supply alone. It had taken a great many words to come to an understanding.

"Ah, yes. Hugh, I mean—Lord Wynnedom, is it?" Aryseeth's voice was still as soft and low and deadly as ever. "Lord Wynnedom and I know each other well." His voice had lost none of its ability to slither down one's spine.

"Lord Wynnedom—" the title rolled off Aryseeth's tongue like a curse "—you have come far in the time you have been away from us."

Hugh bit the side of his mouth to keep from spitting in the man's face. The statement was so bold. So full of double meaning that it was ironically amusing.

"Well, my lords, let us commence with our business." Trust King Henry to get to the point of this meeting. Trade.

Hugh was astounded at the furnishings inside the tent. As an emissary, Aryseeth was well versed in making his contacts feel at ease.

Instead of plush floor cushions and pillows to recline on, there was a table in the center of the room. Not a hastily made trestle table, but a solid carved piece of furniture.

Instead of folding campaign chairs, or benches, there were half a dozen cushioned armchairs, resembling thrones, around the table.

No aroma of sandalwood, myrrh or any other exotic scent filled the room. The light fragrance of lavender and roses wafted through the tent. A purely feminine aroma. One that reminded him of Adrienna. Hugh hesitated. The entire tableau caught him off guard.

And Aryseeth knew it. He slapped Hugh on the back and pushed him toward a chair. "You did not think I understand the English? You underestimate me, my young friend."

Hugh shuddered at the man calling him friend. Never once had he underestimated Aryseeth. He'd not begin now.

After sliding into the seat at the head of the table, Aryseeth leaned forward and narrowed his eyes at King Henry. "You want spices, precious oils and silks. What do you have to offer besides weapons and gold?"

Hugh expected Henry to balk at the emissary's forwardness. Instead the king shrugged, dismissing Aryseeth's aggression as if of no consequence. "Horses. Tin, Herbs and spices of our own."

"We have no need of your horses, nor tin." Now Aryseeth shrugged, letting Henry know that he too could be easily dismissed. "You have no herbs or spices that we do not already accept in trade from others."

King Henry leaned forward on the table. "Your tone suggests that you know exactly what it is your prince wishes."

The glance Aryseeth threw at Hugh before turning back to the king was filled with many things. Amusement. Impatience. And a hatred that no words could describe. Hugh clenched his teeth and willed the foreboding mist to stay at bay.

Aryseeth leaned back in his chair. "Men. Women."

King Henry choked. "My pardon?"

Hugh lurched to his feet. "Over my dead body."

"That can be arranged." Aryseeth's comment reverberated through the tent.

Henry immediately reached across the table and grasped Hugh's wrist in a death hold. "Sit down or leave."

Since leaving was not an option. Hugh bent his rigid knees and sat on the edge of the chair, ready to do battle if need be.

After relaxing his hold, King Henry turned back to Aryseeth. "Now that your humor has been displayed, may we speak seriously?"

Aryseeth threw back his head and laughed.

Henry pinned Hugh with a questioning look. Hugh was still in utter shock. He'd never before seen Aryseeth display any form of humor. If his request for human trade had been in jest, he had made a grievous mistake.

Aryseeth wiped his eyes. "I do apologize. I could not refrain from making an offer your people so obviously detest." He shook his head. "Wynnedom, it was worth it just to see the look on your face."

By gripping the arms of his chair, Hugh managed to control his fury at being the object of such a tasteless jest. He gave Aryseeth a tight smile. "I am glad I could provide you with such amusement." He felt, rather than saw, Henry's sharp glare. The king did not appreciate Hugh's use of sarcasm, however subtle.

Ever the tactician, King Henry drew the conversation back to this meeting's original intent. "Your offer of human trade is not as abhorrent to me as you may think."

Aryseeth did nothing more than raise one eyebrow before he slapped the table and called for wine. After the servant left, he lifted his goblet. "This wine is one thing you can trade." He took a long drink and set the vessel down. "I am certain there are many other items of worth. Shall we begin again?"

Hugh ran his fingers through his wet hair. After returning to the palace, he had requested a hot bath and a cask of wine. The bath had chased away the chills that seemed to have settled in his bones. The wine, which arrived in a small pitcher instead of a barrel-sized cask, had done little to soothe his ragged mind.

It had been a long day and he was glad it was over. Aryseeth was returning to England with King Henry to further discuss the trade and captive release agreement. A leisurely trip was planned, giving Hugh plenty of time to conclude his own business here at Poitiers before joining the men in England.

Exhausted from the tumultuous day, William had fallen into a deep sleep and could not be roused. Hugh had struggled to dump the beast onto the bed in their shared chamber. He glanced at the snoring man. One of them was sleeping on the floor this night and Hugh knew damn well it wasn't going to be him. Hopefully, it wouldn't prove too much of a task to roll William from the bed later.

After closing the door behind him, Hugh left the chamber and headed toward the great hall. Even though he had missed the evening meal, with luck he would still be able to catch Adrienna before she retired for the night.

Just this morning he'd vowed to court her. He didn't want her to think that he'd not meant that promise.

"Ah, but what—what constitutes being in love? How do you know for shertain—certain?"

Hugh paused as he entered the hall. The slurred question hung in the air waiting for an answer. None of those seated leisurely around the table seemed eager to respond to the query.

Not being able to resist the unwitting offer of amusement, and enlightenment, Hugh stepped forward. He leaned his hip against the table. "'Tis simple. It is the way your heart pounds when she walks by. Or the way a sigh captures your soul at just the sound of your name on her lips."

He hadn't seen her, but Adrienna's choked cough easily gave away her location. He walked toward that end of the table and continued, "It is when you lie awake at night thinking of no one but her. Or the way your pulse quickens at just the mere mention of her name."

Adrienna lowered her head, and her hair fell forward to cloak her face from view. He wondered what she was thinking.

"Ah, yes, milord Wynnedom, but those things also occur during moments of desire."

Hugh turned toward the speaker—a young man who appeared to have just recently left his mother's lap. Hugh lifted one eyebrow. This was too good to be true. These people had only their code of chivalrous love to argue with. He had a lifetime of entirely different thoughts on love and desire.

And enough experience to be more than armed for this argument.

He resumed his stroll around the table. "This is true. But there are many levels of desire. Some levels, such as the one you speak of, satisfy only the physical need."

Adrienna looked up. Hugh captured her curious gaze and held it as he continued, "But there is a level that only the soul can reach. Once two souls have attained that level of passion, that much shared desire, is it not…love?"

He paused beside Adrienna, reached beyond her to place a hand on the table and leaned forward. As if suddenly aware of the others eagerly staring at her end of the table, she leaned away from him.

"So, milord, are you implying that sex and love are the same thing?" Adrienna had finally found her voice.

He met her shimmering gaze, then answered her question. "No, not at all. Even the beasts of the fields rut with each other. There is no love required for that."

Adrienna's lips twitched. She fidgeted on her seat. He wasn't sure if she wanted to scream or curse. Either way, her blush was so becoming that he could do no more than patiently await whatever sallied forth.

"Then, exactly what are you saying? What makes the difference?" Adrienna gripped her wine goblet with trembling fingers.

Hugh moved away from her and leisurely circled the table while studying her face. He wondered if her teeth would shatter from the force of clenching them together. He also wondered how she spoke with her jaw held that tightly.

"The difference? Well, if I may be blunt."

Adrienna lifted her goblet toward him. "Oh, please, do."

Again, many questioning glances darted from her to him. But he could not have torn his gaze away from Adrienna had he wished to. He wanted to see the look on her face, he wanted to note the expressions, to see if, or when, they flitted from interest to anger.

While walking closer to her, Hugh answered, "There are times when a man, or a woman, contains a certain amount of tension. A nervousness that cannot be allayed by a walk in the gardens, or an engrossing conversation. But that tension can be relieved by a quick tumble with a willing partner."

A few twitters ran the length of the table. Adrienna

on the other hand was not amused. Her spine straightened. She lifted her chin and glared at him. "For a man that might be true."

To be honest, he had to agree with her. But what purpose would agreeing serve? "Well, yes, to an extent. Women have been known to satisfy their needs, too."

"Married women, maybe. It would be foolish for an unmarried woman to seek ruination in such a manner. Or would it be condoned in your estimation?"

Momentarily taken aback, Hugh wondered if she was threatening him. He pinned her with a steady look and asked, "Is that not why most women are married off at a young age? To prevent them from such foolishness?"

Adrienna rose. "So, it is permissible for a man to spread his seed wherever he may wish, whenever he feels the need. But it is foolish for a woman to risk her chastity because of the same need?" Emerald fire flashed from her eyes.

Hugh instantly realized he should have stopped while he was ahead. Now she was furious with him. Thankfully, he had a month to woo her. This was only the first day.

At his silence, she held her head even higher. She straightened her spine and marched determinedly toward the stairway.

The others at the table sought to apologize for her departure. Sarah flashed him a knowing smile. "This type of conversation takes place all the time."

"Oh, yes," added someone else.

A young lad nodded in agreement. "And every night someone leaves the discussion overwrought."

Hugh cared little for what they thought, or said. He quickly excused himself.

Chapter Five

Adrienna had no need to turn around to know whose fingers caught her wrist. The added heat setting her already overwrought body on fire let her know that Hugh had followed her. Worse, he had caught up with her before she reached the safety of her chamber.

"Adrienna, please wait."

She turned to face him in the torch light, unprepared for what the closeness of his body would do to her. Nothing in the world could have warned her that the sparks gleaming from his eyes would turn her knees weak. How could she have known that just the slightest smile upon his mouth would cause her heart to cease beating and then rapidly resume an erratic pounding?

Who could have told her that the feel of his warm, honey-mead-scented breath would cause her own to catch in her throat?

She placed her hands against his chest and pleaded,

"Go away, Hugh. Leave me be. Toy with me no more this night."

"What is wrong, wifeling?"

With a groan, Adrienna bit back the cry that threatened to leave her lips. *Wrong? Why nothing is wrong. 'Tis merely that I am on fire for you. 'Tis only that I am no longer in control of my body, or my mind. You have bewitched me with your sultry voice. Words that hint at passion and eyes that promise even more. Yet, no promise or even a hint of love leaves your lips.*

Instead, she shook her head. "Nothing. I am simply tired and wish to spar with you no further."

He ran his hands up her arms, and then across her shoulders. He stopped only when his fingers rested alongside her neck. "Adrienna, look at me."

Confused by the sensations his touch chased through her veins, she hesitated to do his bidding. When he threaded his fingers through her hair, she was unable to stop the tremors coursing up and down her limbs.

She stared into his molten gaze, wanting nothing more than to become lost in the liquid desire looking steadily back at her.

"Ah, there is something wrong."

"No, Hugh, nothing is wrong." When she shook her head in denial, he only smiled. His knowing look brought a flash of heat to her cheeks.

He stroked her sensitive skin with his thumb. "No?"

Slowly tracing a path to her ear, he grazed the soft, pale shell. A tremor raced beneath his touch. "Nothing is wrong?"

She stared at his mouth. His deep, seductive voice held her spellbound.

He ran the pad of his thumb along her jaw and at her sudden intake of breath, asked, "If nothing is wrong, why do you tremble beneath my touch?"

Instead of waiting for an answer he claimed her parted lips with his own. Adrienna clung to his shoulders as his warm silken touch caressed her tongue.

Hugh swept one arm down her back, pulling her closer. She wondered if the unsteady pounding against her chest came from her growing desire or his.

Not breaking his hold, or their kiss, he pressed her back against the wall. Adrienna's breath caught in her throat. Which was harder? The solid rock against her back or the hard length of his arousal pressing into her stomach?

He placed his hands against the wall on either side of her head and rested his forehead against hers. "I do not toy with you, Adrienna. Can you not tell that I want you as badly as you want me?"

If the hot throbbing against her stomach was any indication of his desire, then she did not doubt him for a moment. A thrill rushed up her spine at the idea that any man, that *this* man, wanted her and sent her heart aflutter.

Adrienna laced her fingers behind his neck and tried to bring his mouth back to hers. But he did nothing more than brush his lips across her own.

"Nay, wifeling. This is not the way to determine if we wish to remain wed."

Embarrassment at her forwardness chased away the

thrill of desire. She quickly lowered her arms and straightened her spine. "I am sorry, milord, forgive me."

Hugh grasped her chin, forcing her to look at him. "Forgive you? For what? Accepting kisses from your husband? You believe that act requires forgiveness?"

She glanced about the landing. "Stealing kisses in public is not an act of modesty."

"*Modesty*? After the conversation below, do you not think modesty a strange term?"

She could not disagree. Trapped as she was, between the wall behind her and the wall-like body before her, the word *modesty* sounded even more ridiculous. "You know what I meant."

"Adrienna." He breathed her name into her ear. She was unable to still the shivers it caused. "Forget modesty. Forget all that is right and proper. Forget all you think you have learned about desire and love."

After swallowing hard to find her tongue, she asked, "Then what should I not forget?"

Quickly grasping her hands and lacing his fingers through her own, he held them up against the wall. Adrienna frowned. In effect he had pinned her against the stone. A frisson of fear laced with an odd thrill shot through her.

She tugged, but could not break his hold. He had trapped her. Held in place by a strong bond of flesh and blood, she was at his mercy and wondered what he would do next. Before she could form a question about his actions, he shifted his body.

The hardness of his thigh slipping between hers

changed her question to a gasp of surprise. All at once her breasts seemed to swell, her face flamed with heat, her knees turned useless, and she throbbed hot and heavy against his leg.

"Look at me."

She heard his hoarse voice as if through a hazy fog. It came from somewhere above. Able to do little more than turn a misty gaze in that direction, she looked up.

This time when he claimed her mouth it was not with a soft or gentle kiss. This caress was hard, hot and demanding.

She strained against the human bonds holding her to the wall and leaned into him. The movement brought his thigh harder against her. Adrienna did not fight the moan that came from deep inside. She let it escape. Hugh captured it with one of his own before taking a step back from her.

When he released her hands they fell boneless to her side. The night breeze rushed between them. Like a bucket of ice water it raced shockingly cold across her heated body.

"That is what I want you not to forget."

Adrienna fought to catch her breath, trying to absorb his words. She struggled to regain a measure of composure before asking, "What?" Her voice trembled in her ears. "That you can easily turn my thoughts to lust? That I am so weak and easily led that I lose all notion of what is right or wrong?"

He leaned forward and placed a chaste kiss on her cheek. "You did nothing wrong. I care not if you forget or remember thoughts of lust. Just do not come to my bed with only those thoughts on your mind."

She shook her head, seeking to find a tiny grain of self-control. She straightened her spine and lifted her chin. "Lust, sex, what difference would it make when the end result would be the same."

He didn't answer, but his rumbling laugh teased her ears and settled lightly upon her heart. She cocked an eyebrow at him and asked, "Should I ever decide to come to your bed, what would you like me to have on my mind?"

Hugh moved closer and narrowed his eyes. In a deep husky voice, he whispered, "Desire. A burning need to set your soul afire."

Set her soul afire?

Adrienna sucked in a deep breath and felt her nostrils flare with the thought of coming to Hugh's bed on fire. She rested her hands against his chest for support. Would it be possible to burn for him any more than she already did? How?

Was he right? Could it truly be possible that love and desire were not different, or separate? She shook her head, trying to clear the questions from her mind. If she freely gave him the passion he so wanted from her, would they then find love?

The rapid, strong pulse thumping beneath her palm made her weak with longing.

He smelled of pure masculinity. The scent of male laced with desire emanated from him. It wafted around her, swirling across her cheeks, gently brushing her flesh before fanning the still hot embers into another raging fire.

His eyes, so dark and liquid, studied her intently. Twin stars shimmered from their depths. Not a trace of amusement crossed his features. Not a hint of censure flickered from his gaze.

She'd no idea how he'd accomplished so much in so little time. Oh, yes, she wanted him. Yes, she desired him. At this moment her body would settle for sex, for pure, raw lust, and worry about all else later.

Surely the feel of his hands caressing her overheated skin would ease the insistent thrumming that caused her muscles to quiver and her stomach to tighten.

Adrienna did not expect his touch would be gentle. With a certainty she knew his hands would be strong and sure upon her. He would demand a response and she would answer—willingly and without fear.

The mere thought of him commanding her body, guiding her desire, took her breath away.

"Adrienna." His deep voice was strained, his brow furrowed. "If you do not go now, you will lose all chance of winning your annulment."

"I do not care." Her words, a breathless hush, surprised her.

"Ah, but on the morn you will care a great deal."

Briefly locking her gaze on his smoldering stare, she leaned against him and slid her hands up the expanse of his chest, over the breadth of his shoulders. She threaded her fingers through his hair. "We can worry about the morn when it arrives."

His low groan echoed the frustration she felt. He buried his face in her hair, trailing searing kisses down the length of her neck.

Yes. This is what she wanted. What she'd sought for so many long years. Adrienna melted into his tight embrace, shutting out the tiny part of her brain that whispered a final warning. The hot blood rushing through her limbs was louder, silencing her mind's cry.

She wanted more than just the feel of his lips on her flesh. "Hugh, please."

He swallowed her plea by slanting his mouth over hers. And for the endless space of moments she was lost to the wonder of his lips, his tongue and his branding kiss.

Then Hugh jerked away from her as if unseen hands suddenly pulled the two of them apart. He lifted shaking fingers to his deeply furrowed brow. "Go away, Adrienna. Go before it is too late."

His voice, ragged and hoarse, frightened her. More than desire laced his tone. Something deeper, colder, near menacing tinged his words. It sparked through the passion and reminded her of how little she knew about this man. The flame that had shimmered in his eyes flickered and died. In its place glimmered a coldness that seemed to come from his soul.

To ward off the sudden chill seeping into her, Adrienna wrapped her arms about her waist. "Hugh?"

He turned from her, then ordered, "Go."

Hugh heard her quick intake of breath as it hissed between her parted lips. He listened silently as each footstep took her away from him. Away from the sudden surge of anger that swallowed his lust and turned his thoughts of desire into revenge.

To seek relief from the pounding behind his eyes, he tightly pressed the bridge of his nose. Wasn't that why he was here? To teach her passion? To show her what love could be? To take her virginity and lay the world at her feet? To touch her heart? To caress her soul? And then tear it all away?

He leaned his forearm against the wall and rested his head on his wrist. He fought to regain control, and his chest heaved with the exertion to breathe. What was wrong with him? He had nearly thrown away all his well-planned revenge.

Lust he could understand, but when had passion and desire entered the arena? Why did thoughts of revenge cause him pain? What was this sudden self-loathing?

The lurching of his stomach brought him a small measure of peace. Perhaps his contrary emotions were due to that pitcher of wine he'd imbibed before venturing below stairs.

As he wearily headed toward his chamber and his bed, Hugh prayed it was nothing more than alcohol that sought to tear his mind asunder.

"Milord! Lord Wynnedom!"

Hugh rolled over with a groan and parted the curtains surrounding his bed. He winced at the sunlight streaming across the chamber. His stomach rolled. His head throbbed. Every part of his body vigorously reminded him of the honey- and herb-laced wine he'd so easily poured down his throat last night.

Another groan echoed up from the floor. Slowly and with great care, William sat up and held his head. "Please, kill me. Use my sword."

If Hugh didn't so share in the wish for death, he would have laughed. Instead, he released the curtains, letting them shut out the harsh light of day.

Encased in the cavelike bed, he cursed his stupidity. After returning to this chamber last night he'd rolled William from the bed and finished the last of the wine alone. Some evil imp living deep inside his being had convinced him that solace could be found at the bottom of the pitcher.

Obviously a lie. One he would not listen to again.

"Milord Wynnedom!"

Both men again groaned at the loud pounding on the chamber door. It was an obnoxious sound that did not show any signs of ceasing. Hugh called out, "Enter."

After jerking the curtains apart, Hugh blinked to clear the fog from his eyes before directing his muddled stare to a ruddy-faced young page. "What do you want?"

The boy straightened his slight shoulders, bringing him to an immense height of maybe four feet. He looked down his upturned nose, then announced, "The queen requests your presence."

Requests? Hugh again dropped the curtains back into place. At least she hadn't ordered his attendance. He was in no mood to converse with anyone at the moment. "Tell her I will be there as soon as I rise."

"Milord, she said to tell you to attend her now."

Hugh ripped the curtains open with enough force to tear them from the frame. The stone floor was cold against his feet. The morning air rushed across his naked body, bringing with it a strange comfort.

He rose, took one step toward the now pale, trembling lad and asked, "Now? Immediately?"

The stuttering page backed toward the door. "Milord, I think it would be appropriate for you to dress first."

Before Hugh could say anything in reply, the boy raced to the door, pausing long enough to stammer, "I— I will tell her that you—you will be along—soon."

Of all the days to be summoned before Queen Eleanor why this one? Hugh rolled his eyes at his own question. The answer was simple. Because he was at his absolute worst.

While striding purposefully toward the royal chambers, he knew the scowl on his face would keep all others from approaching him.

"Milord Wynnedom."

Hugh sighed. He thought his dark looks would keep all away. He glanced at the blonde by his side, trying to remember her name. "Ah, good morning, Lady…Sarah, is it?"

She lowered her eyes and blushed. "Oh, milord, it is far past morning, but I am gladdened that you remember my name."

He didn't admit to her that her first name was all he remembered. He lifted her hand briefly to his lips and stared into her icy blue eyes. "How could I forget one so lovely as you?"

The woman simpered before him. She fluttered her overlong eyelashes, placed her free hand against his chest and she playfully pushed at him. "Milord, you honor me with your praise."

As if she didn't think she was lovely. He shrugged. "Nay, I speak only what everyone present knows is the truth."

Lady Sarah glanced about before she boldly met his gaze and smiled. "You go to meet with the queen?"

Hugh nodded.

She tipped her head a little to the side. "And afterward?"

He found her obvious ploy for his attention amusing. "I have no plans for this day."

She drew her hand down his chest, stopping only when her fingertips met the leather of his belt. Very slowly, she ran the tip of her tongue across her lower lip. "Perhaps I can think of a way to entertain you."

This woman was more than just bold. She offered herself quite easily and with no shame. In the few days he'd been here, he had watched Lady Sarah track men like a hawk circling its prey. She wasn't here for entertainment. She was trailing for a husband and had added him to her list of possibilities.

Hugh smiled at her blatant suggestion, he then sighed in mock frustration. "First, I must attend the queen."

As if on cue the antechamber door opened and a guard beckoned, "Lord Wynnedom."

Sarah quickly stepped away. "You must go. Shall I await you?"

Hugh shook his head. "Nay, I will find you later."

He watched her walk away, wondering why her proposition held so little interest. Without another thought he set aside his wondering and entered the queen's lair.

"Ah, Milord Wynnedom, so good of you to join us."

He bowed low, paying his respect to the queen. "I apologize for my delay."

Her sharp glance trailed quickly down his body, before returning to his face. "Would you care for a chalice of wine?"

Aye, he did look as bad as he felt. "Nay, thank you, I require nothing."

Queen Eleanor's lips twitched as she waved toward an empty seat. Hugh was thrilled to know he could so amuse her. After resting heavily against the back of his chair, he glanced across the ornate chamber and caught a glimpse of Adrienna's pale features.

"Milord Wynnedom, you seem to have caused quite a stir."

He forced his gaze back to the queen. "My pardon?"

Her eyebrows rose. "Were you so intoxicated last evening that you do not remember the conversation you directed in my hall?"

He swallowed his groan. "Nay, I mean, yes." Hugh cleared his throat and tried again. "No, I was not completely out of my wits. Yes, I remember joining the conversation."

"Tell me, Lord Wynnedom, from where do you obtain your strange ideas?"

He resisted the urge to leave. This was not a conversation he wished to hold with the queen. "Of which ideas do you speak?"

She tapped her nails on the arm of her chair and pursed her lips. "What is love?"

"The meeting of two hearts." He did not add that it was the meshing of two souls. Or that love was the uniting of two separate paths.

Eleanor leaned forward. "And what part does desire play in love?"

"'Tis the physical expression of love."

"But this physical expression, as you call it, should only occur between two parties who are married to each other." When he did not reply, the queen prompted, "Do you not agree?"

Hugh fought to control his thoughts. He was unable to fathom what the queen was after. Instead of arguing, he nodded. "Yes, I agree."

"But love and marriage do not necessarily go hand in hand. So where does this lustful desire fit in?"

He closed his eyes against the dull throb in his temples. "Sometimes familiarity leads to love. Sometimes the sharing of desires helps the seeds of love to sprout."

"What about you, Lord Wynnedom. Will familiarity in your marriage lead to love? Or will it be desire that causes love to bloom?"

His eyes flew open. It was all he could do not to direct

his shocked gaze toward Adrienna. She knew. Somehow the queen had discovered their secret.

The queen leaned back against her own chair before waving toward the door. "All of you may leave."

When Hugh rose, she said, "Oh, not you, Lord Wynnedom."

Reluctantly sitting back down, he watched Adrienna leave the chamber. She held her back stiff, shoulders squared and head high. Yet, the paleness of her complexion gave lie to her show of confidence. Had Queen Eleanor already cornered Adrienna? If so, what had his wifeling said?

When the last person left the chamber, Eleanor rose and shoved a goblet into his hand. "Drink. You will need this."

Chapter Six

The silence in the queen's chamber was deafening. A strong, steady tempo pounded loudly against his chest, before echoing in his ears. And it grew louder with each passing beat.

He wanted to come right out and ask her what she knew. But a sudden flash of wisdom kept his lips sealed. In this case perhaps saying nothing would be best.

Though if Queen Eleanor didn't stop pacing the floor and get on with it, Hugh was afraid all of his wisdom would desert him.

Finally, to his relief, she took her seat and pinned him with a glare that boded nothing good.

"Milord Wynnedom, there were strangers on my land this past day."

She hadn't asked a question, so he remained silent.

"And my husband was with them."

Being seen by any of the queen's men was a possibility Hugh knew existed, but King Henry had waved it away as unimportant.

"And so were you."

He wondered how long it would take her to get to the point.

"I understand you know these strangers."

Mentally, he groaned. Who was providing her information? Henry had sworn to say nothing, and Hugh did not think the king would break his vow. So, who else knew about his past?

Only the three men whose freedom he had fought for and won. William? Nay. He would die before betraying a trust. Guy? Nay. Guy had no reason to carry tales to the queen. Besides, he had his own responsibilities to attend to at the moment and had not the time, nor the opportunity. That left Stefan.

Since the man had proven himself untrustworthy on more than one occasion, his involvement now wouldn't be a surprise. Had it been Hugh's choice alone, Stefan would have remained in captivity. But the plan to rescue the remaining English captives rested on the success of any trade negotiations he could bring to fruition between King Henry and Sidatha's house.

Left behind, Stefan would seek to thwart those plans regardless of the cost. Guy and William had made him see the wisdom in keeping the enemy—Stefan of Arnyll—close. However, Stefan was supposed to be assisting Guy.

Eleanor picked up a stemmed goblet, twirled it between her slender fingers and seemingly studied it intently. "Have you nothing to say?"

He kept his voice steady, reminding himself whom he addressed. "What would you have me say, milady? That your spies are mistaken? That you do not know what happens on your own land?"

She leaned forward. "You may tell me what took place inside the tent of these strangers."

Hugh shook his head at her imperious order. "Pray forgive me, but you will need to speak to King Henry about that. I am not at liberty to discuss his business."

To his amazement, she did not rail at his lack of cooperation. Instead, she leaned back in her seat. "Then explain your presence to me. Lord Wynnedom did not exist before last year. From where do you hail?"

"Out of the country."

"Where?"

"Many places."

Eleanor repeatedly tapped one fingernail on the oak arm of her chair. A steady *click, click, click* that set his nerves on edge. "Do you have a wife?"

Queen Eleanor would not gain her information that easily. He resisted the urge to sigh in exasperation. Even had Stefan supplied the queen with her facts, he knew nothing of Adrienna, so perhaps he was not the spy. Hugh fixed her with his blankest look. "Wife?"

"Come now, Wynnedom, surely you are married."

"Am I, milady? I have been so consumed by King Henry's business that I forget."

"The information is easily checked."

Which meant she had not done so yet. He still had time in which to complete his seduction of Adrienna. "Then by all means, feel free to investigate."

She slammed her goblet down on the side table so hard the wine sloshed over the edge. "This is becoming quite tedious, Lord Wynnedom."

"Then why do you not just tell me what you are seeking?"

"I am seeking to rid my court of you."

Well, he had to give her credit for honesty. "And why is that?"

"Because, Hugh of Wynnedom, you come in here full of dark good looks, a bold tongue and set young women all aflutter."

This time he couldn't contain his surprise. "My pardon?"

"You heard me the first time. I will not fill your head with empty praise."

"Milady, what worries you?"

"It is hard to make a good match when one's belly is filled with another man's child."

He blinked. Honest and blunt. She was slowly gaining respect in his eyes. "I am not in the habit of begetting children. Nor am I in the habit of seducing maidens."

"It is not the maidens I worry about. They fear you. I am concerned about the women here who know something of what you offer."

"I offer nothing."

She threw back her head and laughed. A rich, hearty

sound that for some unknown reason set him on edge. She shook her head. "Horse dung, Wynnedom."

The queen was making fabrications out of thin air. He sought to entice no one to his bed, except his wife. He had never set about to seduce anyone in Eleanor's court. "Milady, I—"

She cut him off with a wave of her hand. "So there is no opportunity for misunderstanding, I will make myself clear. Leave Adrienna of Hallison alone, Lord Wynnedom. I have other plans for her."

Hugh clenched his fingers around the arms of his chair and swallowed back his sudden rage. She had other plans for Adrienna? Plans that did not include him? He shifted slightly in his seat while he mentally gathered the reins of his control. "Is the lady in question aware of these plans?"

"Not as yet. But things were progressing nicely until you arrived. It has been a little difficult for Langsford to continue his suit when you monopolize her time."

Langsford? The name was familiar. It took a few turns around his mind searching before he put the name with a face. It was her suitor, out by the pond. Richard. The one who'd asked Adrienna to marry him.

"This Langsford and Lady Hallison make a good match?"

"Yes. Their lands adjoin and her father is not adverse to having Langsford as a son-by-marriage."

He wanted to snort. Hallison would not be averse to having anyone as a son—as long as the man had enough gold or land. "So, this match is set then?"

"Nearly. There is the matter of her acceptance and the betrothal announcement."

Unable to contain his curiosity, he asked, "What is your interest in this match?"

She narrowed her eyes and resumed tapping her nails on the chair. "Hallison and Langsford combined are a sizable fief."

He knew then what her interest was. Without asking any further questions, Hugh knew where Langsford's loyalties lay. There was no doubt in his mind that Sir Langsford would be more loyal to Eleanor than to King Henry.

"But you need not concern yourself with this matter, Lord Wynnedom." She waved one hand in obvious dismissal.

Hugh had enough problems to sort out with Adrienna. He wanted no part of this ploy to gain support against King Henry in favor of Eleanor and her whelp. Rising, he bowed. "Milady, I wish you well with your matchmaking."

"Keep away from her, Wynnedom, or you will be removed from this court."

Wisely, he kept his thoughts to himself as he headed toward the door of the chamber.

Eleanor offered a final suggestion. "Go home, Wynnedom, and save yourself a measure of grief."

He had every intention of going home—with his wife. He had no choice but to quicken his plans for Adrienna's seduction. The sooner he enticed her to his bed the better.

* * *

The din of so many people gathered for the night's entertainment echoed from one end of the hall to the other. The chatter of countless conversations and the pipers' music raced past Hugh's ears as little more than noise.

His attention had been focused on finding Adrienna from the first moment he stepped into the room. He'd not seen her since she'd been ordered from the queen's chamber with the rest. His welcome at Poitiers was growing thin. He needed to quicken his seduction of Adrienna before Queen Eleanor withdrew her already strained good graces.

Any fool knew that it would not take much investigation on her behalf to fill her in on his background.

And he wished to be gone before she fitted all the pieces together.

A flash of spring caught his attention. In this chamber of overdressed peacocks, the plain green gown unfettered with jewels or needlework was a refreshing sight. He lifted his gaze to the woman's hair and realized he'd found his wife. Who else would use wildflowers as adornment when a myriad other, more flamboyant flowers were at hand?

Quickly checking for the queen's whereabouts, Hugh was relieved to find Eleanor and her daughter, the Countess Marie, absent. From now on, he would have to be very careful, very discreet, when either of the women were present.

Steadily winding his way through the throng, Hugh approached Adrienna. When he stopped behind her the woman she'd been talking to took her leave.

Without turning around, Adrienna asked, "What did the queen say?"

While he was flattered that she knew it was him without looking, his curiosity got the better of him. "How do you know to whom you are speaking?"

She glanced over her shoulder. "My friend Elise warned me of your approach."

Hugh placed a hand over his chest and closed his eyes. "I am mortally wounded, milady. I thought perchance you sensed my nearness."

She turned to face him. "Do not let your pride bleed to death on the queen's floor."

"It may happen." He raised one mocking eyebrow. "Unless you care to tend my wounds somewhere more…private."

"I would be happy to wound you somewhere more private."

"Ah, Adrienna, were you to wound me in such a manner, you would suffer as much as I."

She rolled her eyes toward the ceiling. "Have you always suffered from this affliction, milord?"

"And what affliction is that?"

"A swelled head. A massive amount of pride. An overblown opinion of yourself. These are afflictions you know well."

"And what can one do about them? Is there a cure?"

She studied him intently and then shook her head. "Alas, for you I think it is too late. You will very likely die of this ailment."

He fought the urge to smile. "Milady has a bold tongue when there are others about."

Adrienna shrugged. "Milord, were you of the mind to, you would drag me from here regardless of how many people were about."

"Then what gives you the bravado to spar with me this night?"

She fixed him with an unflinching stare before answering, "'Tis simple. You do not have that look in your eyes."

Hugh frowned in confusion. "That look? What look?" When a light shade of pink raced to cover her cheeks, he smiled. "Ah, *that* look."

She bit her lower lip and dropped her gaze. "I—"

He placed a finger over her lips. "Do not say it. If you apologize I swear, Adrienna, I will kiss you senseless right here in this crowded hall."

He felt her lips twitch beneath his finger. "See, there is your pride again, milord. I was not going to apologize." Each word landed softly, like a kiss against his fingertip.

"Then what were you going to say?" He ran a finger across her lip and felt her tremble, before taking his hand away. He wished they were alone so he could run his tongue across the softness of her mouth and taste the shiver as it raced to meet his own.

"I was going to say that I rather liked it when your eyes were not filled with lust."

"Too late."

When she raised her head, she took his breath away with a hot, shimmering glance. "I see."

"I am afraid, milady, that it will be a lifetime before I am no longer filled with lust for you."

"Not so long, milord."

"You have a cure for this condition also?"

"Aye."

When she did not finish her recipe for his cure, he prompted, "And what would it be?"

Adrienna turned her profile to him. "Your lust will disappear the instant you leave here…alone."

A smile curved one side of his mouth. He shook his head. "You still think you will win?"

"I know I will."

Moments ago she had chided him about pride and self-confidence. Yet, here she stood, a smug smile fixed across her mouth, boldly declaring her win. Her own self-confidence in this matter amused him. "You know nothing."

Her eyebrows rose. "I am surprised you do not choke to death on your own self-worth."

Self-worth. What was he worth? There was a time, not so long ago, that his very life had been worth nothing. It had amounted to even less than a grain of sand from the desert. He doubted if it was worth much more today.

He swallowed back the sudden dryness building in his throat. "I cannot choke to death on something that has already been stripped from my being."

She slanted an odd look at him and frowned. "Hugh?"

His name, issued as a question, hung in the air between them. He would offer no explanation for a question she did not ask.

"What did the queen say?" She changed the thread of their conversation.

Glad to put the threatening thoughts back inside the mist that had given them form, he answered, "She thinks I should return home and wants to know if I am wed."

Adrienna gasped.

"Fear not. I provided her with nothing useful. She knows not if I am or am not married."

"That will not take much to discover."

"I know."

"We cannot talk here." She glanced quickly about the hall. "A stroll in the garden perhaps?"

He shook his head. "No. It has been suggested that I spend less time in your company."

"Why?"

"So that I do not ruin your chances for a favorable match."

Adrienna folded her hands before her, gripping them so tightly that her knuckles turned white. "She knows."

"Nay." He reached out and gently sought to pry her fingers apart. "But if you insist on acting overwrought each time I am near, she will begin to wonder."

"I am not overwrought."

"Then relax your grip," he teased.

Instantly she dropped her arms to her sides. "How can you jest about this?"

"I am not jesting. The queen will be on alert at all times. She will have her spies watch my every move." He pierced her with a hard stare. "We do not have a month, Adrienna."

Her eyes widened. "But you said—"

"If she finds out before our month is up, the game is over. You know that."

He watched the bravado seep from her body. Her shoulders sagged. The shimmer in her eyes dulled. Furrows creased her brow. "I now realize she will be too angry at what appears to be a deception, to ever let the annulment happen."

He couldn't argue with her. Queen Eleanor would be furious to discover that the two of them had made this type of bargain with each other. She would be angrier to have her own plans thwarted in such a manner. "In all likelihood you are right."

"Then why do we not just get it over with?"

Hugh marveled at the sharpness of the stab running through his chest. "Get it over with? Like having a tooth pulled, or a limb cut off?"

No emotion, no feeling. Simply performing a physical act no different from any other bodily function was not in his plans. He didn't just want her body. He wanted her heart and soul, and he knew full well that she wasn't yet ready to give him those things.

"Yes. Just end this charade. Let us go up to your chamber and validate this marriage."

She said it so calmly—as if they were discussing the color of her gown. His first impulse was to throttle her. His next one was to walk away and just keep walking. Instead, he ignored both impulses. He would have all or nothing from her. "Oh, Adrienna, your sweet talk leaves me longing for more. I cannot think of any other words that would entice me into your bed more quickly."

Her fierce glare threatened to lace him. "You know what I meant."

"Oh, yes, I do and it offends me."

"Offends you?" Her voice rose.

"Keep your voice down. I do not want the entire hall to join in this conversation."

"Fine." Her voice was little more than a seething whisper. "What exactly offends you? How dare you be offended? You were not the one left to live a lie for half the years of your life. You were not the one forced to come here to make another *good* match. Do not talk to me of—"

She stopped her tirade the instant he grabbed her arm. "I am offended at the suggestion of swiving this marriage into existence." Releasing her, he gritted his teeth against the anger boiling in his chest. "And never, ever again talk to me of years lost."

Her eyes flashed, but when she opened her mouth only a soft curse issued forth. Instantly following her gaze, Hugh's curse joined hers.

Quickly, before their company could join them, he warned, "Our bargain is still valid and you *will* come to my bed on fire."

"Why you—"

"Lady Adrienna, how are you this fine evening?"

She turned a look of pure irritation on Langsford. Hugh studied the other man. This was the suitor the queen thought would make an appropriate match for Adrienna? Right now, he was of the mind to agree, only because it would serve his wifeling right to be burdened with Langsford. After forming as much of a smile as he could muster, he bid them a good evening before walking away.

Chapter Seven

Adrienna watched Hugh's retreating form and wished for a tiny crossbow. Something small that would fit in the palm of her hand. She could aim for his back, release an arrow and none would be the wiser. Except for Hugh. How dare he walk away?

"Lady Adrienna, would you care for a turn about the gardens?"

Startled out of her depraved daydream, she dragged her attention to Richard. "Nay, milord, it has been a tiring day."

Her exhaustion wasn't feigned. It had been tiring to pace her chamber, waiting for word from Hugh. And when he had not sent her any message, she'd spent the rest of the afternoon and evening anxiously waiting for him to grace the Great Hall with his presence. Where had he been all day?

"Perhaps a seat by the fire?"

How did Hugh expect them to still continue with

this bargain? Not that he would win, but the thrill of the chase was exhilarating. She'd never felt this alive, this eager to face a day. And she'd never felt this desired before.

Nor had she ever been this confused. On one hand she wanted nothing more than to tumble into his bed and end this uncertainty.

But on the other hand something about Hugh made her uncomfortable. His moods changed too fast. At times he looked at her with hatred in his eyes. Yet, before she could discern his true emotion, the look would disappear, as if it'd never existed.

Adrienna frowned. She detested her confusion, but knew not how to make it go away.

"Adrienna, would you prefer to be left alone?" Richard's clipped tone shouted his impatience.

She set her thoughts of Hugh aside and gazed up at Richard's frowning countenance. He was so pale compared to Hugh. One bold, dark and irritating. The other so formal, light and eager to please. And which did she prefer? An image of her husband's face teased her mind. *Cease!*

"Milady?"

Mentally shaking herself, Adrienna motioned toward the fire. "Yes, Richard, a seat by the fire would be welcome."

She sat with her back to the warmth of the flames, allowing her to have a full view of the gathering. And to watch her husband. He had not left the hall. Instead, he was currently engrossed in what seemed to be an entertaining conversation with Lady Sarah. A sight that caused an odd, foul-tasting anger to build in her throat.

"Where are you, milady?"

She focused her attention on Richard, leaving the bothersome sight of Hugh and Lady Sarah behind. "Here. I am here."

He shook his head, sadly. "Nay. You are across the hall, lost to the thought of Lord Wynnedom."

Her cheeks blazed. Had she been that obvious? "I know not what to say."

Richard's hand on her arm was warm. His breath on her cheek even warmer. "Say nothing, Adrienna. Instead, shower me with the looks you reserve only for him."

Why did Richard's touch not set her blood to race? Why had she no desire to lean closer, to feel more than just his breath upon her face? Richard was kind. He was amusing and entertaining. He would never threaten her with lust or desire. Never tempt her beyond her control.

So unlike Hugh, whose mere smile beckoned her to taste the heady elixir of desire. Hugh, whose slightest touch sent shimmering sparks of fire rushing through her veins. Hugh, whose silky words of challenge invited her to follow a treacherous path fraught with danger.

Richard was safe, he would prove a good husband.

Hugh was dangerous. He would bring her nothing but grief.

And Richard was beside her now while Hugh flirted with another. Until this moment, she'd never been at a loss for words with Richard. She dropped her gaze to the table and contemplated lying.

Richard stroked her cheek with the back of his hand. He whispered, "Adrienna, he will use you and leave. Do you not realize this? Your handsome, bold warrior is not dangling for a wife. He is looking for nothing more than a brief respite before setting out on another adventure."

He was wrong. Hugh *was* dangling for a wife—his own. But she couldn't very well tell Richard that. She met his intent gaze and asked, "How do you come to deduce these things?"

"'Tis simple. When he looks at you there is no love in his gaze. Only lust. Only desire." He ran a knuckle across her lips. "I can promise you more than that."

His touch made her lips itch. She resisted the urge to drag her teeth across the irritation. "More than that?"

He stroked the line of her jaw. No sparks, no tremble of passion followed his caress. It evoked no more emotion than a parent's touch.

"Much more. I want to take care of you. To see your every need is met. To protect you from those like Wynnedom."

At first she thought he was jesting. What he described sounded more like a father, not a lover nor a husband. But the seriousness of his tone and the clearness of his gaze told her that he was earnest. "I do not need protecting."

"Yes, you do. You need someone who will worship at your feet. Someone who will give you a place of honor and respect."

His beseeching gaze begged her to believe his words. His eyes were clear, allowing her to see into his very soul.

Something she'd never glimpsed staring into Hugh's eyes. There she saw only mystery and shuttered darkness.

"Adrienna, *I* can do that. I will treat you like an angel."

Her breath caught in her throat. Did she wish to be treated like an angel? To have a man worship at her feet? Would it not be better to have someone who would cater to her, someone she could trust? Someone who would not leave her on their wedding night? Would it not be wiser to follow this, the safer path?

Or did she want someone who could make her forget herself? Make her forget control and respectability. Someone who was not afraid to trap her against a wall with his hard body and kiss her until her knees grew weak and her senses melted. Someone whose slightest touch made her breasts tingle and created hot flames to burn between her legs. Someone who could make her ache for more than kisses.

She swallowed hard against the thoughts that made her mouth dry. Dear Lord above, what was wrong with her? Heat raced across her cheeks. She was thinking like a harlot. A brazen whore with only one thought on her mind.

"Adrienna, marry me." Richard grasped her chin. "Let me show you what a wonderful union we can create." He leaned closer, his lips only a hair away from hers. "I can make you forget him."

Forget Hugh? Never. Not even after he left here, no longer married to her, would she be able to forget Hugh. His dark, brooding frown, his one-sided smile, his passion-laden eyes and his full lower lip would always be in her memory. These things were already as much a part of her as was his touch and his deep, silken voice. She bit her lip, fighting the sudden urge to cry.

Richard pressed a brief, gentle kiss against her mouth before resting his forehead against hers. "Ah, sweeting, I will make you forget."

Hugh stared across the room. He fought the growl building in his chest. And he fought the insane urge to murder Richard of Langsford. If that sniveling court lackey did not get his hands off Adrienna, he would have to die. It was that simple.

"Milord Wynnedom, do you not find it rather warm in here?"

And his death would not be quick or painless. Nay. Hugh would draw it out and make the man suffer the flames of hell.

"Milord Wynnedom?"

He would stake Langsford out in the desert and knick his naked, quivering flesh just enough to draw blood. The sun would bake the man's skin and the smell of dried blood would garner the vultures' attention.

"Lord Wynnedom!"

The sharpness of Lady Sarah's voice startled him out of his growing rage. "My pardon?"

She placed a hand on his arm. "Is it not rather warm in here?"

Why did this woman always find it necessary to touch him? He did not want her touch. He did not welcome her easy familiarity. "Warm? Nay." Seeking to distract her, he nodded toward a group of jugglers. "Let us sit a spell."

The glower on her face was more telling than words. Her eyes flashed like blue ice. Her pouting lips thinned. She removed her hand from his arm. In less than a blink the irritation faded from her face. A pleading half smile turned up the corner of her mouth. She drew the back of her hand across her forehead. "Milord, I am faint and in need of fresh air."

Her plaintive tone sent a chill down his spine. Hugh paused in thought. What was wrong with him? He looked down at the woman by his side. She was everything the troubadours sang praises of—petite, blond and occasionally soft of voice.

Yet, he stood here like a calf-eyed youth panting after one who wanted him not. Where was his control? When had he lost possession of his will? He had fueled his thirst for revenge daily, for many long years. Where was that thirst now?

He stared across the chamber at Adrienna. She and Langsford sat with their foreheads together, like a pair of lovebirds. Every now and then one of them would shoot a quick glance at him before returning to their conversation. Why? Was he the object of their discourse?

Like a vulture perched on his chest, stabbing away at flesh and muscle, their intimate touches, their seemingly easy manner ate at him. Did the flush on her cheeks rise from embarrassment at the intimacies she allowed Langsford? Or was Langsford making her burn with desire? The way Hugh wanted her to burn for him alone? His temples throbbed.

"It will do no good."

Hugh shook himself from his self-torture and looked at Lady Sarah. "What will do no good?"

She nodded her head toward Adrienna. "She is taken, milord. You will not win her hand."

He wanted to kick himself for being so obvious. "So I have been told."

Lady Sarah tilted her head to one side and smiled up at him. "And, she is not the type of woman you should seek to dally with."

He raised one eyebrow. "What type of woman should I seek?"

Lightly placing her hand on his arm, she stepped closer. The skirt of her gown brushed against his thigh. "One who knows what a man desires."

Hugh's gaze skittered back to Adrienna. What kind of promises was she making to Langsford? Did Adrienna know what a man desired? Was she as brazen as the woman clinging to his own arm?

"Lord Wynnedom, I would enjoy a walk in the gardens."

The throbbing in his temples became a dull ache at Lady Sarah's words. Perhaps a brief respite from watching Adrienna and Langsford might help ease the pain.

"I hear that the moonlight is beautiful this night, milord. Someone mentioned countless stars."

With one final glance toward Adrienna, Hugh offered Sarah his arm. As he guided the woman from the hall, he felt a sharp stab at his back. Without turning around he knew that Adrienna's glare had sallied forth to pierce him. Surprised that she noticed anything except Langsford, Hugh was amazed at the sharpness of her response.

The chilled night air helped to cool the anger that had heated his blood. Without the rage, he was better able to think. Since Lady Sarah's endless chatter required little more than an occasional nod, Hugh sought an explanation for his error.

He had planned this quest step by step. Employing all he knew about the rules of courtship, he had been certain that he'd not lose sight of the goal. He wanted revenge, not a marriage. He wanted Adrienna to become dazed by passion and lust. He needed her to be so filled with desire for him that she'd offer her soul freely. A gift he would take and destroy.

His desires were supposed to remain unaffected. So where had he gone wrong?

They'd had the proper introduction. Queen Eleanor herself had arranged that for him.

He'd showered her with attention and gifted her with flowers. Granted they'd been wildflowers, but he'd gathered them himself every morning and deposited them at her chamber door. Surely, since those were the floras she'd worn in her hair on their wedding day, she knew they came from him.

He'd openly spoken of passion and love. So she knew his intentions.

Even though it'd been difficult at first, he'd always looked directly into her gaze, letting her see how much he desired her.

Obviously, by her response last night, he'd succeeded in building her desire to a fevered pitch.

She'd returned his kisses with fiery ones of her own. She'd melded her soft curves against him. When he'd gone a step too far and pinned her against the wall, she'd sought more.

He'd been given many lessons on courtship and passion during his long captivity. Many of the other captives had been from the heathen east and he'd been introduced to ideas and methods that he'd never have learned elsewhere. What had he missed?

Passion was a sensual activity. To fully enjoy the experience, all of the senses required attention. Smell—the flowers. Sight—the eye contact. Sound—his words. Touch—his hands upon her face. Taste—his kiss.

Somewhere along the way he'd permitted himself to also fall under the sensual spell. How would he break it?

Perhaps he was looking too deeply. Did he truly need to break the spell? Once he took this game to a new level would he not then be back in control? Once he won their bargain, he would have the leisure to teach Adrienna how to make love with more than just her body. He would entice her soul to join with his. He would show her a pleasure few enjoyed. Then would he not be the master? And then, once she was under his spell, would he not be in complete control?

Then he would wreak his vengeance on the woman who'd spurned him on their wedding night. The woman who'd lied to a foolish, trusting youth. The woman who'd had her father take all from him—his home, his freedom, his soul.

By falling under desire's spell he was in danger of forgetting all she and her father had done to him. And forgetting the very reason he had come to Queen Eleanor's court.

The touch of a cool hand on his cheek shook him from his thoughts. "Hugh."

His name, breathed on a sigh startled him. But not nearly as much as the feel of fingers stroking down his chest, past his belt—he grabbed her wrist. Quickly tucking Lady Sarah's hand into the crook of his arm, he led her to a bench and sat down.

There was little he could do about their closeness without bolting from his seat like an untried youth. Actually, the feel of her thigh against his held little interest. He had no desire to put his arm about her or to draw her into his embrace. Yes. He definitely needed to complete this seduction of Adrienna.

"Hugh, are you not cold?"

He gazed up at the star-studded sky. There was nothing shy about Lady Sarah. "Actually, I find the air rather invigorating." In truth it was far from invigorating—it was downright frigid.

She snuggled closer to him and slipped her hands up the loose sleeves of his tunic. "I am nearly frozen."

Her hands were like ice where they rested against the fine linen of his shirt. "Would you care to return to the palace?"

Lady Sarah turned slightly. Her breasts rested against

his arm. The intimate contact created no rush of blood, no heat to fill his veins. His lack of reactions amazed him. "Oh, no, milord, I will be warm in a moment."

The last thing he needed right now was for someone to see them like this. Rumors connecting him and Lady Sarah would not sit well with Adrienna. Short of dumping this woman on the ground, how was he going to extricate himself? In another moment, she'd be on his lap.

No sooner had the thought passed through his mind, then Sarah pressed impossibly tight against him. She lifted her face to his, stretched up and grazed his chin with her lips.

Perhaps dumping her onto the ground would not be such a bad idea. But he couldn't lay all of the blame on her. He'd agreed to venture outside with the vixen.

He stopped her unwelcome kisses by grasping her chin with his free hand. "Lady Sarah, this is not wise."

"Milord, we are but stealing kisses in the moonlight." She pulled her chin from his grasp and her hands from his sleeve. "Nothing more." She cupped the side of his face. "Just a kiss."

Her lips closed over his. Hugh fought the sudden urge to push her away. Instead, he again wondered at his own lack of response.

She pulled back slightly and ran a finger over his lip. "Come, milord, I have seen your eyes fill with lust. I have heard your voice deepen with passion. You are a man. A man who desires women. Forget her. She is beyond your grasp." She dropped one hand to his thigh. "I can easily wipe her from your mind."

She traced his lower lip with a fingernail, while caressing the tense muscle of his leg. "Close your eyes, Hugh. Pretend."

Her breathless voice wisped seductively against his cheek. The firm, sure caress on his leg moved higher, coaxing him to surrender to the promise of a stolen moment of pleasure.

The woman, warm and pliant against him, freely offered anything he desired. It would be an easy thing to permit lust to cloud his mind. He'd learned long ago how to detach his mind from his body. There'd been many times in the past when he'd been given no choice over what he'd done or been forced to endure.

But at this moment he had the freedom to choose.

He gently pushed her away. "Lady Sarah, I cannot."

Surprisingly, she didn't rail or curse. Instead she shook her head and stood. She peered down at him. "Cannot, or will not? You are a fool, Wynnedom."

She held out her hand. "Come. I am cold and wish to sit by a fire."

While they walked back to the palace, she said, "You are a man who will be crushed by dreams that will never come true."

"Dreams? What are dreams, but the imaginings of children and fools?"

"Ah, but you *are* a fool. A fool who hungers for a sweet that is beyond your reach."

"You cannot be certain of that."

She tugged at his arm, forcing him to stop. When he looked down at her, he was surprised by the concern etched on her face. It was evident in her pursed lips and furrowed brow. "Hugh. Lord Wynnedom, for your own good, let it go. You will not win your Lady Adrienna. I am as certain of that, as I am of my own name."

"How can you be so certain of anything, Lady Sarah?"

She glanced down at the ground. "Trust me. I am certain of this."

Obviously, she was hiding something. For the second time that evening he grasped her chin between his thumb and forefinger, forcing her to meet his searching gaze. "What do you know, Lady Sarah, that you are not telling me?"

She sought to pull free, but Hugh slid his hand to her shoulder and held her in place. "Lady Sarah?"

Fear brightened her eyes and quickened her breath. She shook her head and whispered, "Please, milord, 'tis nothing. I only thought to save you a broken heart."

She lied. He could see it in her flinching gaze and hear it in her shaking voice. Hugh frowned. First Eleanor and now this. How many more people would warn him away from Adrienna?

Fear would keep Lady Sarah from telling what she knew. He released his grasp, held out his hand and nodded toward the palace. "Your fire awaits, milady."

After sighing deeply, Lady Sarah took his hand and let him lead the way.

Adrienna knew the instant Hugh sauntered back into the hall. Without lifting her head to look toward the door she felt his gaze race across her face.

By harnessing every ounce of willpower she possessed, she kept her own gaze locked on Richard's. It would do her no good to look at Hugh and the harlot she knew would be at his side. Adrienna doubted if she'd be able to keep her rage under wraps if she had to see the two of them together.

It wasn't jealousy. Of that she was certain. But how dare he leave her to fend off Richard's insistent proposal while he dallied in the gardens with the palace whore?

A part of her mind chided her. How was Hugh supposed to know that Richard was going to ask again for her hand in marriage? And wasn't she the one who wanted Hugh to leave her alone in the first place? After all, he would never win this insane bargain of his, so what difference did it make to her who he was with, or where he went?

"Sir Richard."

Not expecting the familiar deep voice, Adrienna nearly jumped from her seat. She swung around to see Hugh and Lady Sarah waiting expectantly behind her.

Richard rose and waved toward the bench on the other side of the table. "Lord Wynnedom. Lady Sarah, please join us."

Adrienna swallowed her groan.

Silence descended on the foursome while they all looked at each other. The air around them grew thick with expectancy. Finally, Richard leaned on the table. "Lord Wynnedom, you were outside in the gardens?"

"Yes, for a bit." Hugh stole a glance at Adrienna.

Fearful of him mistaking her anger for jealousy, she looked away.

Richard draped an arm across her shoulder. "Was it

too chilly for a moonlight stroll?" His gesture of familiarity felt like a heavy weight had settled on her.

Adrienna shrugged his hand off her shoulder. "No, thank you, Richard. If you are thinking of a stroll, I must beg off. It is too late and I am far too tired."

She couldn't help but notice the way Hugh's one eyebrow disappeared under a lock of hair that had fallen across his forehead. His expression made her feel as if he questioned, or judged her. What right had he to judge? After all, hadn't his hand rested easily on Sarah's back a moment ago?

"Ah, yes, my love," Richard soothed. "It has been quite an evening for you, hasn't it?"

Sarah leaned forward. "Oh? And what have you two been doing?"

"Nothing." Adrienna's clipped answer earned her nothing but an indulgent sigh from Richard and a glower from Hugh. She glared across the table at Hugh.

Richard slipped his arm back across her shoulder, briefly hugging her to him. "Silly goose." He smiled broadly at Sarah. "Lady Adrienna has finally consented to become my wife."

Sarah clapped. "How wonderful!"

Hugh's eyebrow again disappeared. But this time, the eyes beneath the dark brows flared to life.

Adrienna pulled away from Richard. "That is not what I said."

He corrected her. "Ah, but it is what you really meant."

It was not what she said, nor what she meant. She'd merely told him that she'd think about his offer. That was all. She gritted her teeth. "Do not put words into my mouth, Richard."

After signaling for a servant, Hugh obtained a pitcher of mead and four goblets. "Shall we drink to your good fortune, Sir Richard?"

What? At any other time, in any other circumstance, having her husband propose a toast to her supposed betrothed might be humorous. But at this moment she found no humor in the situation at all.

"Oh, aye. Let us drink to something that will not take place." Adrienna's comment slipped out of her mouth before she could stop it.

The fingers caressing her shoulder tightened. She flinched under the bruising grasp. "My dear, I can forgive you that now. Perhaps before the wedding though, you will learn better manners."

Her blood froze. Her pulse jumped. The hairs on the back of her neck rose. Something was not right. The charming, friendly Richard she knew would never seek to bruise her. A cross word, or chastisement would never leave his lips. Who was this man beside her? Did he have a dark side that he'd hidden so well all this time? Or had she not paid close enough attention?

"Come, come, Sir Richard, you are among friends." Hugh held out a goblet. "Surely, the lady would never speak so in front of others."

Richard released her and took the vessel from Hugh. "You are right, Lord Wynnedom." He looked down at Adrienna. "Milady, I apologize for my brutish ways." His doleful expression might have fooled another, but she saw the unfamiliar glint of steel in his eyes and suddenly knew his apologetic manner was false.

Sarah asked, "When will the betrothal be announced?" Obviously, she was eager to see Adrienna wed.

"Where will the wedding take place?" Hugh added his weight in gold to the discussion. "Your father must be quite happy with the match."

She wanted to scream. The urge to tell Richard she'd never marry him fought with the urge to tell Hugh where he could take his sarcasm.

"We have not yet informed Lord Hallison of the coming union." Richard added, "But I am certain he will be well pleased."

Adrienna clenched her hands in her lap. "Do you not think it might be best for the two of us to come to an agreement on this union before informing my father?"

Hugh appeared to choke on his wine. He set his drinking vessel on the table, then rose. Did anyone besides her notice that his hand trembled slightly? He nodded to Richard. "I wish you success with your marriage plans."

"Thank you, milord. Are you leaving?" Richard's easy smile made it obvious he would welcome the loss.

"Yes, it has been a long day." Hugh lifted Lady Sarah's hand to his lips. "I thank you for an enchanting evening, milady."

Adrienna swallowed against the tight lump forming in her throat. He was going to leave her to her own defenses. He was also making it very clear that he cared little for her current predicament.

Was it possible that Richard was right? Did Hugh

care nothing for her? His eyes shimmered and his mouth eased into a gentle smile when he looked at Lady Sarah.

Yet when he turned to bid *her* a good evening his eyes blazed with anger and his lips flattened into a formidable line. "Lady Adrienna, I hope you and Sir Richard work out your little disagreement. May you receive all you desire."

Little disagreement? He knew better than that. Yet what could she say? Without giving all away? Nothing.

She could say nothing that would keep him from turning and walking away. Nothing that would set the confusion in her life to right. Nothing that would quell the sudden heaviness settling on her chest.

She prayed that her voice would not break, then met his wintry stare. "Thank you, milord. I am certain that with the grace of God, all my desires will be fulfilled."

Chapter Eight

Hugh pushed into his shared chamber with such force that the heavy wooden door slammed against the wall. The leather hinges creaked and wood cracked, but the metal bracing held the door together.

William jumped up from his seat by the fire, sword in hand. Seeing Hugh, he sheathed his weapon. "Ah, another fine evening, I see."

Hugh ignored the sarcasm. "She thinks to marry that twit Langsford."

"Is that all?"

"All?" The anger evident in his tone took him by surprise. "Is that not enough?"

"Forgive me if I speak out of turn, but it seems to me that the woman is already married."

Hugh waved away his companion's statement of the obvious. He briefly held his thumb and forefinger a hair's breadth apart. "A fact that matters about this much it seems."

For a moment William remained silent. He stared at Hugh before shaking his head. "From what I see, it matters to you. A great deal."

After grabbing a jug and goblet from the small table by William's seat, Hugh leaned against the wall. "Aye, it does." His companion was right—a fact that only added fuel to his anger. "But by the saints above it should not."

"I'll not debate that with you. But the wine will not change anything."

Remembering the previous evening, he commented, "You, my friend, are a fine one to talk." Still, Hugh put the items back on the table. "Perhaps 'tis time to call the game and head for home."

"You will get no argument from me."

He paused at William's deep sigh of relief. The man had yet to return to his own home. Out of some odd sense of honor, he'd willingly stayed with Hugh to offer his help.

It was high time they all returned to their lands. Time to put his plans into action. Time to seek fruition for the revenge he had long contemplated.

He headed toward the door. "The bed is yours for the night. We'll leave at daybreak."

"Where do you go now?"

"To check on the horses and acquire one for Adrienna." Hugh paused and added, "Then I'm off to claim my wife before she finds herself married to another."

"Richard, go to your chamber." Adrienna ducked away from another of his attempts to kiss her. The man either didn't understand her disgust of him, or was too sodden to care. "Leave this for tomorrow, shall we?"

She easily pulled out of his drunken embrace. Lady Sarah had excused herself shortly after Hugh had left. Adrienna had kept Richard at the table by the fire until he'd consumed enough wine to numb his senses.

Her stalling tactic had proved foolish, for the drink had also numbed his ability to reason. Now she found herself fighting off his unwelcome advances in the privacy of a semidark corridor.

She kept waiting for one of the queen's guards to appear, but so far none had. The darkened corridor was strangely empty this evening.

"I cannot go to my chamber. Not alone. The queen forbids it, my Adrienna."

She could barely make heads or tails of his slurred words. What did Queen Eleanor have to do with his retiring for the night?

When Richard blindly reached for her, Adrienna took the opportunity to grab his arm and swing him around to face the direction of his chamber. To humor him, she promised, "We will keep this between us. That way the queen will never know." With a firm push at his shoulder to get him moving, she added, "Go to bed."

"No!"

As if possessed, Richard tore her hand from his shoulder and pulled her back into his arms. "I will not go alone." He started back toward his chamber, with her in tow. "This is the night. No more games or words.

You will spend the night with me and tomorrow we will be wed."

She struggled against him, breaking his hold. Before she could flee, Richard clamped a hand around her wrist and stopped her escape. His near bruising hold burned. When she refused to move her feet, he shrugged. "I can drag you if I must. It matters little to me."

"Richard, cease this nonsense. I will never marry you." Adrienna fought to keep her voice steady. She'd no wish for him to detect even a trace of the fear coursing through her. "There is nothing you can do that will change my mind."

"We shall see." His words echoed in the empty corridor.

"What are you planning?"

"Me? Nothing. I am only following her grace's order like a good and faithful subject."

"What nonsense do you speak?"

While he did not cease their progress toward his chamber, he responded, "I suppose it matters not if you know. It is not as if you can change what will happen this night."

He glanced over his shoulder. "You brought this on yourself, my dear. Had you simply agreed to become my wife, or had you even taken my proposal seriously, we would not have to use these methods."

Adrienna grasped at the empty air for a measure of sanity. "It is you who does not understand. I am not free to marry you or anyone."

"Now who speaks nonsense? You cannot talk your way out of this. You will spend the night in my chamber and be found there on the morn. To save the honor of this court, we will be wed immediately."

"You would force this marriage upon me?" Adrienna gasped as the realization sank fully into her mind. "With the queen's blessing?"

"Blessing?" He shook his head. "Nay. It was her order that I do so."

When he paused before his door, Adrienna clawed at him, fighting to free herself. "No! I will not do this."

"Aye, you will." Richard pulled her forward. "You have no choice."

She took a deep breath and then screamed. Considering the emptiness of the corridor, she'd little hope that anyone would hear and rush to her rescue, but little hope was better than none at all.

"God!" Richard tried to stop her screams by slapping a hand over her mouth. "Cease!"

He pushed the door open with his shoulder and then shoved her inside. Adrienna lost her balance and fell to her knees. She landed hard on a woody clump of dried herbs mixed in with the rushes on the floor. The small bit was enough to send a sharp pain from her knee up her thigh.

Ignoring her gasp of pain, Richard loomed over her. The sneer twisting his face boded ill. "You can do this willingly, or by force. Either way you *will* become my wife."

She gingerly turned around and sat on the floor, rubbing her kneecap. "And you can go to hell, Richard." She debated for less time than a blink before adding, "I am already married."

Suddenly, losing her wager with Hugh seemed a small price to pay. It would be worth anything to avoid becoming Langsford's wife.

Richard laughed. "Do you take me for a fool? Your husband is dead." He reached down, grabbed the front of her gown and hauled her to her feet.

"He is not dead. Let me talk to Queen Eleanor."

"How do you fabricate such lies?"

"It is not a lie. Go, summon the queen. I demand she hear me out."

"Nay, give me no orders. Tell me who this husband is and I will take care of the matter. You will be a widow before the morn."

She knew that Hugh would not be the one dead or injured should the two men come to blows. Earlier, his ability to permanently dispatch men with his bare hands seemed not only odd, but frightening. Now, she thought it a convenient ability.

Hugh was already out of favor with Eleanor. If he killed one of her men at the same time the truth became known, there was no telling what the queen would do.

When angry, Eleanor was capable of anything—including ordering Hugh's death. It was a risk Adrienna preferred to avoid. But perhaps, if she simply admitted all, Eleanor might only be angry enough to order both of them from her court.

"If you will not summon the queen, take me to her and I will divulge all."

When he didn't release her, Adrienna curled her fingers into a fist and swung at him. She contacted with his stomach, then jerked free of his hold while he caught his breath. Before she could reach the door, Richard grabbed a handful of her hair and wrapped it about his hand.

He jerked her away from the door and around to face him. "You bitch!" His wine laced breath rushed hot against her face. His eyes were glazed with rage giving her the impression of a ravenous wild dog closing in on its kill.

Adrienna screamed. While his behavior this night had made her wary, she hadn't truly been afraid for her life until now. She clawed for his wrist, seeking to either gain freedom or prevent him from tearing the hair from her scalp.

He shook her, yelling, "Shut your mouth."

Desperate to escape, she swung at him again. Richard dodged her fist, turned around and dragged her behind him toward the bed.

She moved her feet quickly to keep up with him. It was obvious he'd not stop if she fell. Once there, he pushed her onto the mattress. Before she had the chance to roll out of his reach, he lunged atop her.

"Give in, Adrienna. I am stronger and you do nothing more than waste my time."

"Get off of me."

She squirmed, trying to get out from beneath him, but he only rose up on his knees and straddled her. When she once again tried to escape he pressed his forearm against her throat. "Would you prefer death to becoming my wife?"

Unable to draw breath she could only nod. In all honesty, yes, she would prefer to die than to wed him.

"I truly wish I could oblige you, but it would greatly anger Queen Eleanor were she to find your dead body in my chamber come morning."

While he talked, Richard grabbed a tunic that had been lying on the bed. With his teeth and free hand he ripped the fabric into strips.

Dangling one above her, he smiled. "Since I rather doubt you will remain in this room of your own accord, I will take the choice from you."

If he managed to tie her up she would never be able to thwart the queen's plan. Adrienna knew that with the dawning of the new day she'd end up with two husbands. "Richard, please, there is no need for that. You are correct, there is nothing I can do. So, I will stay right here."

"As much as I would like to believe you, my dear, I am not simpleminded." He pressed his arm harder against her throat. "No, I think we will do this my way."

Unable to breathe, she panicked as a sickly darkness began to cloud her mind. He would in truth kill her. With all of the strength she possessed she kicked her legs and twisted her body back and forth trying desperately to throw him off of her.

"That's right, fight me, Adrienna."

His voice seemed to come from far away. Her head spun and suddenly the strength she'd had ebbed from her, leaving her limp beneath him.

Richard climbed off of her. Too weak to do anything else, she gasped for breath while silently cursing her own stupidity. It gave him the time he needed to tie her wrists together over her head before securing them to a bedpost with another strip of cloth. He quickly moved to the foot of the bed and repeated his actions with her ankles.

Someone tapped on the door, calling out, "Richard?"

Adrienna opened her mouth to scream, but he crammed one of the two remaining strips of cloth in her mouth before she could do more than squeak.

Again, the person outside the chamber door tapped. "Richard, are you in there?"

Through the fog of fear and mounting anger, Adrienna recognized Lady Sarah's voice. What was she doing here at this time of night?

The instant the thought crossed her mind Adrienna closed her eyes and shook her head. Raging emotions obviously weakened her ability to think. It didn't take a great deal of thought to realize why the palace whore would be tapping at a man's door after night had fallen.

Now was not the time to lose her ability to reason. She needed to keep her wits about her if she wanted any hope of escaping this fate Queen Eleanor had planned for her.

Richard secured the gag with the last strip, went to the door and permitted Sarah entrance.

Perhaps she could find a way to gain Sarah's help. Adrienna stared hard at her, seeking a way to miraculously will her thoughts to the other woman.

But to her regret, Sarah showed no surprise at finding someone tied up on Richard's bed. The woman approached Adrienna and only shook her head before looking up at Richard by her side. "I told you she wouldn't agree to this arrangement."

The urge to cry nearly choked Adrienna. Did everyone know of this plan except her?

Richard rubbed his temples. "Yes, she did put up a valiant fight."

Sarah turned to him and rested her palms on his chest. Fascinated by the whore's boldness, Adrienna watched as Sarah smoothed out Richard's surcoat, running her hands up over his shoulders and down his arms.

She tipped her head slightly and looked up at him through her eyelashes. "The important thing is that you proved the victor."

Richard visibly relaxed at her words. A welcoming smile replaced the frown creasing his face. His angry gaze softened to one of desire. He leaned in to her touch. "Was there any doubt?"

"Never." Sarah stretched up and placed a kiss on his chin before wrapping her hands around his neck, coaxing his lips lower to meet hers.

After a few moments, Richard lifted his head. "What shall we do now?"

Sarah trailed one hand down to his chest. Richard's eyes closed and a sigh escaped his mouth.

"I can think of many things we could do now." In a lower, husky tone, Sarah continued, "As much as I would enjoy a tumble in your bed, it appears to be occupied."

Richard slid his arms around the woman, and moved her backward toward the foot end of the bed. "Only a part of it is in use. There is plenty of room for us."

Adrienna closed her eyes briefly to silently plead, *Please, Lord, do not let them come into this bed.*

"Not with your bride-to-be lying next to us." Sarah gentled her comment with a soft moan. "Mmm, but keep me in mind for later."

Hopeful that Sarah's comment would keep them out of the bed, Adrienna kept her wary focus on the two.

While stroking her hair and neck, and frantically attempting to kiss her, Richard obviously tried to change her mind.

Sarah stared up at the ceiling and for a moment Adrienna had the impression that the woman was bored and looking for patience—or a way to escape.

The look vanished just as quickly as it had appeared. *What could that mean? Was Sarah only toying with Richard—manipulating him to do her bidding?* Hope flared in Adrienna's chest. If that were true, perhaps there was a way to gain Sarah's help.

But how?

Sarah murmured something Adrienna could not hear before patting Richard's shoulder. "Later, my love."

Richard closed his eyes and groaned. He then rested his forehead on her shoulder. "Woman, you will be the death of me."

Adrienna wished his death could be that easy.

Sarah stroked his cheek. "Promise that you will not forget me while you meet with Stefan."

Stefan? Who was Stefan? This had to be someone new at court.

Richard straightened and stepped away from Sarah. He physically shook his head and shoulders before plucking at the front of his clothing as if readjusting them. Finally, he placed a quick kiss on Sarah's forehead. "Never, my dear." Heading for the door, he warned, "Do not release her or remove the gag."

Sarah glanced toward Adrienna before asking, "Was it really necessary to gag her?"

"Aye, between her screams, orders to summon the queen and lies about a nonexistent husband, there was no other choice."

"You could find no other way to silence her? Would it not have been easier to make her swoon with kisses and caresses than to tie and gag her?"

Sarah shrugged, then added, "Richard, your wedding night tomorrow would have gone so much easier for you, had you not lost your temper with her this night."

His face twisted with anger. "Watch your tongue, woman. Tell me not how to deal with my bride-to-be."

Seemingly chastised, Sarah glanced down at the floor for a moment. "I apologize, milord." She looked back up at him and smiled, while slowly running a fingertip across her lower lip. "Remember, the sooner you are gone, the quicker we can be back together."

Richard retraced his steps, took Sarah in his arms and covered her lips with his own. After what seemed the longest kiss Adrienna had ever seen, he released the woman and headed back to the door. Pausing, he promised, "I will return before the taste of me leaves your lips."

Once the door closed firmly behind him, Sarah waited the space of about three heartbeats before she scrubbed the back of her hand across her mouth. "Pig."

Chapter Nine

Adrienna stared up at Lady Sarah in amazement. The woman's reaction to Richard's parting kiss gave her budding hope strength.

After peeking out the door, Sarah crossed the chamber, dropped to her knees before a wooden chest and started rummaging through the items inside. "There must be something in here."

Over her shoulder she reassured Adrienna, "I've no doubt that Richard knotted those strips too tight for me to loosen. I need to find a— Thank you, Lord." She rose, holding a dagger.

Sarah knelt on the edge of bed and tried to slide a finger beneath the gag. The material had been tied so tightly that there was little room left for the blade. "If I nick you, it isn't intentional."

The tip of the blade pricking her cheek as Sarah forced the dagger beneath the cloth stung only for a brief moment. It mattered not because Adrienna would gladly suffer whatever scratches or nicks it took to be freed.

The gag fell away and she heaved a heartfelt, "Thank you."

Sarah sawed at the strips tied to the head of the bed. "Don't thank me yet. This blade is so dull we may be here a while. Wait until we make good your escape."

She had a good point. If Richard came back and caught Sarah, there was no telling what he would do to the both of them.

Without pausing at her task, Sarah asked, "Were you telling Richard the truth about being wed?"

Would it make a difference? Adrienna hesitated. What if this entire evening had been nothing but some strange plot of the queen's and Sarah was only carrying out her part?

Had the queen suspected that she was married and this whole fiasco was nothing but an elaborate plan to get her to admit the truth? What would happen then? Without a doubt Queen Eleanor would be angry to have her plans thwarted—the question was how angry?

Not only was her future at stake, but her very life could rest in Eleanor's hands. Worse, not just her own life, but also Hugh's. This useless worry over admitting the truth or lying would get her nothing but an aching head.

The binding holding her arms overhead gave way and Adrienna sighed. Thankfully, she hadn't been trussed up long enough for her muscles to do anything more than burn a little. So, bringing them back down was a relief.

When Sarah started sawing at the strips around her

wrists, Adrienna stopped her. "No, those can wait. Get my feet loosened."

"You never answered my question." Sarah started working on the bindings at the foot of the bed.

If they were caught Adrienna knew she'd need Hugh's assistance. But if nobody knew that he was her husband, nobody would think to inform him of any problem. It would be a risk he'd most likely find foolish, but she had to trust someone.

"Yes, I am married."

The other woman shook her head. "Do not tell me. Let me guess." Sarah stopped working on the bindings long enough to look at Adrienna. "You are married to the Earl of Wynnedom."

Surprise must have shown on her face, because Sarah continued, "It didn't require much thought. The jealousy he displayed because of Langsford could only come from a lover, or a husband. At first I guessed he was an old lover, but the look on your face this evening when he left you alone in the hall with Richard made me wonder."

Adrienna had been angry and not a little bit hurt by his lack of concern over Richard's announcement of the coming nuptials. She hadn't realized the emotions had been that evident.

"Why are you helping me?" It was something she'd yet to figure out.

Sarah hacked through the last of the bindings, freeing Adrienna's feet, before answering, "When I first learned of this plan I thought you deserved whatever the queen and Langsford had in store for you."

Adrienna sat up on the bed and swung her legs over the side. "What changed your mind?"

"Something in the way Richard acted this evening made me wonder if he was hiding another side of himself." She paused, a frown creasing her forehead. "He gave me the impression of a man who would not hesitate, nor regret, harming a woman."

Adrienna stared at her. Shadows played across Lady Sarah's face, making the haunted look shimmering in her eyes more evident. This knowledge of Richard's mood was not the type one just guessed at. Sarah obviously had secrets of her own—dark secrets that made her aware of things a woman should not be forced to know.

"Sarah…" Adrienna reached out her still bound hands and grasped the other woman's fingers. "Sarah, I do thank you for that. But what of the queen?"

"That will be your cost for my help." She tightened their grasp and pulled Adrienna up to her feet. "Take me with you when you leave."

Without a second thought, Adrienna nodded. "Consider it done."

"Good. Now, we must find your husband."

The two women headed toward the door. Adrienna's knee buckled with her fist step and she hit the floor with a heavy thud.

Sarah was beside her instantly. "Oh, my Lord. I did not even think to ask if you'd already been injured."

Rubbing her knee, Adrienna shook her head. "No, 'tis not what you think. I tripped when he pushed me into the chamber and fell onto to my knees."

"Can you walk?"

"I don't have a choice. Just help me up."

Sarah struggled to get Adrienna on her feet. "Loop your arms over my head."

"You can't carry me."

"Maybe not, but you can use my shoulders as support."

They tested that theory and to their relief, it worked. Nearly hanging from Sarah's shoulders, Adrienna was able to step-hop-step to the door.

Sarah opened it and peered out. "Ready?"

"Yes. Do you know where Hugh's chamber is located?"

"You ask the palace whore if she knows where the earl sleeps?"

Adrienna rolled her eyes. "How silly of me. Lead on."

Hugh punctuated the slamming of his chamber's door with a string of curses.

William rose, leaving the warmth of the fire. "She isn't willing to leave?"

"I do not know."

Remaining silent, William stared at him and waited for an explanation.

Hugh stepped away from the door. Running a hand through his hair, he walked to the narrow window and stared out. "I could not find her."

"You checked her chamber?"

"Aye. After searching the hall." He'd checked everywhere at least twice—the hall, her chamber, and even though night had fallen, he'd searched the gardens. She was nowhere to be found.

"Where could she be?" William's eyes widened. "You don't think she and Langsford—"

"Nay. Not willingly." Hugh cut off his friend's assumption. Adrienna would not sneak off with Langsford in such a manner. At least not of her own accord. "But something is afoot."

He knew it. He felt a growing dread in every bone and muscle in his body—something was wrong. The impending doom was worsened by the simple fact that he cared.

And he wasn't supposed to care. He wasn't supposed to have any feelings for Adrienna outside those of revenge.

Yet in the last day or so, he'd experienced a wide range of emotions for her—anger, desire, concern, tenderness, even something close to— He stopped his thoughts before they fully formed. No, surely not that. He could not be that dim-witted.

William sat down by the small table and splashed some wine into both goblets. Handing one out to Hugh, he asked, "What leads you to think that?"

He had to pause a moment to realize William wasn't talking about his wayward emotions. "There are too few guards about the corridors this night." Hugh took the wine, downed it in one swallow, he then set the goblet on the table. "It leaves too many places unprotected—too many dark crevices and corners for mayhem to occur."

No castle or keep would have so many unguarded corridors. No lord—or lady—would leave their guests, or family so unprotected, nearly defenseless.

"Perhaps they deserted their posts."

"No. They seem well satisfied with their lot. And I've heard no rumors or whispers of unrest or treason. It's more likely they were ordered away from their posts."

"Why—"

Their conversation was cut off by a rapping on the door. William rose, pulled both swords from the two scabbards hanging on wall pegs and tossed one to Hugh.

Holding the weapon before him, Hugh opened the door. Stunned, he could only stare at Lady Sarah and Adrienna for a moment before lowering the blade.

Obviously just as surprised, Sarah studied the weapon with wide eyes. "Truly, my lord, we are unarmed and mean you no harm." She ducked her head out from Adrienna's hold.

Spurred to action by the sight of the bindings on his wife's wrists, Hugh scooped her into his arms and set her down on the bed, kneeling on the floor in front of her. "What is this? What is amiss?" He took his dagger from his belt and sliced through the bindings.

William ushered Sarah into the room and closed the door behind her.

"The queen decided Langsford was taking too long to make Adrienna his wife." Sarah sat down by the small table and pointed to a wine-filled goblet. At William's nod, she took a drink before continuing. "So, she dismissed the guards and ordered Richard to keep his wayward bride-to-be locked up in his chamber tonight."

William sat down across from her. "For what purpose?"

Adrienna supplied the answer. "So, that in the morning I would be found in a compromising position and forced to wed Langsford."

"It is unfortunate that she is already wed." Sarah took another drink.

Hugh stared up at Adrienna in surprise. She shrugged. "He had tied me to the bed and she freed me. When she asked if I was wed I could not lie. I knew that I'd need your help."

He heard the slight tremor in her voice. Moving up to sit alongside her on the bed, he pulled her into his embrace. "Tied you to the bed? What happened after I left the table?"

Adrienna admitted, "I kept Richard at the table because I thought he would eventually drink himself into a stupor and leave me alone. I had no idea that he was on a mission for Queen Eleanor."

"You kept him there on purpose? Have you lost all ability to reason?"

"Me?" She stiffened against him. "You think I asked him for this treatment?"

"Perhaps you did not ask him, but you encouraged him by your actions."

Adrienna leaned away from him and was momentarily speechless.

"See, you do not even deny it."

She tried to break free of his arms, but he held her in place. "I? I encouraged him? If anyone did any encouraging this evening it was you."

Was Adrienna jealous of Lady Sarah? He wanted to laugh at the thought, but it would be humorless and hollow since he'd already experienced the same emotion toward Langsford. A fact he'd not share with her. Instead, he asked, "Do I detect a measure of jealousy?"

"Jealous?" Her words came from between clenched teeth. "I think your overblown pride has left you dimwitted."

This argument would take them nowhere but in circles. "Did he tell you anything about the queen's plans?"

"Aye. The same that Sarah told you. They tire of this courtship and decided to trick me into marriage by having me spend the night in Richard's chamber. In the morning I would be found and forced to marry him for the sake of the court's reputation."

Hugh felt as if someone had landed a blow to his midsection. "The queen approved this plot?"

"Approved?" Adrienna snorted. "According to Richard it was her idea. He only followed her order."

Hugh cursed. "You know what this means?"

She returned his look. A sad, half smile tugged at her lips before finally, she nodded. "Yes. It means you have won your wager."

He refused to win her wager this way. "No, Adrienna, that isn't what I meant. I was implying that we need to leave this place immediately. Before they force your hand."

"Oh. Either way, you've still won. I told Richard that I was married. He didn't believe me, but I'm certain he will tell Queen Eleanor."

"It matters not. This giving in on your part was not our wager. You were to come to my bed within the thirty days." He patted the mattress beneath them. "You are not sitting on my bed with any intention of fulfilling our deal. You still have a choice to make and time in which to do so." He leaned his forehead against hers. "Which will it be, Adrienna? Do we go home together as husband and wife, or do we go to beseech King Henry for an annulment?"

She grasped the front of his tunic before whispering, "I do not know, Hugh. I do not know."

Not quite the answer he wanted.

Adrienna realized the instant his lips covered hers that she did know the answer. And when he snaked his hand around her neck and stroked the soft spot beneath her ear, she swore she heard denial from her mind as her heart surrendered.

Without breaking their kiss, he turned her slightly in his arms and brought her more fully onto his lap. He trailed his fingertips across her collarbone. When he lightly brushed his hand across her breast, she thought she'd swoon as the blood rushed from her head to settle hot between her thighs.

It was like floating. Or drowning. She clung to him, not caring which feeling would eventually fight its way to the fore. Either would carry her away.

She heard movement from across the chamber and remembered that they weren't alone. Adrienna reluctantly pulled away from his lips. "Hugh, please—"

He let her slide off his lap. "We can resume this later—perhaps in England?"

"Any place as far away from here as possible."

"Maybe by then you will have decided if we should go to King Henry or not."

She could hardly believe he was still leaving her this choice. But she was grateful for having the option. "I promise, I will decide by then."

"Good. But our wager stands as originally agreed. You will decide by coming to my bed—for more than talking." He flashed her a smile before adding, "I will still win."

He was arrogant, smug and oh, so beguiling when it suited him. "Perhaps. Perhaps not."

"I worry not. You will." He rose and offered his hand. "Come, we need be on our way."

Putting her hand in his, she accepted his help. But when she placed her weight on her knee, she grimaced.

"What is wrong?"

"Nothing of any importance." Unwilling to prevent them from leaving, she lied, "I fell on my knee and it pains me a little."

Sarah dashed her attempt to lie. "A little? Why do you think she was hanging on me when we arrived? She cannot walk."

His eyebrows rose in disbelief. "Let me see."

"No, truly, it is fine."

Before she knew what he was doing, Hugh picked her up, sat her back on the bed and lifted her gown. "It is swollen."

She batted at his hands and tugged at her gown, trying to cover her legs. "I know. It's also stiff from nonuse, so let us be on our way."

He ignored her. Sliding his hands beneath her gown he stroked and probed her uninjured leg. Adrienna closed her eyes. His hands were warm, his caress soothing.

She bit her lip to keep from gasping in surprise at the
sensitivity in her legs.

Hugh paused. "Does that hurt?"

"Nay, it doesn't *hurt*." She opened her eyes in time
to catch a glimpse of his smile before he bent back
down to his task.

He moved to the other leg, caressing, massaging up
to her knee. When he pressed a thumb alongside her
kneecap, Adrienna nearly flew off the bed. "Stop!"

Hugh quickly finished his inspection and patted the
skirt of her gown back into place. "I don't think anything is broken. But neither do I think you did this by
simply falling."

"I could have told you nothing was broken. Can we
go now?"

He took her hand and pulled her up from the bed.
"Can you walk with help?"

"I don't see why not." Adrienna took a few steps toward the door. While the pain wasn't as sharp as before,
it still hurt fiercely, but she fought to not grit her teeth
and claimed, "See, I am fine."

"I would be more than happy to carry you."

She stepped out of his reach. "I am sure you would."
Halfway across the chamber, she glanced at Lady Sarah
and stopped. "Sarah is coming with us."

Hugh lengthened his steps and came alongside her.
"Why would the queen's whore join us?"

Not wanting to be overheard, she kept her voice to
a whisper. "I am not so certain she really is a whore."
Adrienna shook her head. "Or perhaps there is more

to her than just that. She manipulated Richard flaw-lessly and then helped me without question. Some-thing is not quite right with the image she portrays."

"And that itself could very well be a trap for us."

Adrienna knew Hugh could be right. She'd already thought about that herself. But she'd made a vow. "I cannot go back on my word, Hugh."

He tipped his head. "Very well, my lady. Just be on your guard and watch what you say around her."

"I still think we've been wrong about her, but I'll follow your advice until I'm certain."

"Until you are certain? No, you will follow my advice until *I* am certain."

From his harsh tone, she knew he expected her not to argue with his order. She stared up at him questioningly.

"Adrienna, you are not the best judge of people. You've proven that with your Richard. I'll not let you risk both our lives because you *think* someone is honorable."

"I won't argue this with you now. But you are wrong."

He extended his arm as if waving her toward the door. "We shall see."

Lady Sarah rose. "We should be leaving quickly."

To Hugh she sounded too anxious, too worried. "Why is that?"

"I am so sorry." She sat back down with a heavy thud. "I was to be part of this night's plot to see Adrienna wed and you—" She shot a nervous glance toward Hugh, cleared her throat and finished, "And you wed…to me."

Chapter Ten

Surely there were worse things that could happen than being forced to wed the palace whore. Unfortunately, Hugh couldn't think of a single one at that moment.

Adrienna found her voice first. "I beg your pardon?"

"I was to wait until Hugh was asleep, before slipping into bed with him."

"And you'd be found there in the morning, too?"

"No. I was to scream rape just as soon as I was settled in the bed."

Hugh and William both groaned. Dryly, Hugh asked, "The queen was unable to think of something more imaginative?"

"It matters not since I decided not to go along with the plan."

"How noble."

Sarah looked down at the floor. "Everything is not always as it appears, milord."

"Obviously."

Adrienna rubbed her temples, half hoping the action would set her mind to working. "We need to leave this place."

The look Hugh shot her confirmed her own opinion about stating something so obvious.

William cracked open the door and looked out into the corridor. After closing the door, he asked, "Where are the guards now?"

The frown creasing Lady Sarah's forehead sent a cold foreboding down Hugh's spine. "Perhaps you need to explain all, so we can devise a plan."

"The guards should be outside in the corridor any moment now."

Adrienna gasped. "Why did you not say so before we were out of options?"

"I thought I could find a way out of this difficulty before I mentioned anything."

"My husband will not marry you."

If the situation weren't so dire, Hugh would have taken the time to question the outrage evident in Adrienna's comment. She sounded as if she cared. Wasn't that what he'd planned all along? So, what was this odd prick in his chest?

"I know." Sarah's frown deepened. "But if Queen Eleanor doesn't find me in this bed, I will end up in one of her cells." She stared up at the ceiling for a moment. "Yet, if she does find me in bed with him and discovers he is already wed, both of us will end up incarcerated."

"No." Hugh dismissed that outcome. "She would need to explain to King Henry why she confined one of his earls. It's doubtful if my being wed would be a satisfactory explanation."

"Why do we not simply walk out of here?" William looked as if the easiest solution would suit him better.

"The two of you could do that easily." Adrienna nodded toward Sarah. "But we are the queen's charges. While I am wed, giving me leave to do my husband's bidding, Sarah is not. She doesn't have the option of simply walking out of here."

"If they don't realize she's gone—" Heavy footsteps and the clanging of swords echoed in the corridor, cutting off whatever William was about to say.

William cursed, then started pulling off his clothing. He stopped in front of Sarah. "Get in bed with me."

She tipped her head to look up at him. "What did you say?"

He tossed his tunic atop a chest along the wall and pulled his shirt over his head. That garment joined the first. "You heard me."

Her eyes wide and unblinking, were glued to his naked chest. "But—"

Hugh nearly choked. "What in the hell are you doing?"

William grasped Sarah's arm and pulled her toward the bed as he explained, "She needs to be found in bed with someone she can be wed to."

"It was supposed to be me."

Sarah stood as if frozen in place, just watching William disrobe. Her face reddened more with each article of clothing he removed. Hugh realized that Adrienna was correct—this woman was no whore.

"You can't very well marry the woman. And neither can we leave her to spend countless months in one of the queen's cells." He sat down on the edge of the bed and pulled Sarah toward him. Before anyone knew what he was about to do, he took Sarah's hands in his own. "I will protect you. I will keep you safe. Marry me."

She said nothing. But Hugh had to ask, "Why?"

"I owe you my life, my freedom. 'Tis the least I can do."

"You owe me nothing."

Sarah slid her hands from between William's and lifted one as if to ward off Hugh. "I will get into bed with you, but there will be no reason for us to be wed. When the queen discovers us, I will play the simpleton. Perhaps she will believe that I did not know who was in the bed. With luck she will only be angry enough to order us from her lands."

More footsteps echoed from outside the chamber door. Sarah snapped into action. With William's help she shed her gowns, shoes and stockings before they both dived beneath the bedcovers.

Adrienna looked at Hugh. "What are we to do?"

Hugh grasped her hand and pulled her into the small alcove closer to the door. He moved her into the far corner, using his body as a shield between her and the chamber. "They will rush in when Sarah screams. It's doubtful we will be noticed."

"I hope you're right."

"Of course I am." He ignored Adrienna's unladylike snort and snapped his fingers. William's muffled voice floated into the alcove, followed immediately by a heart-rending scream from Lady Sarah.

Adrienna whispered, "Dear Lord, be kind."

They could hear the gathering of men outside the door. Hugh wrapped his arms around Adrienna and pulled her tight against his chest.

Sarah screamed again and the door burst open. The queen's guards filed into the chamber. Then the queen marched by, flanked by yet more guards.

Once they all passed the small alcove, Hugh relaxed his embrace. Everyone's attention seemed to be riveted on the bed. If he wanted it to appear as if he'd just returned, now was the time to slip out of the alcove.

Keeping his voice barely above a breath, he ordered, "Stay here." Then stepped out toward the door. He waited a moment before slipping to the other side of the chamber and chose the perfect location to watch the coming drama unfold.

Eleanor stood halfway between the door and the bed. "What is the meaning of this?"

"Oh, milady, help me." Even though the cry for assistance was muffled by the curtains surrounding the bed, Hugh heard Lady Sarah's panicked, frightened voice. She played her part well. An appendage, he wasn't certain if it was a foot or a hand, poked frantically at the heavy draping.

From the smug satisfaction twisting Eleanor's face, she thought she'd just won. While the queen might be the most powerful piece on a chessboard, she would soon learn she'd lost this match. Not only had Langsford's task in the plot been foiled, this part of her game would be, too.

He understood Langsford's mission. Queen Eleanor had made it quite plain that she wanted a marriage between Adrienna and Langsford because she wanted her man in control of the lands.

He still couldn't fathom foisting Lady Sarah off on him. A forced marriage to one of her ladies would not have gained his allegiance.

Hugh leaned back against the wall and crossed his arms before his chest. He left his questions for the mists— they could wait a time. He'd no doubt that the next few moments would provide unequaled entertainment.

Eleanor nodded at the men closest to her. "Help that woman and hold the scoundrel at bay."

Three men rushed to do her bidding. One tore the curtain back so hard that it came off in his hand and he tossed the heavy fabric to the floor. The second man pulled a disheveled Lady Sarah from the bed. She grabbed her gown from the floor, dropped it over her head and pulled it into place. The third placed the tip of his sword against William's neck.

Lady Sarah staggered forward, falling to her knees before the queen. "Oh, thank you, my lady. I am forever in your debt."

It was all Hugh could do not to applaud her performance.

Eleanor reached down and patted the woman on the head. "It is lucky for you that my men were nearby and heard your cries." She motioned for Sarah to rise. "He did not harm you, did he?"

Sarah's broken sobs were nearly Hugh's undoing. The woman was the most convincing liar he'd ever witnessed.

"Oh, milady, he—he—oh, it was awful." The offended lady shuddered, adding unspoken emphasis to her claim of harm.

"There, there, my child. It is a beautiful woman's lot to suffer the beastlike hunger of men." Eleanor took her time studying Sarah. "I can tell by your demeanor that you fought as best you could."

"What will I do?"

Sarah's pitiful wail brought the queen's attention to the man on the bed. "I warned you, Wynnedom. How dare you not heed my advice?"

"Milady?" The man standing guard over William looked from the bed to the queen. He shook his head in confusion.

Eleanor stepped toward the bed. Her eyes widened and she nearly choked holding back her gasp. "What is the meaning of this?"

Joining her at the bedside, Sarah's mouth fell open in feigned shock. Apparently speechless, the lady could do nothing more than stare at William.

Hugh pushed through the line of men now surrounding the bed. With what he hoped was his most bewildered tone, he declared, "I leave the chamber for a matter of moments and return to find half the palace in attendance." His attention paused on William, "Is something amiss?"

"I am not certain." Holding the covers over his chest

to conceal his nakedness, William sat up on the bed. "I was asleep, until an earsplitting scream awoke me." He peered at Sarah, then continued, "But before I could ascertain where it came from, or why anyone was in my bed, the chamber filled with the queen's men." With a nod toward Eleanor, he added, "And then the queen herself."

A few of the guards shuffled from one foot to the other, each man's attention seemingly drawn to something fascinating on the ceiling. Lady Sarah sank to the floor as if in a faint.

The queen swung her head, glaring from William to Hugh, settling her focus on Hugh. "Rumors of this will be spread far and wide by morning. What do you intend to do about it?"

He knew what she wanted him to say—that he would do the honorable thing and marry the wench. Instead, he took the risk of angering her further. "Nothing."

"This lady's reputation will be ruined."

How one ruined the reputation of someone posing as the palace whore was beyond his imagination. He'd not let on that he knew Lady Sarah's position was a hoax. It would only add to Eleanor's rage. "The lady's reputation is well-known and will remain intact."

Eleanor narrowed her eyes to mere slits. "I warned you, Wynnedom."

"That you did and I have done nothing to incur your wrath, my lady." Hugh shrugged. "Everyone in this chamber is well aware of what took place here this night."

"And everyone in this chamber will swear that you dishonored Lady Sarah."

This was a complication none of them had foreseen. Even were he free to wed Lady Sarah, he would never do so. Another wife did not fit into his plans. He had no idea what he was going to do with the wife he currently had once his quest for vengeance was completed.

At the edge of his vision, Hugh saw Adrienna slip out of the alcove and duck between two of the castle guards. She walked up to the queen and stated, "Not everyone."

Eleanor's frown deepened. "Why are you not—"

"Tied to Langsford's bed?" Hugh cut off her question while motioning Adrienna to his side.

An eerie silence momentarily cloaked the chamber, until one of the nervous guards cleared his throat. Sarah sat up, and renewed her whine as if not a moment had lapsed during her faint, "Oh, milady—"

"Cease!" Eleanor's shout stopped Lady Sarah's complaint.

The queen closed her eyes and took a breath before pointing at Hugh. "I will suffer no argument from you, Wynnedom. You will wed Lady Sarah."

"For what reason?" He wanted her to state what he'd supposedly done to all those present.

"I have ordered you to do so. I need give you no other explanation. But since you insist, it will suit my purposes to have her honor restored and to have you tied fast with a wife."

He had an inkling what her answer would be, but still he asked, "And if I refuse?"

"You would not dare."

"I would dare much."

"If you attempt something so risky, know that you will spend many days and nights confined to a cell."

She could do nothing to him that hadn't already been done before. And King Henry would never permit him to spend too many days or nights in confinement. Still, losing his hard-won freedom was unacceptable.

"Which do you prefer, Wynnedom? The solitude of a cell, or marriage to Lady Sarah?"

Anyone else would have been intimidated by the queen's tone and glare. Not Adrienna. Even though he was certain the king would see to his release, she couldn't let Hugh rot in a cell.

She knew with a sudden certainty that Hugh was the husband for her. There was no longer any doubt in her mind that he would win their wager. But now any thought of winning was senseless. His freedom and life were in jeopardy.

Even though his tactics were unfamiliar and frightening, had he not rescued her in the gardens? Unlike Richard, never once had Hugh caused her physical harm. Did she not, at the very least, owe him something?

Adrienna stepped forward. "He already has a wife, milady."

"He stated that was not so."

Hugh grasped Adrienna's hand and pulled her back to his side. "That is not quite what I said, milady. I believe I gave you no answer."

"Then where is this wife you profess to have?"

Adrienna's resolve nearly wilted under the venom in the queen's tone. But unless she wanted her husband tossed into a cell or forced to commit adultery and big-amy, she had no other choice but to tell all.

And unless she wanted the same forced upon her, it was in her best interest to have Hugh's continued support and protection until they could be free of Eleanor's castle. She turned slightly, stepped closer to him and placed her free hand on his chest. Without taking her gaze from his, she answered Eleanor. "She is here, mi-lady. I am the earl's wife."

A confusing din of noise broke out—Queen Eleanor shouted, Lady Sarah renewed her cries, a few of the guards cursed, while others gasped. But the clamor faded into the background as Adrienna lost herself in the expressions crossing Hugh's face.

At first his eyes had widened in surprise at her con-fession. But now, the look she'd become familiar with curved his lips into a devilish smile.

Instead of gloating at his win, as she half expected, Hugh raised her hand and brushed a kiss across her fin-gertips. "It seems that perhaps you tire of our wager."

His soft whisper was meant only for her. Yet some-thing in the certainty of his voice made it seem as if he'd shouted the words from the battlements.

Ignoring the heat flaring across her cheeks, she nod-ded. "Aye, it appears that way."

"What plot is afoot here?" Queen Eleanor's question broke Adrienna's concentration. She forced her gaze away from Hugh's.

"There is no plot afoot. Earl Wynnedom is in truth the husband I thought long dead."

"I demand an explanation. Ryebourne was no earl."

"No, he was not. But it seems he has risen in status during his lengthy absence."

Eleanor arched one brow at Hugh. "So, Ryebourne, how is it that you appear at my court, miraculously alive with a highly questionable title?"

"Wynnedom, my lady. The Earl of Wynnedom. Despite your concerns, the title is not in question. It was granted by King Henry."

"And you." Eleanor ignored Hugh's answer, turning instead to Adrienna. "Your sire begged my favor under false pretense. I should have him tossed in irons for his part in this."

Before Adrienna could reply, Hugh said, "Such measures are uncalled for, he does not know of my return."

Had he changed his opinion of her father? Relief washed through Adrienna. Perhaps she'd convinced him of her father's and her own innocence in what had befallen him.

Queen Eleanor lifted her chin a notch. "All of you will leave my court." Her voice was low, deadly calm, leaving no doubt as to the seriousness of her order. "If you are still here when the sun rises, I will see you hanged."

The guards parted, letting Eleanor pass between them. When they paused, waiting for Lady Sarah to follow the queen, Eleanor turned around and said, "Not you. Your usefulness in this court is over." She then glared at Hugh. "Wynnedom, take this strumpet with you. I care not what you do with her once you are off my lands."

"I will take her," William called out from his seat on the bed. "But only as my wife."

Eleanor nodded. "So be it. Take her to the chapel this night and she is yours."

Obviously in shock, Lady Sarah stood rooted to the floor as the queen and her men filed out of the chamber.

Once they'd left, Hugh closed the door and turned toward the bed. "William, you did your part, you need not marry the woman."

"Yes, I do. If she leaves here under your protection you will feel honor bound to be responsible for her." With a glance toward Adrienna, he added, "Your responsibility and protection should be to your wife, not some other woman."

He pointed to his discarded clothes. "Hand me those, please."

Hugh tossed the garments onto the bed. But he didn't let the discussion end. "But to marry her?"

"Is she not a lady?" William pulled the bed curtains closed while he quickly dressed, opening them again when he finished.

With an expression Adrienna couldn't decipher, William stared at Hugh and asked, "Did she not only do as her master commanded?"

Something in William's choice of words gave Adrienna pause. As her master commanded...*master commanded.* Not as her lord or lady ordered. But as her master commanded.

Hugh's paler complexion was even more curious.

Why did the comment cause him to blanch? What could have happened to give that seemingly odd word choice the power to affect him so?

Before she could piece little snatches of remembered conversations with Hugh together in her mind, Sarah said, "There is no need for this." Her shock had worn off enough for her to speak, but not enough for her voice to remain steady. "I told you before that you need not marry me, I have not changed my mind."

William rose and stood before her. "Then you need make a choice—wed me, or find someone else to take you from here."

"But, Adrienna promised."

"Yes, I did." She wouldn't let William twist her honor about in such a manner. She had made a vow, one she'd not break. "And Hugh said—"

The twin glares from Hugh and William stopped her argument in her throat.

William lifted Sarah's hand and placed it in the crook of his arm. "Perhaps we can discuss this somewhere more private."

Sarah's frightened, confused look brought Adrienna toward the woman. Hugh stopped her before she reached the other couple. "Leave them be."

While she was to leave them be, *he* made it a point to walk to the chamber door with them. She couldn't hear what he said to William, but it didn't seem to upset Sarah any more than she already was, so Adrienna remained where she stood.

She had other thoughts to dwell upon. One more distressing than the others—what would happen when William and Sarah left and she was alone with her husband?

Chapter Eleven

Once the door shut behind the departing couple, Hugh turned and looked at her. He said nothing, just stared at her as if waiting for her to do, or say something.

Adrienna was well aware of what he wanted. By confessing to the queen, she'd already stated in public that they were wed. But a spoken confession, public or not, was not what Hugh wanted. She glanced at the floor, trying to hide the heat that surely colored her cheeks. No, he wanted their wager fulfilled in the manner they'd agreed upon. She had to come to him.

Her gaze flew to the bed. Nothing in her life had given her the experience she needed to know how to go about this—task. Although of course she knew how the act was performed, she hadn't been that sheltered.

It would have been impossible to go about her daily activities without seeing the rutting animals in the pens. In a keep the size of Hallison there was little privacy and that small luxury was accorded to the lord, her father.

It'd have been a miracle not to come across one of the guards, or guests, and their love of the moment lost in the throes of passion.

Still, witnessing the act left her with no idea how to begin. Should she lie down on the bed? Clothed, or unclothed?

A quick look at Hugh was of no help, either. His steady stare told her nothing. Embarrassment held her tongue silent.

Adrienna's cheeks burned. Taking a deep breath she undid the ties of her gown with shaking hands and let it pool on the floor at her feet.

Her chemise, stockings and shoes were also left in the pile. Without so much as glancing at Hugh, she stepped away from them and crossed the short distance to the bed. Those few steps seemed like miles to her and she nearly fell onto the bed in relief.

She longed to hide herself with the covers. It was a slim hope, but perhaps the flickering torchlight did not reveal all. Or maybe the remaining bed curtains hid her from view.

Once situated on her back, Adrienna cleared her throat and said what she thought he wanted to hear, "This is your bed. I am here. You have won."

Hugh closed his eyes. This was one of the things that could be worse than wedding the palace whore. The future of their shared passion could hinge on this one night. To fuel Adrienna's desire and bring her to bliss only to cause her pain, no matter how brief, was not something he looked forward to this night.

No. He had plans for Adrienna. Those plans did not include frightening her on their first night together. She'd be frightened enough, and angry, later. His chest tightened at the thought.

The sudden clenching made him curse to himself. Why was he feeling this guilt and shame? She owed him. He deserved a measure of revenge for what she and her father had done.

His temples throbbed. Hugh looked at her. Adrienna held her eyes tightly closed. Torchlight wavered across the paleness of her flesh.

Guilt? No. Shame? Yes. While it was true, he was owed much, for his plan to work he needed to make her desire him before moving forward. So for now, he could freely take pleasure in what she offered. And give pleasure in return.

The silent promise of holding the revenge back made the tightness in his chest ease. He crossed halfway to the bed. "Adrienna, I told you once before that I would not swive this marriage into existence. Get up."

She opened her eyes, lifted her head and stared at him. "But I thought—"

"I know what you thought." When she didn't move, he repeated, "Get up."

Slowly she rose from the bed and reached for her clothes.

"No. Just stand up."

Without arguing, she kept her gaze rooted to the floor and stood as stiff and unyielding as a board before him. Ah, but she was a sight to enjoy.

The blush of inexperience covered her face. He would be the only person in her life who would ever witness such a flush. Once she became used to being naked before him, she would no longer feel such embarrassment. It told him more about her nervousness than any words could.

Such nervousness was a good thing. It would keep her senses heightened.

Untried by childbirth, her breasts still jutted away from her body. They would fill his hands perfectly. Without her knowing it, the already hardening tips awaited his attention.

Her narrow waist gave way to rounded hips. Perhaps wider than the beauties of song and story, hers held the promise of a soft resting place. In the flickering light, strands of dark auburn curls mixed with the burnished gold ones at the apex of her thighs.

He'd not realized how long her legs were. Nor how muscular. This was not a woman who sat around the keep ordering others about. The firm curves in her thighs and calves came from working, riding and walking. Her legs would wrap around him and hold him close without tiring.

The mere vision that thought created set heat building in his groin. If he wasn't careful he'd forget that this night was for her.

"Look at me." He kept his voice low and steady, hoping not to startle her.

She shook her head and kept her gaze averted.

"Adrienna—wifeling, you are lovely. You have nothing of which to be ashamed."

When she chanced to look at him, he caught her gaze and held it. He wanted not to teach her of sex, but to lead her into the dance of love. The mind was as much of a participant in this dance as the body. The easiest way to convince her mind to join them, was to talk to her. Soothing her worry with words would permit her mind to envision what he told her.

"You stole some of my pleasure. I dreamed of undressing you the first time. The simple thought of removing your clothing one piece after another and slowly discovering your hidden charms one agonizing inch at a time has given me many pleasurable dreams."

Her face again reddened, but she narrowed her eyes. "You seek to flatter me with lies to make this easier?"

Her defensiveness gave him a clue to what she really thought of her own body. That would not suit, because she truly was a lovely, desirable, albeit inexperienced woman.

"Lies?" Hugh shook his head. "No. You do not see yourself as I do."

She held out her arms. "Then you are blind. I am rounded with excessive fat."

"No, you are not." Why did women think that? One man devises a song about a pale, slight woman and all within hearing believe that was the only picture of perfection. But perfection came in many shades, shapes and sizes and as far as he was concerned Adrienna was perfect.

"You are made to have babies, healthy babies—my babies. You are built to cushion a man atop of you. I defy you to find one curve, one speck of flesh that was not created solely for our pleasure."

Adrienna lowered her arms with a sigh. "I give, Hugh. I have not the words, nor the knowledge to argue with your illogical notions."

"Soon, wifeling, soon you will know just how logical my notions truly are."

She had no reply. Instead she apologized, "Then I am sorry for ruining your dreams."

Now she was headed in the right direction. "You can make up for your grievous error."

"How?"

She was curious. Good. Curiosity would allow her to take an active part in this dance. It would also allow her the opportunity to become familiar with his body. "You can undress me."

Her mouth fell open. She blinked once—twice, before sputtering, "I—I can't do that."

"You can and you will, once you let go of the fear."

"I am not afraid."

"Now who lies? Everyone is fearful of the unknown. It takes bravery to force oneself beyond the fear." He crooked a finger at her. "Come to me, Adrienna. I will help you find your bravery."

She approached him slowly like someone condemned. Hugh swallowed a smile at the pathetic look of confusion and trepidation crossing her face.

When she stopped before him, he lifted her chin with the tip of his finger. "Kiss me. I need to taste your lips on mine. I want you to not be afraid."

She stretched up and placed her lips briefly against his.

He rolled his eyes heavenward as if seeking help. "Have I not yet taught you to kiss better than that?"

Adrienna bit her lip for a moment before leaning against him, placing her arms about his neck and lowering his head toward her.

While her lips covered his Hugh kept his arms at his sides, unwilling to take the lead from her in any way. That resolve was nearly shattered when she parted his lips with her tongue and tentatively beckoned him to return the kiss.

Aye, this wifeling of his had learned well. He closed his eyes and savored the feel of her soft body pressing into his chest.

She deepened their kiss, strengthening her silent plea for his response. Hugh answered by sliding his lips over hers. Adrienna nearly melted against him. The hammering of her heart matched his own rapid pulse.

She moaned and he raised his mouth from hers. Staring down into her passion-laden gaze, he asked, "That was not so bad, was it?"

"Only the stopping."

Her breathless voice prompted him to offer reassurance, "Oh, fear not, there will be more." He led her over to the bench near the lit wall torch. He wanted to see every expression cross her face.

He sat on the bench and pulled his tunic out from beneath him. Hugh longed to feel her hands on his flesh, to hold her close, her soft breast pressed tightly against the muscle of his chest.

Keeping a controlled rein on his own desires, and not wanting to rush her, he stuck out his feet. "Boots first."

Adrienna knelt before him. She was relieved to find only short cuffed shoes and not high boots. At least these she could easily slide off his feet. The boots would have required her to turn around, bend over and put his leg between hers….

The mental image forming at that thought caused the heated flush to return to her face. What was he doing to her? Would this constant burn of embarrassment ever give her peace?

Quickly reaching beneath his tunic, she undid the garters holding up his stockings and removed them. Using his thighs for support, she rose. Halfway up her swollen knee threatened to buckle.

"I'm sorry. I forgot about your knee." Hugh grasped her arms. "Are you all right?"

She could well believe him, since she'd forgotten about it, too. "No, it's fine. I shouldn't have stood so quickly."

"We can retire to the bed if it would be easier."

Good heavens, not yet. "No." She eased herself upright. "This is fine."

He'd already loosened his tunic, so she only had to gather the hem in her hand and pull it over his head.

His quick intake of breath froze her in place. Adrienna looked down. With her arms stretched overhead, her breasts were so close to his face she could feel his hot breath against her flesh.

Overwhelmed, she shuddered. Her emotion was not

as much fear of the unknown as it was an uncomfortable shame.

She lowered his tunic before her. "Please, Hugh, no more. I will perish from humiliation."

He captured her between his knees. Holding her firmly in place, he tugged the garment out of her hands and tossed it to the floor. Before she could cry cease, he covered the tip of one breast with his mouth.

"Oh!" Surprise at his touch faded as quickly as the shame and humiliation. A hot wave washed through her. Adrienna threaded her fingers through his hair and held him close.

A light scraping of teeth across her nipple sent a flash of need to settle low in her belly and drew a moan from her throat. "Hugh…" Unable to identify what she sought, Adrienna rubbed her cheek across his hair.

A tremor rippled the length of her. If his hot, moist caress on her breast could make her this weak with need, what would he do to her once they were in his bed? Adrienna gasped with anticipation at the thought. She'd never imagined that a man's touch could make her want to cry for him to stop and plead for more at the same time.

When he moved to her other breast, she lifted her head and arched her back as pleasure fogged her thoughts.

Hugh ceased just as suddenly as he'd begun. Taking her hand in his, he placed a kiss on her palm before placing it against her chest. "Do you feel that?"

The light above them shimmered in his eyes. A fine sheen of sweat covered his brow. She could only nod her answer. Oh, yes, she felt the hard drumming through her whole body.

He trailed their hands down her abdomen and belly to rest over springy curls. "And do you feel the pulsing here?"

She closed her eyes and nodded again. Feel it? She wondered if it would consume her.

Hugh moved their clasped hands to his chest. "And this, do you feel how hard my heart pounds?"

"Yes." Her whispered answer sounded breathless to her.

He stroked their hands down his abdomen. Adrienna bit her lower lip, but did not ask him to stop. When the hard length of his erection pulsed against her palm, she closed her eyes.

"No, Adrienna, look at me."

Still worrying her lip between her teeth, she met his eyes. She hadn't known what to expect in his expression, but his heavily lidded gaze of desire chased her concerns away.

He pressed her palm harder against his erection. "And do you feel the pulsing here?"

"Yes."

Hugh lifted her palm briefly to his lips before releasing her hand. "Ah, wifeling, do you now see that what I do to your body, you do to mine?"

He brushed wayward strands of hair from her face and stroked her cheek. She leaned into his touch and answered, "Yes."

"If our bodies respond so passionately to each other, how can there be any shame in what we do?"

She had no answer for him, but there was a strange logic to his way of thinking.

He sighed, then gently circled the tip of one finger around her breast, bringing the circles closer to the nipple. When she moaned softly at his touch, he asked, "Do you like the way that feels?"

She arched her back. "Oh, yes."

He sat back and relaxed his knees. "There is more. Much more." Hugh plucked at his shirt. "But alas, I am still clothed."

Adrienna grasped his finely pleated shirt and nearly tore it when she jerked it over his head. Then she reached for the ties on his braies, only to have him grasp her wrist.

"Do you not wish to inspect what you have uncovered?"

She stared at him. Actually, the only thing she wanted was for the wild throbbing between her legs to be appeased.

"Adrienna, slow down. Take the time to be as familiar with my body as you are with your own."

Suddenly it all fit together in her mind. He was doing everything he could to keep her from being distraught. While she was nervous, she was not some silly frightened girl to run at the thought of being with a man.

Still, his unwarranted consideration lent a gentling warmth to the unchecked fire coursing through her veins. If he kept this up, she would easily surrender her soul to him.

She stroked a finger down the center of his chest,

tracing the fine line of dark hairs to his belly before splaying both hands across his chest.

The muscles beneath her touch were as solid as stone, unyielding beneath his sun-darkened flesh. She stroked a fingertip along one long narrow scar, then another and another.

Desire faded beneath growing confusion. "Not all of these are from a blade." She whispered to herself as she traced one from the front of his chest, along his side and after pulling him away from the wall followed it halfway across his back.

No. Her mind refused to comprehend the visual proof before her. "What caused these scars?" When he didn't answer, she stepped back, ordering, "Stand up."

With nothing more than the raising of one eyebrow he did as she bid. Adrienna walked behind him and gasped at the multitude of fine white lines crisscrossing his back.

He was a living, breathing man. Nobody with a heart or soul would abuse another in this manner. Prisoners were treated better than this. Dear Lord, not even an obstinate animal would be handled this badly.

It was no wonder he worried so about frightening, or distressing her. She placed her lips against each puckered scar marking his back. Standing before him she asked, "How did this happen? What was done to you? Was it from your father?"

Hugh's throat convulsed as he fought to hold back a snarled response. His father? No, it was because of hers.

But something kept him from telling her that. He

didn't know what that odd something was, nor did he know why it was suddenly so important to shield her from the truth.

It only mattered that they get through this night first. He wanted her bound in some way to him—even if only by passion—before telling her about his captivity.

Instead, he brushed the tears from her cheeks before pulling her into his embrace. "Wifeling, not everyone has an easy lot in this life."

"Would that I could make it better for you."

"But you have, you are."

She pulled out of his embrace. "Hugh, hold me."

"I was."

"No. Not that way." She took his hand and led him toward the bed. "You said my curves were made to cushion a man. Show me."

Ah, so his wifeling was no longer too embarrassed to take her part in this dance. Good. Because he was as ready for her as she thought she was for him.

Chapter Twelve

Hugh padded barefooted across the floor as he followed her to the bed. She released his hand, debating whether she should finish removing his clothes, or climb into the bed. The instant she made her decision and turned around, he tumbled her onto the bed already naked.

Within the circle of his arms she snuggled against his side. To her satisfaction, their bodies fit well together, her soft curves resting easily against his hard muscles.

His warm, spice-scented flesh beckoned her to be bold. She stroked his chest, pausing over each scar, before trailing to the next. She longed to ask again how and why he had received so many wounds, but held her tongue. Instead she concentrated on the softness of the dark hair dusting his chest and abdomen.

The mind-numbing urgency she'd felt only moments ago ebbed to smoldering hunger. Now she was content for the time to learn his body, and to become familiar with the feel of him beneath her.

She traced circles around his flat nipples, and they tightened beneath her touch. When Hugh inhaled softly, she realized that the stroking gave him pleasure. Just as his touch had done to her.

Hugh caressed her back and hips, then drew her leg across his to gently probe her knee.

Adrienna tilted her head and nipped at his stubble-covered chin. "I told you it was fine."

"I was just reassuring myself."

Should he not be thinking of something other than her knee? She slid her leg farther across him and came up over him. "See. It is fine."

Her intent had been to prove that her knee was intact and not seriously injured. But straddling him wiped all thoughts of her knee from her mind.

A sensual half smile curved his lips. She stared into his heavily lidded eyes and wondered at the control he seemed willing, near eager to give her.

Anticipation tightened her muscles. But his sure touch on her breast and his hand steadily caressing her exposed inner thigh urged her to relax.

Without thought Adrienna arched her back, seeking relief from the insistent throbbing between her thighs. He drew in a slow, shaking breath before sliding his hand higher.

Hugh caressed her shoulder before pulling her closer. Against her lips, he whispered, "I want to touch you."

"Please." Her voice rasped harsh and hoarse in her ears. But somehow, he understood her need and found the teasing caress that dragged a near frantic moan from her.

A moan Hugh swallowed with a harsh kiss of desire and bewilderment. All of his well-built plans were shattering around him. By God he wanted her for himself, not for any scheme of revenge.

There was no artifice in her reaction to his touch, no false moans of pleasure escaped from her kiss swollen lips. Only an honest response to the overwhelming desire driving her toward completion.

He craved her honesty, desperately needing it to bring a glimmer of light to his black heart. Later, he would despise himself. Now, he wanted only to lose himself in shared passion.

Hugh enveloped her in his arms. "Adrienna—"

Beyond speech, she gasped at the loss of his touch and pushed up out of his embrace. Before he could roll her beneath him, she reached down and placed his near burning hardness at the opening to her womb.

Slowly Adrienna took him into her body. Hugh grabbed the covers beneath him. She flinched once, but didn't stop. Never had he felt anything as erotic as this untried woman freely taking what she wanted.

He marveled at the speed in which she found the right tempo for the two of them. He closed his eyes and let himself get lost in the haze of passion.

"Hugh, please." Adrienna's fingernails dug into his shoulders, jerking him out of his haze. He met her fevered, frustrated stare and curved his arms around her before rolling them over in one fluid move.

Without coaxing, she wrapped her legs around his waist and held on tightly. No matter how hard he tried to be gentle, Adrienna demanded more. She met him thrust for thrust. And when he brought his lips hard over hers, she returned his kiss and dug her nails into his shoulders.

This union in no way resembled the acts he'd been required to perform in the past. No master ordered him to this woman's bed. And the woman now beneath him demanded nothing.

He was supposed to be initiating her into this mating dance, binding her with physical pleasure. Instead, she'd become an equal participant in an act that had become much more than simply physical.

Acceptance, trust, sharing—the things he'd hungered for, longed for, needed for so many years were embodied in the woman he was supposed to hate. He couldn't put a name to the emotion tightening his chest at this moment, but it was nowhere near hatred.

Soon their joined cries echoed in the chamber. Hugh knew he was in danger. Grave danger. His already shattered plans for retribution became jumbled in the hazy fog of passion.

Once his body stopped throbbing, he collapsed beside her. The unfamiliar urge to rage, cry and laugh all at the same time overwhelmed him.

Adrienna cursed beside him. Then her trembling, choked laugh made him smile. He slipped an arm beneath her and pulled her to his side. While he'd fought the insane urge to release his emotions, she'd given in to it.

"Hugh?"

"Aye?"

"What would you like to wager now?"

"I am not certain. Perhaps together we can think of something."

A knock at the chamber door stopped their conversation. Hugh rose from the bed and pulled the covers over Adrienna before retrieving his tunic and dropping it over his head.

The knock was repeated. Before he reached the door, Sarah entered with William right behind her. "Forgive us for intruding, but we need to leave here immediately."

Hugh took one look at William's tightly drawn face and knew something was seriously wrong. The only time he'd seen a look that desperate was when the two of them had joined King Henry at Aryseeth's tent.

"What is it?"

"Stefan is here."

That short declaration was enough to jerk the floor from beneath his feet. "Stefan of Arnyll?"

"Aye."

Hugh motioned William to follow him and they sat down at the small table.

He poured both of them a measure of wine. "That isn't possible. Stefan is with Guy."

"No." William shook his head. "He is here. I saw him with Langsford."

Langsford and Arnyll—a match of which the devil would approve. And one that boded ill for him and William.

"It would be interesting to discover his reason for being here." Especially after he'd sworn to assist Guy.

"He's been here for two days."

Hugh paused. Two days? Without him knowing about the man's arrival? He glanced at Adrienna. Obviously he'd been too consumed with other matters.

William beckoned Sarah to the table. "Tell Hugh what you told me."

"There isn't much to tell. This Stefan arrived two days ago demanding an audience with Queen Eleanor."

"Were you privy to this audience?"

Sarah smiled. "Of course. My…position…does afford some benefits."

Her slight hesitation gave Hugh more proof that her position wasn't the palace whore. Leaving him to wonder exactly what tasks she did complete for Queen Eleanor.

"He was looking for you, Lord Wynnedom. But not as a friend."

Hugh's attention peaked. "I can imagine not."

"He wanted to bargain with the queen, offering gold in exchange for her silence when you turned up missing from her court."

It would have been hard for Eleanor to refuse the deal. "And she accepted this bargain?"

"No." Sarah shrugged. "Eleanor has little use for more gold."

Surprised, Hugh leaned forward. "If she truly wanted me gone from her court, she should have grabbed the chance with eager hands."

"Ah, but, Lord Wynnedom, you are Henry's man and she knows this. It was your only saving grace. While she'd willingly plot to see you destroyed, she'd not thwart her husband so easily."

Disbelief crowded out his earlier surprise. "I can't imagine Queen Eleanor being worried about thwarting King Henry."

"Perhaps not. But she had no liking for this Arnyll. She said he was hiding far too much, something too dark for her to become involved."

"Dark?"

"I'm not sure, but it seemed to me that while he was full of fine words and sweet compliments, his eyes appeared to be made of a strange green ice." Frowning, Sarah paused a moment as if remembering the event. "After he left her chamber, even the queen commented on his lack of soul and how rehearsed his offer appeared."

He knew exactly what she spoke of. Arnyll was soulless and cold. But Stefan couldn't be faulted for that. Not when Hugh had to search for his own soul at times.

"How did he become acquainted with Langsford?"

A wry smile curved Sarah's lips. "Eleanor requested that I introduce the two. She thought they'd suit each other perfectly."

"So, instead of being forthright, she gave them the opportunity to plot and plan my demise seemingly behind her back."

"Aye."

Hugh wanted to leave this place immediately. And do so without coming in contact with Stefan. "Where are they now?"

"In the hall, drinking and discussing you."

He asked William, "Did Arnyll see you?"

"No."

"Good. Then he doesn't yet know we're aware of his presence." Hugh nodded at Sarah. "Help Adrienna dress." He wanted to talk with William alone.

Watching Lady Sarah approach the bed, Adrienna wished Hugh had used a bit of tact with the woman. A hard frown creased Sarah's brow. Her lips were little more than a tight, thin line.

She stopped alongside the bed and lifted her chin. "I am not your servant."

Adrienna swung her legs over the side of the bed. Yes, Hugh did need to be more careful with this woman. "Nobody called you such." She leaned closer and lowered her voice. "I think the men just wanted to converse in private."

"He could have said that."

"True." He could have said many things, but from the flat tone of his voice and harsh, drawn expression, Adrienna doubted if being kind, considerate or even slightly tactful was at the forefront of his mind just this moment.

In the short time she'd known him, she knew for a certainty that Hugh of Wynnedom was not a fearful man. He was far from being a coward. But this Stefan put him on edge. She didn't know why, but if forced to guess, she'd say they had spent some time together…time that had been far from pleasant.

In truth, she didn't know her husband well enough

to guess. *Husband*. Lord above, what had she done? Her body warmed with recent memories. She had no complaints, other than to wonder why she'd waited so long. If all did not turn out for the best, it was too late now to change her mind.

"I'm here to help you dress." Sarah broke into her musings. "Where are your clothes?"

Absently pointing to the other side of the bed, Adrienna asked, "When will you and William wed?"

With a soft, dismissive snort, Sarah left to retrieve the clothing from the pile. She returned and answered, "We have already exchanged vows."

"And?"

"There will be no *and* until I grant him permission. If I ever do."

While Adrienna bunched up her under gown and dropped it over her head, Sarah added, "I was promised a titled lord. I will not settle for less."

"Perhaps you should make do with what you have."

"And perhaps you, Lady of Wynnedom, should keep your thoughts to yourself."

Adrienna paused before snatching her gown from Sarah's extended hand. She pulled the clothing over her head and laced up the sides before asking, "Why are you being so nasty now? Why did you bother to free me from Richard's chamber?"

"Would you rather I'd not?"

"I'd rather you answer my question."

"I freed you from Langsford's bed because the man is a swine. He has no care for a woman's pleasure and thinks pain should suffice. I would subject no woman to his twisted desires."

Adrienna's stomach rolled. Before she could thank Sarah, the lady reached down the neck of her gown and pulled out a pouch. "These are yours."

Taking the pouch, Adrienna looked inside and found the few pieces of jewelry she'd brought with her from Hallison.

"We stopped by your chamber to gather some of your belongings for our journey. Elise gave us this pouch and wishes you well."

Adrienna would miss the only female friend she'd ever truly had. And she hoped Elise found a husband she could care for, and not come to regret the time spent in Eleanor's court.

"Are you ready?" Hugh approached and touched her arm.

"Aye."

"Then, ladies—" he included Sarah in his glance "—let us be gone from here. The sooner I can set foot on English soil, the happier I will be."

William agreed, motioning for Sarah to join him. Hugh waved toward the door. "Shall we get under way then?"

There was nothing Adrienna wanted more than to leave this place. "Yes. Please."

Stefan of Arnyll leaned into the crenellation of the stone curtain wall and watched the four figures ride through the outer bailey.

"Are we not going after them?"

He looked at Langsford and shook his head. "Not yet. We have time. Plenty of time, since we know their destination."

"Aye, but we could take them on the road and be done with it."

This man the queen trusted did not deserve to live. He seemed to take great pride in showing his lack of wit to the world. His stupidity would either get him killed—Stefan smiled to himself—or perhaps it would gain him a position in Aryseeth's slave quarters.

Stefan nodded. Aye, the slave master always seemed to need countless fools to use as bait.

"And what if someone came to their rescue while we attacked them on the road?"

"I didn't take that into consideration." Langsford sighed as if he was greatly disappointed. "I suppose the odds would be a little more in their favor."

A little more? If Langsford fought with his wits, the odds would be greatly in Hugh's favor.

Although Stefan had to admit, if only to himself, he, too, was eager to confront Hugh. It would bring him great pleasure to turn the man over to Aryseeth and witness his final humiliation.

Far from stupid, Stefan knew that Hugh had only petitioned Sidatha for his release with others to keep an eye on him. After suffering their scorn for years on end, how could they have thought he'd be glad to be welcomed into their fold?

Nay. The only welcoming aspect about freedom was the gold to be gained from returning all of them to their rightful place—captivity.

Chapter Thirteen

Adrienna had been around her father and his men often enough to know when something was wrong. Even though she could not yet determine all of Hugh's moods, she was well able to decipher the sense of foreboding his overalertness conveyed. His uneasiness cast a pall of doom that chilled Adrienna despite the warm sunshine.

Yet, she could not understand his caution. If one did not count waiting for the white-capped channel to calm enough for a crossing, the six days journey from Poitiers to Southampton had been uneventful. Yet, both Hugh and William had been wary since the moment they'd left Eleanor's castle.

Wary and…curt. Hugh had responded to her questions with single-word answers that more resembled grunts than human speech. Even when they'd stop for the night, whether alongside the road, in an empty hunters' lodge or a well-tended inn, he'd barely spoken.

It wasn't so much that he seemed angry. While his jaw

was tense and his manner brusque, his eyes did not blaze with rage. It seemed to her that he was consumed by a worry and concern she could not name, nor see. Eventually, she'd simply given up trying to hold a conversation.

Now, the man who'd killed another with nothing but his bare hands had his weapons at the ready. One sword hung in a scabbard from his belt, with another strapped to his back. The daggers were not encased in scabbards. Instead one was tucked in the top of his high boot, while the second one hung from a looped thong on his saddle.

If for any reason he fell, or was thrown from his horse, he would likely impale himself with his own weapons. William had armed himself in the same manner. They appeared to be headed toward a battle.

If the men expected to be attacked, who was the enemy? And why would anyone attack this small party?

Not robbers. Anxious to leave the castle they'd not taken the time to pack all of their belongings. So, their possessions were meager…only the basic necessities. As far as she knew they carried nothing of value that would cry wealth or riches to any who spied them on the road.

She could stand it no longer. Adrienna urged her palfrey ahead. When she was alongside Hugh, she asked, "What worries you so?"

"Nothing." He scanned the trees lining the road—an act that had been repeated countless times before.

"If nothing worries you, what are you looking for?"

Without taking his attention away from the forest, he asked, "I cannot survey our surroundings?"

Adrienna grimaced at the unwarranted harsh tone of his

voice. But she'd be put off by his surliness no longer. "You can survey the surroundings all you like, *my lord earl.*"

Her clipped answer caught his attention. He turned his gaze to her. She held his stare and continued, "However, if someone is going to jump out of those trees to attack us, I would prefer to know beforehand."

Hugh's shoulders rose then fell with an exaggerated sigh. "I was trying to be discreet."

"You are failing miserably."

"So it seems." He checked the road ahead. "Is it odd for me to be this concerned for your safety? Would your father not do the same?"

In truth? No. Her sire would not be as concerned for her safety. His horse and men would come first. Men…Adrienna paused…there were no men. No guards protected the Earl of Wynnedom. That level of lack was unheard of and quite possibly foolish. But from what she knew of Hugh he was no man's fool. She looked behind her at William and Sarah before turning back to ask, "Where are your men?"

He shrugged, as if her question was of little consequence. "Perhaps you now understand the reason for my attentiveness to our surroundings."

"You have no guards, or men in your employ?" Surely King Henry would not have given the title to one without the means to afford such a rise in stature.

"I did not say that."

Truly confused, she asked, "Why are they not with you now?"

"They are—"

His answer was cut short by a series of shrill whistles. Hugh shouted, "Ride!" before grabbing the reins of her horse.

Instantly grasping for a secure purchase, Adrienna kept from falling backward off the horse by grabbing the beast's mane with one hand and the pommel of her saddle with the other. When righted, she tore the reins from Hugh's possession with a muttered curse.

He may have taken lead of her horse instinctively, but she was not some weak, fainting maid to be led from danger. She easily kept pace with Hugh. Their companions, William and Sarah, were close behind.

When Hugh urged his horse faster, Adrienna leaned as far forward as the high pommel of the saddle would allow. Her heart beat in rhythm with the thunderous pounding of the animals' hooves. Trees seemed to whoosh by them at a dizzying pace. The wind tore the covering from her head, permitting her unbound hair to stream behind her.

They quickly covered what seemed like miles to her before coming to a halt just beyond a small clearing. Quickly dismounting, Hugh breathlessly ordered, "Into the woods."

On foot he led his animal into the more protective cover of the woods, away from the road. She, William and Sarah did the same.

Sarah pushed another small tree branch out of her way. "I see no one. Why are we leaving the road?"

"Simply because you see no one about, does not mean they are not there," William explained.

"So we are running from someone we cannot see?"

Wondering the same thing, Adrienna frowned. Who were they running from and where exactly were they headed? She'd been so anxious to leave Poitiers behind that she'd never questioned Hugh about their destination.

William lowered his voice and said something to Sarah that Adrienna could not hear.

When the party resumed their slow foray into the woods, the areas between the trees eventually became wider. Adrienna urged her tired horse a little harder and caught up with Hugh. They hadn't stopped for a long while. Not since early this morning and now the sun was getting lower in the sky. "Hugh?"

He spared her a glance before hacking more underbrush out of their way. "Yes?"

"Are you not tired?"

"Of course." Without stopping he swung his sword in an arc before him. "But where would you like to make camp for the night?"

He was right. It would take hours to clear an area in which to bed down for the night. But that wasn't what caught her attention. "Ah, I am truly heartened to know that you can still use more than one word at a time."

He frowned before nodding in agreement. "Aye. Perhaps my concern with this journey has made me a little short with you."

In an attempt to lighten the mood a little, Adrienna slowly studied his profile from toe to head and back down. "Curt perhaps." She swallowed hard against the butterflies winging against her stomach. "But nay, my lord, never short."

The return of his frown let her know the attempt had been in vain. "The men following us wish us ill…or worse. I have no time for teasing, Adrienna."

That answered her most pressing question about his uneasiness. "Why did you not say so before now?"

Intent on watching his face, she stumbled over a fallen log. Hugh grasped her arm, keeping her upright. "Be careful. Breaking a leg would not help us any." He released her before asking, "What would you have done had you known about the men? Worried along with me?"

"Perhaps."

"It would have served little purpose."

"Except to explain your need to be so—distracted." When she'd made the decision to truly become his wife the last thing Adrienna had expected was to be as thoroughly ignored as she'd been the last few days.

"Distracted?"

"Aye, very much so."

"Inattentive?"

She couldn't disagree there, either. "Most assuredly."

He glanced sideways at her and Adrienna caught a hint of a smile twitching at the corner of his mouth. Was he baiting her? Had she lost this argument before it'd begun? She took a deep breath and quickly defended her position. "You have been ignoring me."

"I know. I realized that fact when you slept on the hard, cold ground every night. And again when you went through the day with nothing to fill your belly."

She cringed at her pettiness. Aye. She'd lost this argument. Not one night had she slept on the hard, cold ground. In fact, he'd been the one who took the brunt of the coldness—she'd spent the nights sprawled mostly atop his chest with their only cover tucked securely around her.

And there hadn't been one day, morning nor night, when they'd gone hungry.

Adrienna closed her eyes and shook her head before placing a hand on his arm and apologizing. "I am sorry for sounding so petty."

Hugh couldn't help but smile. When they'd first started this journey he *had* been distracted. But noticing her increased bewilderment at his one-word answers had only prompted him to intentionally goad her more.

If Adrienna's attention were directed toward seeking to figure out his supposed foul mood, she'd not notice his men surrounding them, or the enemy closing in. He didn't expect that tactic to last forever, but he had thought she'd complain before now.

Either to his credit, or her own, she'd remained in good temper much longer than he'd expected.

He glanced behind and found that William and Sarah had stopped a short distance back. They seemed to be deep in conversation. It gave him the opportunity to turn to Adrienna.

Cupping her chin, he stroked his thumb across her lower lip. Her shiver at his touch told him more than any words could. "There is no need to apologize."

"I have been petty and churlish in my complaint."

"No. 'Tis I who should apologize for intentionally

baiting you so much. You have only acted as I wanted you to act."

Her forehead creased in confusion and for a moment he thought she'd move away to consider his brash statement. Instead, she leaned into his touch. While her mind thought through what he'd just said, her body sought only contact with his. Hugh drew her closer.

"The men following us wish to take us hostage."

Adrienna's frown deepened. He knew that in her world being taken hostage was more of an inconvenience than horror. Hugh silently cursed his inability to explain in a manner that would not convey his terrors to her.

"Wifeling, this man Stefan knows not the meaning of honor or chivalry. He cares not about laws or decency."

"He would kill us instead of taking us hostage?"

Her breathless question made him wish it could be that simple. Death would be a preferred end to what Stefan possibly planned. "No. He will make us pray for death."

Adrienna's eyes widened. Sidatha's words echoed in his head…*bring no harm to the innocent.* He nearly choked on the sudden urge to protect her from the evils of his world.

Pulling her against his chest, Hugh rested his chin atop her head and wondered how he'd permitted her so completely into his soul.

Forgive…forget…were Sidatha's suggestions. At the time Hugh had fought against the idea. Now?

He was no longer as certain.

While his thirst for revenge had not been quenched, the pain wasn't nearly as sharp. And while memories of the years lost had not evaporated, they lacked the teeth to keep him awake nights.

Yet a small part of his mind still asked the same question, *are you not owed something for those years and what was done to you?*

He closed his eyes against the raging debate. This was not the time, nor the place, for serving his own end. Danger lurked too close. A danger that could toss all of them into an unending nightmare.

Hugh lifted his head and promised, "He will not succeed."

She gave him a half-hearted smile. "If we stand here conversing, he just may."

He scanned the forest before assuring her, "We could safely stand here all day if you like."

"That's what you've been constantly searching for all this time." Adrienna narrowed her eyes at him. "You *do* have men in attendance."

"I never said otherwise. My men had been waiting for my return to Southampton. They'd already had their orders." He released her, but stroked her cheek before stepping away. "There are twelve forming an armed, breathing wall around us."

"Eleven, my lord."

Hugh swung around to the voice behind him. Alain, the man temporarily in charge of the others, stepped into view.

William joined them at the same time, asking, "Eleven? Who is missing?"

Watching William with the man and noticing the way

he responded to him gave Hugh pause. Had the captain for his new guard been beneath his nose this whole time and he'd not realized it?

Alain gave William his full attention. "Young Osbert took an arrow. It was fatal."

William sighed. "At least he was not taken alive."

Silently Hugh agreed. While young Osbert had been training hard and would have become a competent guard, he was not made of stern enough backbone to survive more than a week in Aryseeth's care.

"His body?" William scanned the horses now entering the area. "We need return it to his family."

Hugh forced himself to remain silent. Another might take offense at the way William controlled the situation at hand. He'd not yet been assigned to this task and in truth did overstep the bounds of simple friendship.

But Hugh now realized that William was well suited to this position. For right now, he needed to care-for, be concerned for, others. It was a task that somehow made him seem more alive than anything else.

Of a certainty, he would need to officially make William the captain of Wynnedom's guard.

"Sir…" One of the other men stepped forward leading a horse. "We have his body."

Lady Sarah gasped. But before she could settle into a horrified scream, William pulled her to his side and held her close. To Hugh's astonishment the tactic seemed to calm her instantly.

After inspecting the form draped across the saddle,

William nodded. "Good. His mother will thank you. What about Arnyll and his men?"

"Arnyll still lives, but his men now number only three." Alain straightened in well-deserved triumph as the others voiced their prowess. "Your suggestion to use bows instead of swords worked to our advantage."

Since there had been fifteen men in Stefan's party, Hugh had to agree—using the bows had proved a smart move. It kept his men out of arm's reach and in such close quarters none of the men had to be true archers.

William raised a hand, signaling silence. "And what of Arnyll?"

"He kept to the north road. We followed for a short distance. But I thought it'd be a mistake to leave you, the earl and the women unprotected."

Hugh stepped in. "Well done. After a decent night's sleep, perhaps we will be able to make good progress tomorrow. With luck and God's continued blessing maybe we will be home by the end of the week."

Alain pointed toward the setting sun. "There is an empty hut straight ahead, my lord, with a stream behind it. The men and I can scavenge some food."

Both women sighed, drawing soft chuckles from a few of the men. Hugh waved Alain ahead, "Lead on."

He glanced down at the woman walking beside him. Even though she hadn't said so, Adrienna looked tired. The smile she turned toward him lacked her usual vibrancy. The circles beneath her eyes looked like smudges of dirt. Her hair had come loose during their race through the forest and now lay in tangled knots down her back.

It was imperative that he have a discussion with William this night. He only hoped it could be finished quickly. He wanted to spend the rest of the evening wrapped in a shared embrace with his wife.

Chapter Fourteen

To Adrienna the neglected hut in the forest looked like the grandest of castles. It was nothing but a wood framed two-room wattle-and-daub house.

Whoever had built it had most likely used the trees cut from the clearing for the framework. The branches and twigs would have gone into the wattle, with the mud daub holding it in place to fill in the frame.

What mattered most to her was the central hearth. There would be not only shelter from the night, but much welcome warmth.

While Hugh talked with the men, and William turned his attention to Sarah, she took the opportunity to put the stream to good use.

Clouds had rolled in with the setting of the sun so two small campfires had been lit behind the hut. They provided just enough flickering light to see the way to the water's edge.

The men tending the fires dipped their head as she

passed by. Sitting on a large, flat boulder Adrienna removed her soft leather boots and stockings. She dipped a toe into the stream and shivered as the icy water threatened to freeze her flesh.

Once accustomed to the coldness, the water felt good rippling over her feet. She slid closer to the edge of the boulder and tapped her toes on the pebbles covering the bottom of the stream.

The clouds parted enough to let the light of the moon shimmer across the surface of the water. The stream moved quickly, carrying the sparkles of light with it before rushing into the darkness of the forest.

Adrienna sighed. She longed to wade into the stream and let it carry her growing tension away. There were things Hugh was not telling her. She knew by the seriousness of his voice. And by the worry peering out at her from behind his gaze.

He thought he hid his concern so well. Did he not realize that she had witnessed his many changing moods? She did not need him to tell her when all was not right with him. It did not require a great deal of skill to compare one expression with another, or one tone with another. She could see the change, could hear it. She could almost taste its presence upon her lips.

Without a doubt, something *was* wrong. And it was something more than just this Stefan of Arnyll who had followed them from Queen Eleanor's court.

How was she to get him to talk to her? He would need to trust her before that could happen. So, how could she gain his trust, when she wasn't at all certain she fully trusted him?

This husband of hers was one contradiction after another. He could kill a man with his bare hands, yet those same hands gently and surely led her into the throes of passion.

His words could be harsh, cruel and cutting one moment, and then softly lull her into a cocoon of warmth and safety the next.

He would discuss something as important as battles or strategy with other men, while at the same time strip her clothing away with nothing more than a glance.

She was not used to this. Nothing in her past had brought her in contact with one so...aggravating. The men she knew were either strong, hard and mean, or soft and weak. They were not combinations of both.

Even Richard had only hidden his cruelty beneath a false mask. Had it not been for Hugh she may have discovered Richard's true face too late.

"Where are you, Adrienna?"

Startled, she would have splashed into the icy water of the stream had Hugh not caught her in his arms before she fell off the boulder.

Pressing a hand to her thudding heart, she admitted. "You frightened me. I did not hear you approach."

"Since I called your name twice, that is obvious." He released her long enough to sit down beside her and pull her onto his lap. "What were you thinking about so intently?"

"You." She slipped off his lap and sat between his

legs, her feet in the water and the back of her head resting against his chest.

"Comfortable?"

She snuggled tighter against his chest. "Very much so."

"I thought you might want this." He handed her a wide-toothed comb, asking, "So, were you thinking good thoughts of me?"

"Oh, nay." She pulled her hair in front of her and started untangling the knots at the ends. Glancing quickly over her shoulder, she smiled before admitting, "My thoughts of you are far from...good."

Hugh leaned his head down and whispered against her ear. "Then I hope they were wicked, lustful thoughts." He slid his arms around her, holding her close.

Her trembling had nothing to do with the coldness of the water. It was because of the heat of his breath against her ear, the strength of the arms embracing her and the feel of his chest beating against her back.

She forced herself to focus on combing her hair. "You removed your armor."

"And you are seeking to change the subject."

He brushed his thumb against the swell of her breast, chasing her interest in unsnarling her hair to the furthest reaches of her mind. She closed her eyes and wrapped her arms over his.

"Of course I am changing the subject." Adrienna sighed when he slid his lips lightly from her ear to her shoulder. "Talking about your lustful ways would never suffice."

"No? Then what do you suggest?"

The huskiness of his voice sent another tremor down her spine. She knew exactly what she would suggest if she was bold enough. She'd tell him to take her in his arms, kiss her senseless and then…Adrienna's cheeks flamed with heat at her thoughts. Never would she possess that much boldness.

"Do the words escape you?"

Before she could answer, Hugh pulled her up from the boulder, across his lap and then he lowered his lips to hers.

Was there anything more wondrous than being kissed so thoroughly by the man who could summon her passion with little more than a glance? Nay, but they were not alone. Even though his men had doused the small fires, giving them a measure of privacy, the guards were still mere footsteps away.

This was not the time—but his lips, his touch, were so warm and inviting. Nor was it the place—but his unspoken desire begged her for a response in kind.

Adrienna moaned in frustration at the ceaseless banter winging round and round in her mind. Seeking a way to still the demons, she laced one arm around Hugh's neck and drew him closer.

At her invitation, he parted her lips and deepened their kiss. She relaxed against him. It would require little coaxing to remain here, in his embrace, for an eternity.

The night breeze floated against her calves. The warmth of his stroking caress inching ever so slowly up her thigh chased away the coolness.

Lost in the fires his touch created, Adrienna clung to him. Her pulse quickened, she trembled in anticipation.

Yet, when he stroked the heat near the center of her body, she froze.

The bantering grew louder. They were not alone. Embarrassment and shame nearly choked her. Pulling away from his kiss, she cried, "No. Hugh, I cannot."

Hugh slid his hand from beneath her gown and wrapped both arms tightly around her, holding her on his lap. While nuzzling her neck he tried to calm her, "Hush, Adrienna, what is the matter?"

She buried her face against his shoulder. Now, feeling more of a fool than embarrassed, she tried to explain. "There are others around. I cannot. If they saw…I cannot…I…oh, Hugh…" It was all she could do not to burst out in tears of humiliation and frustration.

Adrienna turned her head, resting her cheek on his chest. "I am sorry."

He stroked her back and kissed the top of her head. "There is nothing to be sorry about."

"But you came here expecting…love play." She rolled her eyes at her hesitant word choice. "And were sadly mistaken."

"Look at me."

She leaned away and looked in what she believed was the direction of his face. The clouds had again covered the moon, leaving them in complete darkness.

He touched her cheek. "What do you see?"

"Honestly?"

"Of course."

"Nothing."

"So, what then did you think my men were going to witness?"

Instantly grateful for the deep darkness of the night and the cool breeze against her heated cheeks, Adrienna shrugged.

She heard his sigh and felt it warm against her cheek before he turned her face to his and kissed her.

Once she relaxed again he broke their kiss, but his lips brushed against hers as he spoke. "You can talk plainly to me, wifeling. You can tell me your most passionate thoughts. You cannot shock me. Nor will you disgust me."

Adrienna leaned her forehead against his. "I thought they would see us naked, lost in the throes of passion."

"On this hard, cold boulder?" He cradled her head in his hands. "I only came out here to kiss and caress my wife until she became senseless, that is all."

"Oh. I thought—"

He covered her lips with his thumb. "I know what you thought. Just because I kiss you…" His lips briefly touched hers.

"Or touch you…" He lowered a hand to her breast, causing the still sensitive peak to swell.

"Or caress you…" He grazed his knuckles down her ribs, across her belly until his hand rested between her thighs. "Does not mean I need to tumble you onto a bed."

Even through the layers of her gowns she could feel the heat of his touch. She gasped before softly moaning at the quickening of her body and the desperate pulsing beneath his kneading fingers.

He drew his hand away, bringing it up to brush the hair from her face. "Do you still have the comb?"

"What?" Breathless, her voice nearly trembled. Adrienna cleared her throat. "The comb?"

"Mmm, yes, the comb." His lips were against her neck. The feel of his tongue on her flesh did little to quiet the pounding of her heart.

"What do you want with the comb?" She tipped her head to the side, giving him better access.

Hugh trailed the tip of his tongue along the offered flesh, stopping just below her ear. "Since I can think of no other use for a comb, I thought I would help you untangle your hair. Was that not what you were going to do with it?"

"I guess." She sighed. "I think so."

He threw back his head and laughed. Adrienna leaned away and crossed her arms against her chest. "It isn't that funny."

She heard him sniff before he agreed, "Of course, you're correct. But I told you I wanted to drive you senseless and I think I have succeeded."

"Next time you will fail."

"If you say so." The humor in his voice was still evident.

Even though he couldn't see her, she narrowed her eyes at him. "I am permitted to do the same?"

He shouted for one of his men to bring a torch and to rekindle the campfires, then answered, "Oh, yes. I await the day."

She slid off his lap and returned to her position sitting on the boulder, between his legs, with her back pressed tight against his chest. When the torch's light fell across them, she handed him the comb over her shoulder. "Milord, your comb."

He pushed gently at her shoulder. "Milady, lean forward a little."

Adrienna dunked her toes back into the frigid water while Hugh worked the comb through the ends of her hair. The icy stream would have done more to cool her well-lit passion if his fingers weren't running through her hair, or stroking her scalp.

To her surprise, the silence that had fallen between them was comfortable. She felt no need to break the companionable quiet with idle chatter.

His gentle touch against her scalp soothed and quelled her heated passion. Now, the warmth of his chest against her back lulled her nearly into slumber. She stretched and yawned, fighting to stay awake.

Hugh rested his hands on her shoulders. "We should head back to the hut."

"Not yet, please. I am too comfortable to move."

"We have a long ride ahead of us come morning. You should rest while you can."

She'd almost forgotten. "Where are we going?"

She felt his shoulders rise and fall behind her in a shrug. "Where would you like to go?"

In truth she wanted to stay right here. It would give her the opportunity to come to know this husband of hers. "If we cannot stay here, I suppose Wynnedom, or even Hallison would do."

It was barely perceptible, but against her back

Adrienna felt the brief stiffening of his body, and the quickening of his pulse before it returned to a more normal rhythm. She frowned. Did he not want to return to Wynnedom, or was it the mention of her father's keep that put him on edge?

When he didn't respond, she offered, "If those places do not suit, anywhere you want to go is fine with me."

"No, Hallison is on the way to Wynnedom. We should stop and visit your…sire."

His slight hesitation made her frown. "Hugh?"

"Yes?"

Even the timbre of his voice had changed. No longer raspy with passion, it became tighter—more of the clipped tone she'd come to know these last few days.

Adrienna sat up straighter. She kept her gaze trained on the rushing water. "What is wrong?"

"Nothing. Why do you always ask me that? If something was wrong, I would tell you."

If nothing was bothering him, if nothing was wrong, why did she tingle with dread?

"Come, it is time to return."

She did not offer to disagree. Rising, she picked up her boots and stockings and then followed him silently to the path. Her stomach churned, but not from the lack of food. She truly was not hungry. Her temples throbbed.

At the start of the small path that would lead them to the hut, Hugh paused. When she kept walking, he grasped her arm and brought her around to face him. "Adrienna, I am sorry."

She glanced up at him. The angry coldness she had

sensed in him was gone. His gaze on her was soft, his voice low and husky. He did appear to be sorry. She touched his face. "Is everything well, Hugh?"

He rubbed his stubble rough cheek against her palm. "Aye, wifeling. I am simply overtired and hungry."

Something deep in the pit of her stomach warned her to be careful. She had no way of determining if he spoke the truth, or lied. So her only choice for the moment was to accept his explanation.

"Then you should eat something before we retire."

His forehead furrowed in a frown. He parted his lips as if to say something, but closed them before taking her hand in one of his own and kissing her palm. "I will."

His frown disappeared as quickly as it had formed. He held her hand as they returned to camp.

The smell of roasting meat over the campfire made her stomach growl. Perhaps she was just a little bit hungry.

A few of the men made room for her and Hugh on the log before the fire. She sat down next to him and gladly accepted the fare offered to her.

The meat was greasy, tough and unflavored with any spices, but it was hot and filled her belly. She looked around at those gathered by the fire. Hugh's men and William were present. But Sarah was missing.

Between bites she asked, "Where is Lady Sarah?"

William waved toward the hut. "Tomorrow will be a long day. She is already taking her rest."

One of the men made a comment that Adrienna could not hear. But she did recognize the heavy sarcasm in the tone. She shrugged her shoulders. "Think what you will, but keep your words to yourself. Lady Sarah saved my life and for that I will always be grateful."

The man who'd spoken hung his head and apologized. William nodded. "Thank you, milady."

Adrienna stared up at him and blinked. "Milady?" She looked around in pretend interest. "Where do you see a lady? 'Tis simply Adrienna, William."

"Nay." He shook his head. "I have sworn fealty to the Earl of Wynnedom. As his wife, you are my lady."

The Earl of Wynnedom. It sounded odd to hear the title spoken by someone else. And to be the Lady of Wynnedom sounded even stranger.

"So, you have sworn allegiance to the earl have you?" She glanced sidelong at Hugh. This was something he could have shared with her. He only bit off another hunk of meat and gave her a half shrug as an answer.

Adrienna turned her attention back to William. "And what pray tell does the earl have you doing?"

Alain answered, "Sir William has thankfully taken charge of the guard." He and the others cheered.

Eyes wide, she stared at Hugh. He only extended one hand toward the men as if to say they seemed completely satisfied with his decision.

She shook her head. It most likely was a good choice. After all, William did seem to have a way with the men. She just could not imagine Lady Sarah married to Hugh's captain of the guard.

She sucked in a deep breath. That meant she'd be living with Sarah.

Chapter Fifteen

Adrienna leaned closer to Hugh and whispered, "We do need to talk about this."

He swallowed hard before whispering back, "We do not need to talk about my men. But I imagine you are referring to William's wife?"

"Yes, milord."

"Tomorrow will be soon enough I trust."

Adrienna smiled as sweetly as possible before agreeing. "Yes, that will be fine."

Adrienna looked up at William and said, "I can think of no man better suited to ensuring the safety and security of Wynnedom keep and those residing there."

He tipped his head. "Thank you. I hope your trust will not prove to be misplaced."

Once he returned to join the others, Adrienna finished eating and rose. "I beg your leave to retire, milord earl."

"Granted," Hugh said. He then waved toward the hut. "I will join you shortly."

Unable to resist the urge to tease him, she lifted her chin and stated, "There is no need."

He grasped her wrist before she could escape. Tugging her closer, he turned her hand over, leaned forward and ran the tip of his tongue across her palm.

Shocked at the frisson of icy fire shooting up her arm, Adrienna looked over her shoulder. The men paid them no heed. She tried to pull free, but he easily held her before him.

Gritting her teeth, she whispered, "Hugh."

He only smiled and answered back, "Wifeling."

Her heart stuttered at the slow, deep, graveled way he called her *wifeling*. Would she ever become accustomed to his easy seduction of her senses? In a way, she hoped not.

Sighing, she conceded, "You win." She traced a finger along his jaw. "I will await you inside."

To her surprise he growled at her and lightly nipped her fingertip before releasing her hand. Uncertain how to react to his response, she turned and nearly ran for the safety of the hut.

Hugh watched Adrienna race toward the shelter. Teasing her was a bit like playing with a double-edged sword. While he admittedly enjoyed bringing the easy telltale flush of embarrassment to her cheeks, the dismay on her face always pricked him with guilt.

And that only made him long to take her in his arms and apologize for acting so childish. Perhaps it was time to leave the childlike entertainments behind.

On the other hand, she'd started it. Besides, this was

an amusement he'd not been able to indulge in for a great many years.

Hugh stared back at the fire. If he were to leave anything behind, it should either be his need for revenge…or Adrienna.

He was not yet ready to make that choice. At this moment it would be far too easy to forget his vow of vengeance for a time. But if he did so, what of the future? Would he awaken someday, look down at his sleeping wife and be consumed with regret?

Or, if he carried out his plans would he awaken alone some night and be overwhelmed by grief at the thought of what he had given up in the name of revenge?

Damn him for being such a fool. Hugh cursed himself. He would drive himself mad with this womanly indecision. The path to his destiny, to his future, was up to him. Yet he stood at a crossroad unable to ascertain the right direction.

He was not used to this uncertainty. Even though his battle experiences had not been like others of his acquaintance, he was still a warrior. As such his life depended on his ability to make quick decisions.

One false move, a slight moment's hesitation could be the difference between life and death. So, why was he permitting a mere woman to bewilder him so?

Was it the passion they shared? Had he somehow let physical desire cloud his judgment?

No.

If he were to be honest with himself, he had to admit

this confusion had nothing to do with desire. It was deeper than simple lust.

He had come to care about this woman, her safety and her welfare far too much. It was an error he had vowed not to make. But it was done.

The men gathered around the fire sharing tales and jokes. It would be impossible to sort out his thoughts amidst their merriment. He rose and headed toward the hut.

To lie next to Adrienna, to gather her into his arms and hold her close, would be a mistake. A mistake he knew he would make tonight and then repeat over and over in the nights to come.

It would be one more thing to live with should he decide to strike out at Adrienna. The question was—could he? Would he be able to break her spirit, crush her soul and walk away?

Hugh paused and rubbed his pounding temples. They would be at Hallison in three or four days. By then he would have to come to a decision. Forgive and forget as Sidatha encouraged, or satisfy his need for vengeance.

Seeking not to awaken Lady Sarah, Hugh entered the smoke-filled hut as quietly as possible. An ensuing conversation from the bedchamber stopped him outside the archway.

"I care not for this plan of theirs." Sarah's voice carried more than a touch of anger.

There was a moment of silence before Adrienna asked, "Is there anything I can do to help?"

"Help? Why would you wish to help me?" Sarah spoke to his wife in a tone Hugh found unacceptable.

"I owe you for helping me escape Richard. And it is not hard to see how unhappy you are with the way things have happened of late."

"Unhappy? This is not what was supposed to happen."

"I know…" Adrienna paused. "You were supposed to wed Hugh."

He breathed a silent sigh of relief that had not occurred.

"I was promised title and wealth. I received neither."

"But William is a good man." Hugh was surprised to hear his wife defend his friend. She had known him but a few days and had already seen the good in him. "Perhaps in time you will come to care for him and he for you."

"What difference would that make? He is my husband, nothing more."

Nothing more? She said that as if William's selfless act in wedding her counted for less than little. William did not have to marry her. He had not been forced to do so. Nobody would have faulted him for leaving her to fend for herself. Did she really see his honorable act was worthless?

"Would it not be easier to live with someone who shared your feelings?"

"Adrienna, you have listened to far too many tales of starry-eyed lovers. Marriage is an arrangement made for wealth, land or power. That is all."

"Nay. You are wrong. I would gladly give up all the wealth, land and power for just a chance at love."

Hugh's chest tightened at the wistful longing in his

wife's statement. It echoed the sudden awakening of his own longing for the same.

"If you think your earl will fulfill that wish, you are doomed to be disappointed."

"Only the future will tell if that is true or not."

"Oh, Adrienna, you are a fool. In the end you will be burned to a cinder. Do you not realize that your husband is not a man given to tender feelings? You are wed to a man with fury in his blood. Are you truly unable to recognize his moods and thoughts?"

"I am not a fool." He was taken aback by the forcefulness of Adrienna's words. "Do you think I know my husband so little? If so, you are wrong. I am well aware that he does not love me."

"And how do you, with so little experience, know this?"

"I can feel it in his touch, and see it in his eyes when he looks at me. Sometimes there is desire, sometimes a strange longing and other times a hatred so strong I want only to run away."

"And yet you do not."

"No. I cannot."

"Why not?"

Hugh closed his eyes, and over the rapid, loud pounding in his ears, he forced himself to listen to his wife's hushed answer.

"I…I do not know."

She lied. Even without seeing her face, he knew that she lied by her hesitation in answering.

"You are more of a fool than I thought, Adrienna."

He heard the rustling of covers as one of the women

rose. Quickly, before he could be caught, Hugh crept to the door of the hut. Once outside, he moved away from the door before releasing the breath he'd not realized he'd been holding. Why had he not taken Adrienna's perceptiveness into consideration?

In the short time since he'd found her, she'd easily learned to read his expressions and judge his emotions. Wasn't that what he had planned all along? That she learn to know him so well that he became a part of her?

So why now was he surprised that she seemed able to peer inside his mind and know his thoughts? Why was he not overjoyed to know that this much of his plan had been successful?

This did not bode well for him. Instead of recognizing this as a step toward his long-awaited revenge, he sensed a newly formed bond, just one more strand in a silken web that drew and held the two of them together.

If he had any wisdom whatsoever, he would pack up his wife and head for Wynnedom posthaste, altogether avoiding her father and the memories that would surely feed his thirst for vengeance.

But how would he explain that decision without divulging all? It was best that they continue on to Hallison. Right now, however, he wanted nothing more than to take Adrienna into his embrace and hold her close.

After Lady Sarah left the hut and joined William by the fire, Hugh reentered the dwelling and crossed to the bedchamber.

His wife was curled beneath the covers in the middle

of the narrow pallet. He placed his sword on the floor alongside the makeshift bed before removing his belt, boots and tunic.

Without a sound, Adrienna stretched out on the pallet and moved closer to the wall, making room for him. He slid beneath the covers and she came willingly into his embrace.

Snuggling against him, Adrienna rested her cheek on his chest. He stroked her back. "Comfortable?"

"No. I'm not used to sleeping on the hard ground."

Hugh smiled as he pulled her atop him. "Better?" It was how they'd slept each night since leaving Poitiers. And he, too, had become used to the odd arrangement.

She kissed his shoulder. "Does this truly not bother you?"

He tightened his arms around her. "Would it matter if it did?"

At first she stiffened and said nothing. He thought for a moment she would think him serious. But she quickly relaxed. "No. It wouldn't matter in the least."

With their legs entwined, the softness of her breasts pressed against the hard plane of his chest and her head cradled against his shoulder, it was easy to let the tension of the day ebb away.

She tipped her head back and kissed the side of his jaw. "What are you thinking about?"

Their closeness would make it almost impossible to lie. Still, it would provide him the opportunity to see how good her perception of him was. He said, "Nothing. I am trying to go to sleep."

"Then why did your heartbeat quicken? Why did your breathing change?"

That answered his question about her perception. "I was thinking about you and our journey north."

"How long will it take to reach Hallison?"

"Are you anxious to see your father?"

Her nose bumped against his cheek as Adrienna shook her head. "No. Maybe." She sighed. "We did not part on good terms."

There was something else they had in common. Hugh kept that thought to himself. "Did you argue about going to Poitiers?"

"In a manner of speaking. I felt as if I were being sent to a public market to shop for a husband I did not want."

He couldn't help but smile. "Yet you found one."

"I would say he found me."

From the back of his mind came a question he could not bring himself to ask. *Do you want this husband, Adrienna?* Instead, he drew the conversation back to her father. "Was he angry that you did not want to go?"

"Very. Although he did give me a choice. Find a husband, or leave Hallison for good."

Hugh shook his head. What father would condemn their only child to certain death in such a manner? Besides Hallison he could think of none that cruel.

Knowing the man's heartlessness, he had to ask, "Why then are we going to Hallison?"

"Because he is still my father. I have to believe he had good reasons for his actions. I want him to know that I do indeed have a husband."

To his amazement, he was able to hold back a strangled choke. "Aye, you do have a husband. But do not be so certain your sire will be happy with your choice."

"I don't see why not. He was the one who made the original betrothal between us."

This conversation had suddenly swerved toward territory he wished not to enter. She was obviously still denying her father's involvement in her young husband's disappearance. "Either way, we have a long ride ahead of us and should be thinking about sleep."

She laid her head back down on his shoulder and yawned. For a few moments she said nothing, then asked, "Hugh, are you satisfied with your choice?"

He waited until her breathing slowed and he was certain she slept before answering her, "Well satisfied, my love."

Chapter Sixteen

Hallison Keep—June 1171

Finally. Adrienna reined in her horse, stopping to stare down at the valley below. The green rolling hills gave way to her father's keep. The wooden structure surrounded by a wall made of fieldstone had once been home to a Roman fort.

While the fort no longer stood, the existing keep served the same purpose—protection for the valley and its inhabitants. For an act of bravery she couldn't remember the Earl of Richmond had rewarded her father with this honored position.

In her opinion, he'd done his job well. Never once had they been attacked. So, her life growing up had been for the most part free of war and battles. She'd only experienced the darker, more dangerous part of life through stories shared by passing visitors, or tales of battles related by her sire and his men.

Until Hugh arrived at Eleanor's court.

Hopefully, now that they were safe at Hallison, he and his men would be able to relax by letting down their vigilant guard.

She glanced at Hugh. He'd unsheathed his sword and rode with the weapon in hand. The five men he'd brought north with them had done the same. Sidling her horse closer to his she touched his arm. "You've no need for your sword."

The look he turned toward her took her breath away. An expression of pure hatred twisted his face into an unrecognizable mask of evil. Some demon from her worst nightmare had taken form inside her husband.

Four short nights ago he'd called her his love. He'd incorrectly assumed she'd been asleep. He'd been wrong.

How could that same man look at her in such a fearful manner? Adrienna twitched her horse's reins, putting some distance between her and Hugh.

He shook his head and blinked, as if awaking from a dream. "I am sorry. What did you say?"

She looked away, gazing down at the peaceful valley instead. "It was nothing." Half-afraid to look at him again, she took a deep breath before tearing her gaze away from the idyllic scenery below them. Her breath escaped on a loud whoosh. The mask had disappeared. Now only a questioning glance marred his face.

He squinted against the sunshine, but his blue eyes still pierced her from behind narrowed lids. "You look at me as if afraid I might bite you. What did you say?"

Had she mistaken his hate-filled stare? Had the sun

played tricks with her eyes? Adrienna looked away. "Truly, nothing of any importance. I simply wondered why you appear ready to go into battle."

Hugh tapped his weapon. "I have not been at Hallison in many years. There is no way to know what my welcome will be like."

"I am certain that my father will welcome you with open arms."

He arched an eyebrow at her. "Your certainty does not outweigh my instincts. I would prefer to be prepared for the worst."

"So, you will arrive at my father's gates with weapons drawn?" While her sire might welcome him, the men guarding the gates would take offense at the approach of armed riders.

"Until I am positive you, my men and I are safe, yes, the weapons will remain at hand."

"So be it." Adrienna urged her horse ahead. Over her shoulder she added, "But if you are attacked from the walls do not blame me."

Easily catching up to her, Hugh called out, "Adrienna, stop."

She was anxious to be within her home, but something in his voice made her bring the horse to a halt.

He came alongside. "Are you seeking my death?"

What had put such a notion into his head? "Of course not. Why would you ask such a thing?"

"What will Hallison's guards do if it seems I am chasing you to the walls?"

She'd not thought of that. The guards would protect

her if they thought she was in danger. She eyed his weapon. "If you and your men would sheath your weapons my father's guards would have no reason to think I was in danger."

He looked at her and said nothing. But the hardness in his eyes let her know that he would not be swayed.

She could not wait to see her father. Not because there was any great depth of love between them, but because she wanted him to explain his innocence. She knew without a single doubt that he had had nothing to do with Hugh's capture the night of their marriage. Maybe once her husband discovered the same, he could set aside this bitterness toward her father.

For now, she would ride at Hugh's side like the dutiful wife and not mention the subject again.

Adrienna pointed toward the small river running behind the keep. "If we are here long enough, I would like to show you the waterfalls."

"I hope to be here long enough to rest the horses and the men before heading out toward Wynnedom."

"We can stay here as long as you like."

"And now you speak for the Lord of Hallison?"

Adrienna wanted to scream. No matter what she said it circled back around to her sire and Hugh's nearly tangible hatred of him.

An icy cold knot formed in her stomach. She swallowed hard against her growing sense of dread. Perhaps coming to Hallison had been a mistake. Each step closer to the gates only darkened Hugh's disposition. By the time they reached the hall, he would be ready to shed her father's blood.

Nay. Surely he would do nothing so foolish. Hallison's guards would cut him down the moment he but threatened their lord.

She looked at him, trying to see the man she'd come to care so deeply for, and past the stark anger evident on his face. "Hugh, I wish no harm to come to you or my father. We need not stop at Hallison if you do not desire to do so."

Hugh forced the growing rage down. Frightening Adrienna beforehand would do him little good. "We are here now."

She reined in her horse and faced him. "Yes, we are. But tell me what you plan. Need I fear for your safety?" She glanced briefly toward the keep. "Need I fear for my father's?"

A part of him wanted to reassure her that all would be well. It was natural for her to wish safety for her father. But a niggling voice in the back of his mind wondered if she was as guilty as he.

Hugh had come to believe that was not the case. He'd turned the past over and over in his mind concluding that her cry of innocence was true. She'd told him that she'd only gone to her father seeking assistance in securing their future.

Until these last few miles he'd believed that had been the case. Now he was no longer as certain. He wanted to simply ask her outright if she'd played a part in his capture. But right now he would suspect whatever she told him.

Payment for the years stolen from him was now a matter of honor. He would not back down. But neither could he bear the worry and fear etched on Adrienna's face.

He reached out and cupped her chin. "I will make you a bargain."

A small half smile crossed her mouth. She rubbed her cheek against his palm. "And what do you propose this time, milord?"

"If your sire can swear to his innocence, I vow not to provoke him."

"And if he cannot convince you?"

Hugh ran his thumb across her lips before removing his hand from her face. "At one time I sought only his death. Now, I do not know, Adrienna."

"You once mistakenly thought I participated in your— removal from Hallison that night. Did you seek my death, too?"

Her hesitation caught his attention. When Adrienna lied, or sought to hide the truth, she hesitated. He considered his answer a moment, before saying, "Your death? Never. I had other plans for you."

"Other plans?" She moved away from him. "Something worse than death?"

Hugh silently cursed himself. He'd said too much already. With a flick of the reins, he urged his horse forward.

After a moment he heard the pounding of her horse's hooves on the ground behind him. She shouted at his back, "Hugh, what about now? What are your plans now?"

Thankfully, the gates of Hallison were within hailing

range. He slowed his animal so she could catch up with him. "Make yourself known."

Adrienna shot him a glare that would have sliced through his flesh had he not been wearing armor. But she did his bidding and hailed the guards at the gate tower.

An older man leaned over the side. "Lady Adrienna?"

"Aye, Osbert." As they passed beneath the portcullis, she asked, "Is my father here?"

"Nay. We were not aware you were returning home." Osbert's answer was breathless as he clambered down the ladder. "He and a few of the others left this morning to go hunting. They will not return until tomorrow morning, milady."

Adrienna slid off the horse and handed the reins to a young lad. She nodded toward Hugh. "Osbert, this is my husband, Hugh, the Earl of Wynnedom."

For a moment Hugh wondered if the man would somehow recognize him. It was unlikely, since he'd only been at Hallison for mere hours and had been nothing more than a boy.

The servant's mouth opened and closed like a fish out of water and Hugh realized that he'd worried for naught. Osbert stared from Adrienna to Hugh, and back a time or two before tipping his head toward Hugh. "Milord, welcome to Hallison." He then swung back to Adrienna. "You did not tell your father of this marriage did you?"

She asked, "Is that not why I was sent to Poitiers?"

"Aye, but Lady Adrienna, your father has not blessed this union."

The man's tone had turned accusatory, so Hugh dismounted, handed the reins to the waiting stable boy and made a point of brandishing his sword before slipping it into the scabbard. "I doubt if Hallison would naysay having an earl as his son-by-marriage."

Osbert backed away. "Nay, my lord, I did not mean any disrespect."

"I am sure you did not."

Adrienna's eyebrows rose. She started to explain, "It will not matter, Osbert. Hugh and I were already—"

Hugh grasped her elbow, turning her toward the keep, and completed her sentence. "Acquainted. We were already acquainted."

A light tug prompted her to walk alongside him across the bailey. Hugh paused and looked back at Osbert. "See to my men."

"Aye, milord."

Once they resumed their progress across the yard, Adrienna pulled her elbow from his hold. "There was no need to be so high-handed with Osbert."

"High-handed? I simply gave him an order."

"You intimidated him on purpose."

"Of course I did. He thought to scold my wife and needed to know that would not be permitted."

When he reached toward her, Adrienna sidestepped away from him. "Why did you not want him to know we were already wed?"

Hugh paused and glanced behind them. "What are they doing?" When Adrienna stopped to look, he reached out and laced his fingers through hers. "That's better."

Unable to free her hand, she ordered, "Release me."

He raised their clasped hands to his mouth and brushed his lips across the back of her hand. "Never."

Sufficiently flustered, she sighed before asking again, "Why didn't you want Osbert to know the truth?"

After tugging her closer to his side, Hugh admitted, "Because I want to see your father's face when he learns I am not dead."

"You said you would not provoke him."

"And I will not break my vow to you. But I will learn more from his initial expression than I will from any speech he has had time to prepare."

She fell silent. But her flushed cheeks and furrowed brow told him much. "Adrienna, do not plot to inform him before I do."

The flush on her cheeks deepened. Finally, she nodded. "I know that he will prove his innocence, so there is no need."

Her certainty made him feel guilty. He had made that vow to her knowing full well Hallison was guilty. He'd not imagined the man's presence in the stables that night. No more than he had imagined the years lost.

"How many men guard Hallison?"

Adrienna's frown returned. "You think to attack?"

"Attack?" If he desired to attack Hallison he'd have done so by now. Hugh shook his head. "No, I seek to turn the conversation to something safer."

"Six men reside here. Fourteen others split the duties here and at their own homes."

"So, at any given time only thirteen men guard Hallison?"

"Aye. There used to be many more men, but my father found he had no need of such a number."

Hugh studied the keep. It sat unprotected in the open like a willing target. The stone-and-mortar curtain wall was shabbily constructed and had most likely been built by those residing here instead of a professional stone-mason. A single barrage from a loaded trebuchet would fell the structure.

He trailed his perusal across the bailey. Buildings appeared to be erected haphazardly. Stables, the single well, a kitchen and a small smithy lined one side. He assumed the churned-up ground in the center of the bailey was the practice area for the men.

The other side of the yard housed six huts. Small plots of land around each dwelling were planted with vegetables. A woman raced about the plots shouting and flapping her apron at the three pigs rooting in the gardens.

"Who planned the layout?"

"Nothing here was planned."

That much he had already guessed. "How has your sire held Hallison for so long?"

"In truth I think since we are never attacked and pay our taxes in a timely manner, we have been forgotten. Hallison is not near a seaport, we have no main road nearby and there is nothing in the area of any import."

That explained the need for so few men. "You have never been attacked?"

She shook her head. "Nay, not that I can remember."

"How does Hallison support itself?"

"Sheep."

He looked around. "Sheep?"

"Not here," Adrienna said. "They don't live in the keep. The village is on the other side of the stream. I will show you later."

They stopped at the steps leading up the earthen mound on which the keep was built. Hugh took in the three-story wooden structure atop the mound. "A well-placed flaming arrow would destroy Hallison."

"Milord, contrary to appearances, the wall was placed with care. I do not know how far you can send an arrow, but our strongest man could not hit the keep from the other side of wall. Not even with a crossbow."

"Flaming pitch from a trebuchet would do the job."

"How would they get the trebuchet here?"

Hugh paused. The path to Hallison had been steep. From what he remembered all of the hills surrounding this valley were just as steep. An enemy would have to build a weapon of war right outside the walls within sight of the guards. From all appearances, Hallison did not look to be worth the effort.

"You father is not the fool he appears."

Even though he'd only made an observation and had not asked a question, she said, "No. He is not."

Hugh waved up the mound. "Show me your home."

Adrienna leaned her head against his shoulder. "I would rather show you the waterfalls."

"The day is still early, is there a reason you cannot do both?"

* * *

The lengthening shadows surrounding the racing stream bespoke of nightfall. It had taken more time to show Hugh around Hallison than she'd planned. Adrienna tugged his hand toward the path that would lead them behind the falls. "Come, hurry while there is still light."

He let her lead him down the embankment to the water's rocky edge. They followed a series of flat-topped boulders closer to the falling water.

None of the many waterfalls dotting the river were immense by any means, but this was the largest near Hallison and behind it was a cave. Adrienna knew that if they hurried, she would be able to show him a beautiful view of the setting sun from behind a curtain of falling water.

At the edge of the falls, he hung back. "Where are we going?"

Feeling ten years younger than her age, Adrienna asked, "Do you not trust me?"

"That depends." He eyed the cascading water. "If your intent is to drown me you may succeed."

"No. There is a cave behind the water." She tugged at his hand again. "We may get wet, but I vow not to drown you."

This time he let her pull him along behind her. When they reached the rock face, she released his hand and said, "Keep your head up."

Adrienna pressed her back against the rocky wall and shuffled her feet along a ledge, ducking into an opening behind the water.

Hugh followed. Ignoring her order, he looked down—and received a drenching. Quickly pulling his head up, he shook the water from his hair and ran a hand down his dripping face.

He ducked into the mouth of the cave and was greeted by Adrienna's smug smile. "I told you to keep your head up."

"Wench, you could have told me why." He shook his head like a dog after an unwelcome bath. Hugh unbuckled his sword belt and dropped it where he stood. He then pulled his soaking wet tunic over his head to toss it onto the floor of the cave. It landed with a loud plop.

She nearly choked on a laugh.

He glared and threw back his shoulders before stalking her toward the back of the small cave. "Oh, think that's funny do you?"

Unable to speak, Adrienna nodded and brushed the tears of humor from her eyes.

Hugh pressed her against the damp cave wall and stared down at her. "Do you still find it so funny?"

The cold dripping water from his clothing soaked through the fabric of her gown. But the shiver coursing down her spine was not caused by the icy water.

She reached up and wound her arms about his neck. While toying with the damp hair at his nape, she looked up at him and whispered, "Nay, milord, 'tis not funny in the least."

Hugh pulled her into his hard embrace. Nuzzling the

sensitive flesh beneath her ear, he hoarsely whispered, "I want you."

The desperate need evident in his tone echoed the longing burning inside her. "As I want you."

She reached between them and tugged at the ties holding up his braies, while he loosened the laces along the sides of her gown. Adrienna felt the tremor in his fingers and knew that her own hands shook at their task.

Hugh paused, asking, "You do have another gown?"

"Yes, but…" She closed her eyes against the sound of fabric being torn. "This *was* one of my favorites."

He pushed it off her shoulders, letting it pool at her feet. "I will buy you another to call favorite."

"For your carelessness, you will buy me two."

When he grasped the hem of her chemise, Adrienna grabbed his wrist. "Let me."

She had to have something left to wear on the walk back to Hallison. While she removed the loose-fitting undergown and placed it on a dry rock, he tugged his boots off and then the rest of his clothing.

She had no more than turned toward him when he pulled her hard against him. Hugh nudged her head back and covered her mouth with his own.

There was nothing soft about his kiss. Only a desperate, driving need that threatened to take her breath away. Without ceremony, he lifted her in his arms and lowered both of them to the floor of the cave.

The damp, coldness of the rock beneath her was no more than a momentary discomfort forgotten the instant he knelt between her legs.

Bathed in the reds, oranges and golds of the now setting sun, Hugh stared down at her. An expression of wonder and bafflement crossed his features, leaving a slight frown in their wake.

Adrienna reached up and stroked the furrows from his brow. Even with all of his dark looks and changing moods, she knew that she loved this man. And right now, she wanted nothing more than to share that love the only way she knew how.

She breathlessly coaxed him. "Hugh, love, I need you now."

Without taking his gaze from hers, he leaned forward and entered her in one fluid movement.

Adrienna closed her eyes and moaned as a flash of white-hot desire flooded her senses. She locked her ankles around his waist and rose up to meet him.

Gentleness had no place in their lovemaking. They both took and gave until the stars bursting behind her lids took on the colors of the sunset.

Hugh collapsed atop her. After catching his breath he rose up on his elbows and cradled her head between his hands. He cleared his throat, then whispered, "If this is love, I will have more of it."

Adrienna smiled. Rubbing her cheek against his palm, she whispered back, "You can have all you wish, milord."

Chapter Seventeen

The singing of birds woke Adrienna from her slumber. She rolled over with a groan. The night spent on the floor of the cave had left her feeling bruised and battered.

A slow smile twitched at her lips. It wasn't as if she'd noticed the coldness, nor the hardness. When they hadn't been furiously sharing their passion, they'd been slowly and leisurely making love.

If she remembered correctly she'd been the one to fall asleep first. Her last coherent thought had been of Hugh's lips on hers.

Reaching out, she touched empty air. "Hugh?"

"I am here." His voice came from outside the mouth of the cave.

"What are you doing?"

He entered the cave, this time without getting wet. "I took a bath in the stream, dressed, found us some food, you a gown and now I am just waiting for you to awaken."

In his arms he carried a leather wrapped bundle that he placed on the floor next to her. Still bent over, he leaned closer and kissed her before asking, "And how are you this fine morning?"

Adrienna touched her still tingling lips. "I am well, milord, and you?"

"I have never seen a better morning and would be quite anxious to start the day."

"What prevents you from doing so?"

He glanced meaningfully at her, before suggesting, "We cannot leave this cave if you do not rise."

She was torn between beckoning him to her side and bathing. The heated flush on her face and Hugh's smile decided her.

Perhaps she could have both.

Rising, she walked slowly to the mouth of the cave.

"Where are you going?"

Over her shoulder, Adrienna asked, "Did you not bathe? I am going to do the same."

"The stream is cold."

"So is the waterfall." Pausing at the entrance she added, "But at least it is not out in the open."

She stuck her hands beneath the tumbling water before stepping forward. Someone unaware would have been knocked to the ground by the force of the falls. But she'd done this many times in the past and planted her feet securely on the rocks.

Hugh swallowed past the sudden dryness of his mouth. He rooted through the bundle and retrieved the damp tunic he'd used after his bath and strode toward Adrienna.

Unaware of his nearness, she nearly shouted, "See, you did not need to go out to the stream."

He pulled his tunic and shirt off in one tug, and then reached through the water to tease the rosy tip of one breast.

Adrienna jumped in surprise at his touch.

He pulled her out of the flowing water and whispered against her ear, "Is this not what you wanted?"

Turning around in his embrace, she nipped at his chin. "Of course. I was just waiting to see how long it took you to—"

He swallowed her words with his lips. His hands slid easily over her wet skin. The coldness of her flesh quickly warmed against him.

At one time a near unquenchable thirst for vengeance urged him to steal her heart and soul. He had planned to train her body to his touch, and leave her wanting.

Now as Hugh groaned against her mouth he would sooner cut out his own heart rather than awaken without her at his side.

He broke their kiss and eased out of their embrace. "Come, let me help you dress."

Adrienna reached out to pull him back into her arms, but he easily evaded her. "Hugh, we have all the time in the world."

"Aye." He used the damp tunic and began drying her body. "We have the rest of our lives."

She leaned forward and dropped a kiss on his cheek. "That we do."

When he finished, she retrieved the bundle from the

floor and pulled out a gown, asking, "How did you come by this?"

Hugh tossed her chemise to her and took the bundle. While taking out bread, cheese and an apple, he said, "My men were searching for me and I sent them back to Hallison for these supplies."

She pulled her clothing over her head. "Your men know we were here all night?"

Hugh looked up from slicing the apple. "We are wed, Adrienna." He watched her struggle with the laces of her gown for a moment, then set the apple down. "Come here."

After he helped her finish dressing, he offered her food to break their fast. Knowing this quiet contentment would not last for long, Adrienna let him hand her slices of the apple, followed by small chunks of the cheese and bread.

Once the food was gone, he gathered up the bundle and his still wet tunic from the floor. "Ready?"

With a loud sigh, she took his offered hand. "Yes."

A heavy weight seemed to press on her chest with each step they took closer to Hallison. The dread she'd thought gone slowly formed in her stomach.

At her growing silence, Hugh asked, "Is all well?"

Afraid her fear would show in her voice, Adrienna only nodded.

He stopped just outside the gates and turned her to face him. "Perhaps later you can show me the village?"

She nodded.

Hugh brushed her wayward hair from her face. "Is there a cave anywhere near the village?"

His question brought a smile to her lips. "No. But we must cross the steam to get there."

He pressed his lips to her forehead. "That is better, my love."

"Hugh—"

"Lady Adrienna!" One of the guards shouted over the wall, cutting off her question. "Your father awaits you."

She grasped the front of Hugh's tunic. "Hugh, please."

He gently disentangled her fingers from his clothing. "Adrienna, you have my word. Leave me my honor. I made a vow to you and I will not break it."

Something she could not name clawed at her stomach, making her dizzy. She swallowed hard as the food they'd shared threatened to race up her throat.

A small voice asked, *What if your father is not innocent?*

She watched Hugh walk toward the keep unable to force her legs to carry her after him. What could she say to sway him from seeking out her father?

What would she do if Hugh's angry retribution could not be tamed and he killed the Lord of Hallison?

Adrienna gasped. What would she do if the Lord of Hallison, or the guards, somehow killed her husband?

She closed her eyes and prayed, "Dear Lord, please. Please keep them both safe."

After taking a few deep breaths, she willed her suddenly leaden feet to follow Hugh into the keep. One agonizing step after another carried her to what she was certain would be the most decisive day of her life.

* * *

Hugh forced himself to walk, not run across the bailey. He measured his breaths.

He wished to face Hallison with as much composure as possible. Anger would only distract him from his purpose.

Adrienna caught up with him as he stood before the doors leading into the Great Hall. Unwilling to turn his attention from the task at hand, he said nothing.

She stood at his side as he opened the door and placed a hand on his arm. "I have to know, Hugh. Come what may, I must know the truth of what happened that night."

He wondered what had caused this change of heart, but only nodded his consent.

They entered the hall together. A servant tipped his head toward a private chamber at the other side of the Great Hall. "His lordship is in there."

Without pausing he crossed the wood planked floor. Adrienna fell a step behind him. He could smell her fear, the acrid scent leaving a bitter taste in his mouth.

But she held her tongue and did not cry. For that he was thankful.

They stopped before the closed door and knocked before entering. Adrienna rushed around, ducking out of Hugh's reach.

"Father, 'tis good to see you."

The urge to strangle her was tempered by the welcoming smile on Hallison's fleshy face. If this was how she normally greeted her sire, then by all means, let her lead him to believe all was well.

Hallison rose from his seat by the lit brazier and wrapped one arm around Adrienna. "I understand you found a husband." He released her and turned toward the door.

Hugh was surprised by how old the man had grown. Hallison wasn't as tall, or imposing as he'd once been. The man's hair, or what was left of it, had grayed. The muscular chest had…fallen…to a now rounded belly.

As he drew near, his gaze flew to Adrienna. She stood next to her sire and lifted one eyebrow.

"Come, come, my boy. Let us talk." Hallison waved to a seat on the other side of the brazier. "We should have talked before this, but I remember how impatient the young are."

Hugh stood before Hallison and looked down at him. "We have met before."

"Oh?" Adrienna's father squinted up at him. "Perhaps you do look a little familiar. Do I know your father or liege?"

"My liege is King Henry." He glanced at Adrienna. She hadn't moved, but her eyes were closed. "My father was Sir Gunther of Ryebourne."

"Nay." Hallison literally fell onto his seat. "That is not possible. Ryebourne is dead."

Adrienna's eyes flew open. "Oh, father, no. You didn't."

Hugh's heart clenched at the horror and disbelief etched on her face. He longed to gather her into his arms and take her from here, from the truth that would hurt her so much.

She knelt before her father. "Tell me you did not hire men to kill my husband all those years ago."

He pushed her away. "What have you done, girl?"

"Me?" She rose. "What have *I* done?" Her voice broke on a cry.

Hugh pulled her to his side. "Be still."

Lord Hallison glared at his daughter. "Aye, you. How could you bring him here? Do you seek my ruination?"

Hugh led Adrienna over to the other seat and pushed her down onto it, ordering, "Stay right there. Do not move."

He then turned to face Hallison. "Why would my presence be your ruination? Other than stealing twelve years from my life what other vile deeds have you done?"

"Stealing twelve years?" Hallison leaned back in his seat. "It appears to me that you are here, are you not?" He pointed at Hugh, asking, "How do I know you really are Ryebourne?"

Not wanting to see her face while he explained, Hugh positioned himself behind Adrienna and rested his hands on her shoulders. She reached up one hand and clung to his. Just their shared touch lent him calm as the memories broke through the barrier he'd so carefully built.

"How do you know? Let me remind you of what happened that night."

"Why?" Hallison snorted. "My memory does not fail me. My daughter does not need to hear this."

"Yes, father, I do. I need to know what depths of hell

you were able to sink to in order to gain what little Hugh possessed."

Her father waved his hand in the air before picking up a goblet from the floor alongside his chair. "'Tis a fine thanks I get for seeking to protect you."

"I did not ask for your protection. I asked only for your help until we could find our own way."

Hugh briefly tightened his grasp. Adrienna fell silent.

"I was just a boy, milord. A boy trying to make it in a man's world. When I entered our marriage chamber I found my new wife sitting atop our marriage bed, her wedding finery around her, clutching a doll to her chest, while she screamed at me to go away."

Adrienna lowered her head and looked away. Hugh slid his hand along her shoulder and brushed his thumb against the side of her neck. This was not her fault. If he did not know that before, he did now.

Hallison's bushy eyebrows rose. "And you ran because of a doll, a screaming woman? 'Tis a fine man you were."

"Yes, I ran." He refused to let the comments goad him into rage. Instead, he continued, "I ran because I wished not to further frighten the child I'd wed. The only hiding place I could find to spend the night was in your stables. Obviously the men you hired had been following me, because I'd no more than sat down when they grabbed me."

As if it'd happened only yesterday, the memories became more vivid. "That was when you came in and silenced my pleas for help."

Hallison shrugged. "What did you expect? How could I let my daughter go away with a boy who had nothing?"

"So you thought my death would be a better choice?"

"Aye."

"I wish they had killed me. It would have been easier."

"Hugh." Adrienna snaked her hand up his arm. "Do not say such a thing."

He ignored her. He had no choice. Now that the words had come, he could no more stop them than he could stop his heart from beating.

"How much did you pay them for my death?"

"Not much. A few pieces of gold," Hallison defended himself. "It matters not since you are obviously hale and hearty."

Hugh shook his head. "They made more gold by selling me into captivity."

Adrienna gasped. "No."

"Captivity? What nonsense is this?"

"Nonsense? Ask your daughter about the whip marks covering my body. Someone skilled with a whip can do much damage without bringing death."

Hallison frowned. "And where were you held in such a manner?"

"Far from here. A world away. A place with more wealth and luxury than you can imagine. A place where inhumane acts are commonplace."

Faster and faster the memories swirled around his mind. The terror of a young man. The pain of the lash. The twisting and knotting of a long empty stomach. The thirst of parched lips.

"Obviously you could not have been treated too harshly. You are here. You grew into a man."

"A man? Is that what I am? A man? You are sadly mistaken, milord. A man has a soul. He has a conscience. I no longer have either."

After taking another swig of his drink, Hallison asked, "'Tis a rather fanciful declaration, is it not?"

"Is it? Tell me, how many men have you killed over the years?"

The older man shrugged. "A few dozen perhaps."

"I have killed hundreds. It is what I was trained to do."

Adrienna shook beneath his touch. He knew she was remembering that night in the queen's garden. She had insisted on being present for this conversation. Soothing her would have to wait until later.

"One does not become a killer against their will, Ryebourne."

"No? If one is tortured enough, starved enough, abused enough, one will do anything to stop the abuse."

How many nights had he prayed to lose a battle. To die at another's hands just so he would not be forced to take yet another life? Yet each time he entered the arena the will to live and to fight on made him forget his own humanity.

"So you killed others." Hallison shrugged. "Men die in battle every day."

Hugh had suffered enough of the man's nonchalant attitude. He released Adrienna, stepped around her and grabbed the front of Hallison's tunic with one hand. The man's eyes widened as Hugh easily lifted him from his seat.

"I am not talking about men dying in battle." He wrapped his free hand around Hallison's throat. "I am talking about killing men in an arena with my bare hands—for nothing more than a few moments of entertainment."

He could feel the man's throat work beneath his palm. A red haze clouded his vision. It would be easy to squeeze the breath from him and let him fall lifeless to the floor.

Adrienna screamed. "Hugh!"

He released her father, letting the older man fall back down onto his seat. Hallison grabbed his neck and stared up at Hugh speechless.

"Oh, my God, Hugh, I am so sorry." Adrienna's voice broke on a cry. Before he could stop her, she raced from the chamber.

Drained from spent anger, Hugh took the seat she had just vacated.

Hallison eyed him warily. "Are you going to kill me?"

"I was going to, yes." Hugh glanced around the room. "Is there any more wine?"

Rising on shaking legs, Adrienna's father retrieved another goblet and a full ewer of wine from a side table and handed them to Hugh.

After he sat back down, he asked, "And now?"

"I should." Hugh took a long drink of the wine. It slid easily down his throat. "Your death would bring me a great measure of peace."

Hallison nodded. "I can understand that. You owe me no favors, but I do ask one of you."

"What?"

"Use a sword."

Hugh leaned back and looked at his wife's father. The man's hands shook and sweat beaded his brow. Hugh's handprint around his neck stood out starkly against the paleness of his flesh.

He felt sick to his stomach. What had he become? Was he truly the monster he'd thought he was for so long now? It would be no sport to kill this old man. Neither would it ease his thirst for vengeance.

Then what would?

Hugh frowned. His mind raced back to Sidatha's lessons.

He had his wife. Her touch brought him peace of mind. Their nights together gentled the pain.

That was his revenge. Hallison's daughter loved him against all odds. He'd thought only to mark her with his desire and somehow, by some miracle, she'd come to love him.

He still had a question he'd like answered. "Why did you never see her wed to another?"

Hallison eyed him warily. "There was no need for quite a few years."

"My land brought that much gold?" It was only a guess, but by the older man's hesitancy, Hugh assumed the land he'd held free from the king had been sold. It'd been the only thing his father hadn't lost in the war between Stephen and Matilda.

"Yes."

Hugh sighed at Hallison's reddened cheeks. "It matters not. I had intended to do so myself, but knew not how at the time."

Seemingly comforted by that admission, Hallison continued. "When I petitioned King Henry for a future betrothal, he claimed that he would not grant Adrienna another betrothal until your body was discovered."

Hugh frowned. "She was at the queen's court. Did my body suddenly appear?"

Hallison picked at the arm of the chair. "In a manner of speaking, yes."

"How?"

"While hunting, I and my men found a decomposed body in the woods and I sent word to Henry that it was you."

"Without bothering to discover who it truly might be?"

Hallison shrugged. "The finding was too opportune to pass up."

"And you also thought it fitting to lie to Adrienna by having a missive sent telling her of my death?"

"What would you have done? The deed was complete. My daughter needed a husband. King Henry needed a body."

Hugh rose. "And you needed more gold." He'd heard enough. It was time to leave this hall before he again lost his temper.

He glanced at Adrienna's father and took little pleasure in the way the man flinched away from him. "I need to find my wife."

Lord Hallison's sigh of relief echoed in the chamber. He waved toward the door. "By all means, go."

Chapter Eighteen

The wind whipping against Adrienna's face dried her tears as they fell. Crying had not eased the heaviness of heart. The thunderous pounding of the horse's hooves had not lessened the sickness in her belly. Both had only made her feel worse.

Now that Hallison Keep was well behind her, she reined the animal in and dismounted. After tying the reins to the saddle, she slapped the horse's rump. As she knew would happen, the beast headed for the keep and its food in the stall.

She needed some time alone and would enjoy the solitary walk back to the keep later. For now, she sat down against a tree. Twirling a blade of grass between her fingers, she tried to sort through all she'd learned this day.

How could her father do such a thing? While he was not the most demonstrative man she'd ever encountered, he'd never before shown her the true blackness of his soul. And the sight sickened her.

How could he have paid men to kill her husband? Worse, why had he never thought to ensure they'd carried out his plans?

If he'd at least have queried the men the next day, or even the day after that, he might have been able to save Hugh the terror of his unholy captivity. Her father had been the only one who could have helped. Hugh's father was deceased. He had no brothers, no one to search for him, or to offer any ransom in exchange for his release.

Her sire's actions were unimaginable.

They were unforgivable.

And the things Hugh had had to endure. She shuddered. It was no wonder Hugh despised her father. How could he not? If he chose to murder the Lord of Hallison, she could not blame him. She could only pray her husband still believed in mercy.

More in question, how could he love her? Did he love her? Adrienna's thoughts drifted back to last night in the cave. Aye, Hugh loved her. She did not believe his touches or kisses lied.

However, when she compared the kisses and touch of his hands last night to those mere weeks ago, he had lied at first. There was no doubt in her mind that he had intentionally sought her out at Eleanor's court.

The knowledge stung.

Then, she'd also been a target of his need for revenge. She remembered their conversation in the queen's garden that first night. She'd complained about him leaving her on their wedding night and basically accused him of desertion, of abandoning her.

As if he'd walked out on her of his own will.

Humiliation heated her face and Adrienna hid her flaming head in her hands. Dear Lord, she'd called him a liar, and sworn that she hated him. Her breath hitched. She'd defended her father.

How could Hugh love her? How could he forgive her?

An odd gentleness stole over her, calming her with the knowledge that Hugh did indeed love her. It mattered not how, or why.

He'd touched her with his love, marked her with all the passion and desire he possessed. And no matter what it took she would make herself worthy of his love, and his desire.

Adrienna rose. It was time to return to the keep. Time to find her husband and help him, if not forget his past, perhaps lessen the sting of its memory.

The sound of horses galloping toward her made her turn and stare across the clearing. She smiled. It would be like Hugh to either come looking for her, or send a couple of men to do so. Leaning against the tree, she waited.

Adrienna gasped when they were close enough to see their faces. The one man, the darker one was a stranger to her. But the second one was familiar. *Richard!* Frantic to find an escape, she looked around, finding none.

It was too late to run. She was too far away to scream for help.

Her heart froze in her chest. Why had he followed them here?

The men paced their horses back and forth in front

of her. Richard smirked down at her. "Well, well, what do we have here?"

Adrienna pressed her back harder against the tree. She bit her lip to keep from saying anything that would tip his sarcasm to anger.

The other man asked, "Where is Hugh?"

"Yes, where is your husband, my dear?" Richard's gaze hardened.

She swallowed. Hugh was safe at Hallison. If she sent these men there, he and the others would easily take care of them. "He is at the keep."

"Good." The darker man nodded at Richard. "Take her. He will come for her."

When Richard brought his horse closer, Adrienna moved to the other side of the tree. "Hugh will kill you if you touch me."

"Stefan, a little assistance will make this easier."

The second man had to be Stefan of Arnyll. Her mouth went dry. Hugh and William had insisted on leaving Poitiers rather than come face-to-face with this man.

Stefan dismounted. "Can you do anything by yourself?"

Adrienna stepped away from the tree and started running toward the keep. Her escape was short-lived when Stefan grabbed a handful of her hair.

He wound the length around his wrist and jerked her against his chest.

Adrienna screamed.

"If you are wise, you will not do that again." Stefan dragged her toward his horse.

She screamed again. Her effort gained her a bruising slap across her mouth.

"You were warned."

Richard rested his forearm on his knee and leaned toward them. "My dearest Adrienna, it would be in your best interest to simply do as you are told. We don't want you. We want your husband. You'll be released as soon as he gives himself up."

"For what? Why do you want him? He did nothing to you."

Stefan shook her. "Stupid woman. We don't want him. His master does."

Adrienna's stomach rolled. "Oh, God, no." She pleaded, "Please, Richard, for the love of God don't do this."

Richard shook his head. "I am sorry, my love. But he is worth far too much gold for me to change my mind now."

Hugh slapped the flat of his sword against his leg. Where was she? He'd searched for Adrienna all day. Now the sun was sinking low in the sky. Soon it would be night and he'd have no choice but to call off the search.

He cursed himself for not following her out of the chamber. He'd known how upset she'd been. In her state of mind anything could have happened. She could have fallen into the stream, bashed her head against a rock and been carried away.

She could have stumbled down the side of one of the

hills surrounding Hallison. This very minute Adrienna could be lying injured with no one around to help her. He twisted the reins in his hands.

"You will drive yourself mad, cease."

Hugh turned around and glared at Hallison. "Had I gone after her instead of staying in the chamber with you, this would not have happened."

"Blaming yourself will not help. She is a smart girl. She will be fine. It is nothing new for Adrienna to take herself off and fume in solitude."

Hugh suddenly wished he had dispatched the man to his maker. "She was not fuming. She was upset."

"Oh, aye and that is something new. 'Tis the first time a woman has ever been upset."

When breathing deeply did not help, Hugh looked at his men and ordered, "Take his lordship back to the keep and make sure he stays there."

Once the others left, Hugh headed back toward the stream. He would spend the night in the cave. Perhaps Adrienna would eventually make her way there. If not, then in the morning, he would begin his search anew.

Every fiber of his being told him that she was alive and in trouble. She needed him, yet he knew not where to find her.

The sky opened up and rain poured down on him. It was as if the clouds shed the tears he could not.

He tied his horse in the dense shelter of the trees before taking refuge in the cave. Hugh leaned against the back wall and waited. He had to believe that she would come, otherwise he'd be lost.

"Milord!"

At Alain's shout, Hugh rose and left the cave, hoping his man brought word of Adrienna's return.

"Milord, you are needed back at the keep."

His heart fell. Not wanting to know the answer, he asked, "Is it Adrienna?"

"We have word of her, yes."

Instead of waiting for his man to explain, Hugh mounted his horse and took off at a gallop for the keep. All the way there his mind played out horrible endings to this news. Each one worse than the one before.

By the time he raced into Hallison's chamber, his dread nearly choked him. Hallison's drawn face, red eyes and shaking hands only strengthened the dread.

"This came by a messenger."

He handed Hugh a rolled piece of parchment. If Hallison's appearance were any indication, the news would not be good. Hugh unrolled the missive.

The words etched on the page took the breath from his body. He sank down heavily onto a bench. "When did this arrive?"

"While we were out searching." Hallison handed him a portion of wine.

Hugh waved it away. The drink would only sicken him more. "Did anyone see who delivered it?"

"I am told it was a young boy. He handed it to the guard at the gate and left."

Hugh stared back at the missive. Tears borne of rage and fear blurred his vision. But he did not need to see the words again. *Your wife will make a fine addition to my household.* It was signed with nothing more than the letter *A.* Somehow Aryseeth had his wife.

"Hugh?" Hallison leaned forward and asked, "Who is this A?"

Hugh rose and headed toward the door. Over his shoulder he answered, "It is my old slave master."

Hallison's strangled cry and the clattering of the man's goblet hitting the floor followed Hugh out into the Great Hall.

Before he reached the entrance doors, Hallison caught up with him. "What are you going to do? How will you free her? You will free her, yes?"

Hugh stopped with his hand on the door, but did not turn around. "Yes, I will see her freed. She will return to you soon."

"Do you need my men? Is there anything I can do?"

"No. I do not need any men." He turned around and looked at Hallison. "But there is something you can do."

To his amazement, Hallison knelt before him. "Anything."

For as harshly as this man had treated him and as harshly as he'd treated his only daughter, Hugh could not find it in himself to hate the man. He obviously cared a great deal for her. Hugh had not the time to discover if this caring was something new, or if it had always existed.

He pulled a ring from his finger and held it out to her father. "Send this and my men to King Henry. He will see to it that my wife is well cared for and lacks nothing."

"I will. I swear to you that I will see it done." Hallison took the ring. He rose, asking, "What are you going to do?"

Hugh shrugged. "The only thing I can. Exchange my life for hers."

By mid-morning the next day Hugh had found the encampment. He sat on his horse staring down at the tents dotting the valley beyond Hallison's village.

An overwhelming emptiness filled him. It chased away the cold dread that had kept him moving through the night. And it swallowed the fear he'd experienced at Adrienna's disappearance.

The familiarity of the emptiness was almost welcome. Like a numbness settling over him, the lack of feeling would see him through whatever the future held.

"My lord."

Even though he had not heard the rider's approach Hugh did not need to turn his head away from the scene below to know who had joined him. He recognized William's voice as easily as he would his wife's. "What are you doing here? Were you not ordered to Wynnedom?"

"We never made it there." William flanked his right.

"Do they have your wife, too?" Guy of Hartford took the position on his left.

At Hartford's question, Hugh did turn in surprise. He nodded. "Yes. I would say it was good to see you, but under the circumstance…"

Guy shrugged. William only grunted in agreement.

"The two of you should leave. There is no need to sacrifice yourselves when it is I who they want."

"I am heartened to know you have not lost your lofty opinion of yourself." Guy glanced beyond Hugh toward William asking, "Has he been like this for the last two years?"

"Aye. The earl has not changed a whit."

"Oh, the earl is it? I'd heard rumors of your rise, but had not the time to investigate the truth."

Hugh clenched his jaw as the numbness faded. The emptiness filled with anger. He was in no mood to bandy words about. His brief taste of freedom made the thought of what was to come nearly unbearable. How could these two jest when it was all he could do not to shout his rage?

"Gritting your teeth together will only gain you a sore jaw." Guy leaned toward him. "Hugh, my friend, we seek only to goad you out of this foul mood."

"Anger is all I have."

"Your anger will get us killed."

"I cannot look on my last moments of freedom with anything but anger and regret."

When Hugh made a move to leave, William tore the reins from his hands. "No. Forgive me, but I will not let you do this alone. Not like this."

Guy moved his horse in front of Hugh's, blocking his way. "Anger and regret? Do you think you are the only one who is suffering?"

"No." Hugh shifted his glare from Guy to William. "Our wives are suffering while we sit here conversing."

"They will wait." Guy shrugged a shoulder. "They can do nothing else."

"And in the meantime?"

William's eyes widened as if shocked by Hugh's question. "In the meantime we must plan what to do."

Guy added, "Unless of course you have already formed a plan of action."

"I intend to offer myself in exchange for my wife."

"Like hell you will." Guy slid Hugh's sword from the scabbard and waved toward William. "Get him away from here until we can discover where he left his common sense."

Hugh's anger grew at being led away like an unthinking youth. But now his rage was directed at Guy and William—men he'd thought were his friends until this moment. So angry he could hardly speak, he swung his mail-covered fist at Guy.

The other man could have easily ducked the blow, but he took it full force in the center of his chest. Guy swayed in his saddle, but righted himself and said, "That is somewhat better."

Something sinister in Guy's breathless statement gave Hugh pause. He stared hard at both men. By all outward appearances nothing of any importance bothered them. They appeared calm.

But someone who knew them well could see the barely perceptible tick in William's jaw and the heightened brightness of Guy's eyes.

Even someone who did not know them well would have noticed the additional weapons strapped to their backs and saddles. They would have seen that instead of chain mail the men wore short leather jerkins.

Dressed not in the typical long Norman tunic, these men wore unadorned vests. The bulging muscles of their arms bare beneath the edges of the fabric. Instead of hard-soled boots, theirs were soft and cross-laced to their knees.

Guy and William came prepared to fight. Hugh hung his head. There was no fight left in him. He didn't know where it had fled, but he could not dredge it up from whatever depths it had sunk.

"Hugh…" Guy's low, steady voice drifted through the mist of worry and anger shrouding him. "Listen to me. I know we thought these days long gone. But we cannot change what is before us. We can only face it and win."

William grasped Hugh's shoulder, adding, "Or die together trying."

"You cannot trade your life for your wife's. Think."

"I have thought. She is all to me."

"Her life is of more value?"

Hugh looked at William and nodded. "Yes, it is. You do not understand."

"Nay," Guy answered, "'tis you who does not understand. While it may be true that William does not yet have a great depth of feeling for his wife, I have been married for nigh over ten years now. Although I have cared deeply every single one of those days, I only thought I loved Elizabeth. On the day I arrived home, I found her giving birth to another man's daughter."

Guy paused and took a ragged breath. Hugh's heart ached for his friend. Thoughts of his wife had kept Guy sane and alive the years they'd spent captive. How had he ever been able to forgive her?

With a sigh Guy continued, "Love was a hard learned lesson in the ensuing weeks…for both Elizabeth and myself. And now, not only is my wife held captive, our daughter has been kidnapped. Perhaps it is the newness of this love that makes it worse. But I do know your fear. What you feel right this moment is fear for another. That is why it is not familiar to you."

Hugh frowned. Was Guy right? Is that what had made him feel so helpless, so damn afraid? No. That could not be the cause of this despicable weakness. "I have known fear before."

"Yes." William tightened his grasp. "But only for yourself. Hugh, you were but a boy when they brought you to Sidatha's palace. You had not known love. You had never had the chance to be a man. Never were you responsible for the lives and welfare of others as you are now. King Henry did you no favor in making you an earl with land and men. He gave you added responsibilities that you'd never had before."

"I see to my responsibilities."

"Yes, too well. You cannot tell me that you are not concerned about Wynnedom and the lives of those who live and work there. You could never convince me that you are not terrified for Lady Adrienna's safety."

"Your terror will see her killed."

The truth in William and Guy's words hit him like a falling tree. Hugh closed his eyes. Offering himself in exchange for Adrienna would not suffice. Aryseeth would lie and in the end have both of them.

Hugh would rather ensure both of them died, even at his own hands, than to permit either of them to fall into Aryseeth's power.

Hugh unlaced his helmet and tossed it to the ground. He unbuckled his sword belt and handed it to Guy. Without thinking twice, he ordered William, "Help me out of this mail."

Guy took the scabbard and turned his face to the sky. "Thank you, lord."

Once the chain mail was removed, Hugh said, "I need a fighting dagger and a short sword." He knew he'd chosen his captain wisely when William handed him a well-honed notched-edged dagger and a blade only about the length of his forearm.

While William secured the horses to a tree, Hugh slipped his shirt over his head and ripped the material into strips. After tugging off his boots, Hugh used the fabric strips to cross wrap his legs from ankle to knee. His stockings and cross-laces were not much, but they would provide a little more protection for his legs than just the flesh covering them.

Certain the wrappings would stay in place, Hugh stood upright. He stepped into the sunshine. Taking his dagger in one hand and the short sword in the other, he raised his head, squared his shoulders and flexed the muscles in his arms.

With his face turned toward the light of the sun, he closed his eyes and let the warmth wash over him. As was their old custom, the other two men flanked him and did the same.

Every deep breath Hugh drew into his chest and slowly released took a portion of his fear and hot anger away. A cold determination replaced the rage and fear.

Certain his resolve would not fade, he lowered his face and looked from one man to the other. "Ready?"

Once before, they had fought and won their freedom. They would do so again. More than just their own freedom depended upon their success. Failure would not be an option—they would most definitely succeed.

William grunted. Guy's lips curved into the evilest smile Hugh had witnessed in many months before nodding toward the path. "Lead on."

Chapter Nineteen

With her arms wrapped tightly around her bent knees, Adrienna sat on the dirt floor of the tent rocking back and forth.

Since Richard and his companion Stefan had brought her here, nobody had disturbed her. After ordering her not to leave the tent under any circumstance, Richard had suggested she take comfort knowing they didn't want her.

How could she have been so very wrong about Richard? She'd thought he'd been her friend. Outside of Elise, he'd been the only person at Poitiers that she'd trusted.

It was hard to swallow the fact that she was such a poor judge of people.

Comfort? He thought she should take comfort knowing the men who'd once held Hugh captive wanted him back in captivity?

What sort of comfort was that to provide her?

If they succeeded in their plan to recapture Hugh, she

would rather die. Adrienna rested her forehead atop her knees. It was a sin to commit suicide. She wasn't sure, but it was most likely a sin to even contemplate such a notion.

Granted, every day some woman learned to live without the love of her husband. But she could not imagine how. Just the thought made her chest feel as if someone were squeezing it tightly. It made her head throb and her stomach churn even more that it already did.

Obviously, they were much stronger than her.

A loud vehement cursing broke out in the tent alongside hers. Once before the occupant had raised a commotion, only to be quieted. She didn't want to know how.

This time however, Adrienna paid closer attention. Something in the voice rang familiar. It was a female. She uncurled her arms and crawled to that side of the tent.

"Get out of here! You whore son of the devil, my husband will geld you and then rip your head off with his bare hands!"

Sarah. How had she been captured? Did that mean they already had William? Or, please Lord, was William with Hugh?

Adrienna lifted the bottom edge of the tent and peeked underneath. The next tent was less than an arm's length away. Scraping the ground she found a few stones, gathered them in her hand and waited.

Soon, she saw feet march toward Sarah's tent. The woman's shouts where silenced by a loud crack.

Adrienna flinched, but kept her mouth shut. She waited until she saw the feet leave the tent. After counting to twenty, she prayed fervently that it was now safe and then tossed a few of the stones at Sarah's tent.

She waited a moment and tossed a few more. At her fifth toss, the edge of Sarah's tent lifted. To her relief, Sarah's blue eyes stared warily out at her.

"Adrienna?"

"Shh, yes. Is William with you?"

"No. When they snatched me, William was off gathering firewood and giving me a chance to come to my senses." Sarah's voice trailed off as she added, "We had...argued."

"Oh, Sarah, I am sorry." She did feel sorry for the woman. Being forced into an unwanted marriage couldn't be easy, especially for someone who had never really had anyone to rely on before.

"William wasn't truly angry, he would have returned shortly."

Not normally given to prayer, Adrienna briefly closed her eyes and whispered, "Oh, thank you, Lord."

"And Hugh?"

She shook her head. "No. He was at the keep."

Sarah's bloodied lip shook. "Do you think they will come for us?"

"Of course they will. Just try to be quiet until then." Adrienna heard voices approaching. She waved Sarah away, dropped the edge of her tent and sat back up.

Stefan and Richard entered carrying a length of rope. "We thought you might like to watch the entertainment."

Adrienna eyed the rope. "No. In truth I am fine here."

Stefan crossed the tent and unceremoniously hauled

her up from the floor. Without saying a word he pulled her arms behind her and tied one end of the rope around both of her wrists.

Richard stepped forward and traced a fingertip down her cheek. "My dear, if you would but act the part of a meek and dutiful wife it would be easier for you."

"Meek? Dutiful? Go to—"

Anything else she'd been about to say was cut off when Stefan wrapped a gag around her mouth and tied it behind her head.

Richard grasped the front of her gown. "Did I mention you were part of the entertainment?" He rent the fabric to her waist exposing most of her breasts.

For a moment he just stood there and stared at her flesh. Then he sighed. "It is too bad Hugh came. I would have enjoyed tasting your charms in his absence." He ran a fingertip across the top of one breast. "Who knows, I still might."

Adrienna screamed, but the gag effectively cut off any sound.

Stefan tugged the free end of the rope, jerking her backward. "If you fall, I will drag you."

She stumbled, but managed to stay on her feet as he led her like an animal out of the tent.

Their weapons drawn, Hugh, William and Guy marched side by side into the encampment. The tents formed a circle, leaving the center area clear.

Hugh stopped in the middle of the clearing, facing the largest tent. "Aryseeth, I come for my wife."

His heart thudded fast and hard in his chest, but he'd not let his concern for Adrienna cloud his thinking, or actions ever again.

Guy was right. The all-consuming fear had been for Adrienna. Instead of centering his energy on gaining her freedom, he'd wasted it on useless worry.

Sidatha's old slave master walked out of his tent holding what appeared to be a leg of mutton. "Who disturbs my meal?" He glanced at all three men and smiled. "Oh, I see the lost lambs have returned to the flock." He chortled at his own ill-spoken jest. Waving the meat around, he asked, "You don't find that humorous?"

"Where is Adrienna?"

"And Sarah?" William's voice was hard and low.

"And Elizabeth?" Guy's voice remained emotionless.

Aryseeth raised his hand and snapped his fingers. The three women were dragged from separate tents. He carefully watched each man, waiting for an expression. Something that would give him any hint to their emotions.

Hugh kept his face immobile and was certain the other two did the same. They knew Aryseeth well. He would find their weakness and use it against them.

No longer a frightened boy, Hugh would not so easily divulge his innermost feelings—especially not to this son of the devil.

Hugh gave Adrienna nothing more than a passing glance. It was all he needed for him to know she was not truly injured. The blaze of ire in her eyes did not speak of fear. She had not been as abused as her appearance would lead one to believe.

The bindings, torn gown and gag were nothing more than an artfully created mask meant to goad him into reacting.

It would not succeed.

"What will you give me in exchange for the lives of your women?"

"Exchange?" Hugh raised an eyebrow. "There will be no exchange. You will give them back to us, or we will take them from you. I killed the last man who tried to capture her, a few more will not matter."

"Ah, I wondered what had happened to the imbecile I sent to find you at Poitiers. It should have been an easy enough task to snare the woman who had charmed you and use her as bait to dangle before you. He received his just due for failing. However, it appears that your temporary freedom has given you a sense of humor." The smile left his face, to be replaced with a fierce glare. "I will personally see it removed."

Hugh beckoned him forward with his sword. "My day would be complete if you tried." He knew the slave master would never think to attack him. At least not without chains securing his ankles and manacles on his wrists. Aryseeth was a coward.

"So, the three of you think to battle my entire camp for the release of your women?"

Hugh and his companions nodded.

Aryseeth reared back as if in shock. "I have fourteen men at hand."

"Make it sixteen and let the battle begin."

"Sixteen?"

Hugh waved the tip of his dagger toward the two men standing behind Adrienna. Stefan and Richard. "Aye, those two would make your force sixteen." He would be glad to take either or both of their lives. He had no doubt they had brought Adrienna here, so it would be just payment.

Richard paled and backed away. "No. Thank you, I do not fight hand-to-hand."

Aryseeth lifted his hand and crooked a finger. Two of his men grabbed Richard before he could make his escape. They bodily dragged the struggling man to Aryseeth and dropped him at the master's feet.

Aryseeth pulled a thin bladed knife from beneath his robe, grabbed Richard's hair and held the blade to his throat. "Fight and die bravely, or die like a dog."

"But I cannot—"

Hugh silently cursed as Richard's voice ended on a gurgle of blood as the knife was drawn swiftly across his throat.

Aryseeth released the dead man.

Hugh heard one of the women hit the ground, but refused to look. Instead, he kept his focus on Aryseeth. "Fine, then make your force fifteen."

Stefan rushed forward and dropped to his knees before Aryseeth. "My lord, I am a freeman who has served you well."

"And you will serve me well in this. For if you do not, you will forfeit your freedom."

"These men will kill me."

Aryseeth stared down at Stefan in amazement. "You have betrayed them. I would expect them to do no less."

He beckoned two men forward. "Take him and prepare him for battle...on the morrow."

William asked, "On the morrow?"

"Yes. You heard me correctly. On the morrow. My men have toiled hard today and need rest. This night you may spend with your women, or alone, I care not."

Hugh's mind spun. What was Aryseeth up to this time? Keeping his thought to himself, he demanded, "As an earl of this realm I want a tent, food and privacy for myself and each of my companions."

Aryseeth waved toward the tents. "Of course. I would never mistreat one of King Henry's men...at least not here. Naturally, you will not mind if the tents are guarded?" He paused a moment, then added, "Just to insure your safety."

Hugh shook his head. "No. There will be no guards. Since you know my importance to the king, I expect to be treated as a guest."

Aryseeth glowered, but acquiesced. He headed back into his own tent. Stopping at the flap, he added, "Sleep well."

As the three men approached their wives, Guy asked in a whisper, "What do you think he's planning?"

Hugh offered, "I think he knows we will not sleep tonight. Either we'll sit up all night contemplating the battle, worrying about being attacked in our sleep, or bedding our...*women.*"

William sighed, before admitting, "I am not sure about your women, but I fear mine will kill me before morning even arrives."

Hugh glanced at Adrienna. She'd not yet had enough time with Aryseeth to become truly afraid. The only emotion coursing through his wife at this moment was rage. And from the look on her face it seemed to be directed solely at him.

Little did she know that the worst was yet to come. Stopping in front of her, he held her hot stare as he reached behind her back and grabbed the free end of the rope.

William did the same with Sarah while Guy gathered his unconscious wife from the ground. He then nodded toward Hugh and William. "As Aryseeth said, sleep well. Until the morning." He waited for a guard to point him in the right direction.

As if uncertain what to do, William lifted his eyebrows in question. Hugh shrugged before tugging on the rope in his hands. "Come, wife."

Her eyes widened, but she followed him back to the tent.

Once inside Hugh placed his weapons on the dirt floor, turned to her and raised his hands as if to fend off the look she gave him.

"Turn around." While working at the bindings on her wrists, he leaned close and whispered in her ear. "We may not be guarded, but they are listening. If they get even the slightest idea that I care for you, all will be lost. They will use you to defeat me."

He freed her wrists from the bindings and dropped the rope to the floor, before turning her around and removing the gag. He gathered her into his arms and held her against his chest. "Berate me if you must, but keep your voice down."

"He killed Richard."

Her harsh whisper sounded odd. Hugh leaned away and looked down at her. "Adrienna, look at me."

The gaze she turned on him was over bright with unshed tears. He cupped her cheek. "Did Richard deserve to die?"

"Yes, but not like that."

"Then what are these gathering tears?"

"Hugh, I am so sorry for what my father did. And for what I did. How can you love me? How can you bear the sight of me?"

So her look didn't hold anger directed at him, rather anguish at the pain her family had brought him.

"Do not talk nonsense now. You hold my heart and soul in your hands. What happened before is in the past and will stay there." He tightened his arms around her. Still keeping his voice low, he said, "God, Adrienna, I thought I would never find you."

Her shoulders shook and the hot wetness on his chest told him she'd lost her fight at holding back the tears. Lifting her in his arms, he crossed to the center of the tent and sat down. "Shh. Wifeling, hush."

She wrapped her arms around him. "Hugh, what if we have no tomorrows?"

"No. Do not even think like that. Adrienna, I need you to be strong. I need you to believe in me, to trust me."

Adrienna did believe in him, she did trust him. But

she didn't know how she could find the strength he required from her.

"Hugh, love, I can do anything you ask. Give you anything you need, but I cannot be strong."

"Aye, you can." He leaned away from her. The depth of the love shining in his eyes evident for her to see. "It is easy. All you need do is be quiet."

She didn't understand what he was talking about. "Be quiet?" It made no sense.

"Tomorrow we will battle for our lives and for yours. You will be forced to watch. I need you to make no sound. No gasps, or shouts of victory or dismay. No sound at all."

It still did not make sense. "Why?"

"Wifeling, I will hear your voice over the din of combat and be distracted."

Now his reasoning made sense. One hesitation, one slight distraction could spell disaster. "I will be quiet."

"No matter what."

"You make it sound as if there will be something more than just a battle."

"There will be. They will torment you."

Her breath lodged in her throat. "Torment me?"

Hugh brushed the hair from her face and tucked it behind her ear. "Just torment. They will not torture you. But they will lead you to believe that they will. They will make you think that at any moment you will be violated and harmed. But, Adrienna, they will not do so while I live."

This is where the believing and trusting in him came into play. "What if you do not live?"

"I will, but just in case," Hugh slid a thin handleless blade from the wrappings covering his legs. "This is yours."

She took it from him carefully and looked at it. "If I carry this around I could stumble and kill myself."

"Aye." He rested his forehead against hers. "That is the idea."

She stared at him, unable to believe what she'd heard. "You want me to take my own life?"

"If I die, yes."

"Does that mean they will make my life not worth living?"

"The threats of violation and harm they make tomorrow to torment you will become in earnest if I should die."

Adrienna sucked in a deep breath. "Then, my love, you had better not fail."

"I have every intention of walking away from here tomorrow with you at my side."

Not if she kept him up all night he wouldn't. She slid off his lap and patted the ground. "Lie down. Sleep."

He stretched out on the dirt floor and pulled her down alongside him. "I did not have sleep on my mind."

Adrienna smiled. "Oh, I nearly forgot, did I not hear you mention something about bedding your woman?"

"You know I did not mean it that way." He cupped her breast and brushed his thumb across the nipple.

She sighed with pleasure before grasping his wrist and sliding his hand to her hip. "Sleep."

Easily shaking off her grasp, he rolled her onto her back with a near animal-sounding growl. Lying atop her, he cupped her head between his hands and stared down at her. "Wifeling, I need you this night."

Adrienna snaked her arms around him. "Then, my love, I am yours."

Before she could convince him of the wisdom of sleep, they were naked. Hugh's slow and gentle touch on her body brought tears to her eyes. Oh, how she would mourn him if anything were to happen.

Chapter Twenty

Hugh awakened just as the sun peeked through the seams and cracks in the tent. Adrienna was no longer in his arms.

"Go back to sleep."

He turned his head and saw her sitting up at his side with his sword across her lap. "How long have you been there?"

"Since you fell asleep."

"Why?"

"For all my trust and belief in you, I do not trust them." She pointed the sword at the tent flap. "They tried to open the flap twice."

His chest swelled with pride and love for his wife. "So you sat up all night to protect me."

It wasn't a question, but she answered nonetheless. "Aye. You will risk your life this day for mine. I could do no less."

He sat up and slowly stroked a line from beneath

her ear along her jaw to her chin. "You would make a fine warrior."

"I would much rather be a wife."

"Then I suppose I should see to that, shouldn't I?"

"Aye, you should."

Her voice trembled. Hugh paused, wanting to say something to reassure her, but feared he would choose the wrong words.

Instead, he rose. "Then I will gather the other two and make certain our plans are set."

Adrienna held his sword up to him. "Will I see you before the fight?"

"It is doubtful."

She stood up and wrapped her arms around his waist. Holding him fiercely, she whispered against his chest, "Hugh, be strong, but do nothing foolish. Tonight, when the sun sets, I want to see the reds and oranges flame off your chest as you lie atop me in our cave."

He kissed the top of her head. "I can think of nothing better to see me through this day."

"Go." She pushed him away. "Go, before I start crying."

He added, "Again."

Adrienna only waved toward the tent flap.

"I love you, wifeling."

She gasped and turned away. Hugh smiled before turning her around and swiping at a tear with his thumb. He lifted it to his lips. "This falls for me, for us. There is no shame in such a show of concern. I could tell you not to worry, but it would do no good. So, worry and cry now, my love. Do so in private so that later there will be no tears left to shed."

She leaned against his chest and promised, "I will."

The sun was not yet a third of the way into the sky when Aryseeth ordered one of his slaves to ring the gong calling the combatants to the makeshift arena.

Adrienna stood between Sarah and Elizabeth at the edge of the clearing. Two armed men stood guard at their backs.

Sarah kept looking over her shoulder as if she were trying to figure out a way to escape.

"You are wasting your time." Adrienna's statement went unheeded.

Sarah scanned the hills surrounding them. "Surely there is a way out of here."

"Only if your men live." Aryseeth came up behind them. "But I would not count on that happening. Instead, I would count on you joining my household."

"Your household?" Sarah's belligerent tone would likely get them killed before the battle began.

"Ah, yes." Aryseeth focused his gaze on Sarah's breasts. "I keep a well-disciplined supply of females at my private quarters."

Elizabeth's eyes grew round. "And what is this supply used for?"

Adrienna refrained from shaking her head at the naiveté of the woman's question.

"Used for? Why what else is a woman used for except to bury oneself between her legs?"

Elizabeth bit her lips and averted her attention to the field.

Aryseeth continued, "And the women in my household are rigorously trained to excel at pleasing a man." He sighed before saying, "You will not much enjoy the training at first. In fact, in the beginning it could seem rather brutal, a few frail women have died under my guidance. But the three of you appear strong and once you become accustomed to my methods, you will fight among yourselves to share my bed."

It wasn't so much what he said, as the way he said it. To Adrienna his veiled threats were made worse by the low, not quite seductive voice he used. The tone rang false to her, as if it was forced.

She said nothing. But she did note that Elizabeth and Sarah had also fallen silent. Obviously their husbands had warned them of the coming threats, too.

When the men finally entered the field, Adrienna could not rip her stare away from Hugh and his companions.

As long as she ignored the evil-looking weapons in their hands, they were a sight to behold. The muscles on their chests and arms glimmered in the sunlight, as if they'd applied oil to their skin.

"My, my, my." Sarah's hushed whisper echoed Adrienna's thoughts.

As if the men heard Sarah, or read Adrienna's mind, all three of them flexed the muscles in their upper arms, before pulling their shoulders back and expanding their chests. The sudden flash of heat on her face had to be from the sun. It had to be. Otherwise everyone would know that the vision of these three had made breathing difficult.

The men stopped in the center of the clearing. They formed a small circle with their backs to each other. Hugh raised his sword and waved it as if urging the enemy to come forward.

Aryseeth whistled and ten of the fifteen warriors entered the clearing.

Sarah grasped Adrienna's hand. Adrienna reached out and took Elizabeth's hand. Each woman stiffened her spine and stared straight ahead, forming a bond that would hopefully be strong enough to get them through.

Hugh had told her to trust him, to believe in him. He had explained more than once that he'd been trained to be a killer of men.

Adrienna hadn't realized what that meant until this moment. Even though she stood at the edge of the clearing, the distance was not great. She was close enough to see the shimmering promise of death in his eyes. And near enough to smell the stench of already spilling blood.

Hugh, William and Guy took down six of the men before Adrienna's heart could resume beating.

They were quick and they were strong. And wielded their weapons with sure and certain destruction.

The four remaining men regrouped. Aryseeth whistled again and the last five entered the field.

To Adrienna's amazement, Stefan rushed ahead of the other newcomers and approached Hugh with his back turned. She wanted to ask what he was doing, but held her tongue.

Aryseeth cursed and shouted, "Kill the traitor!"

Hugh nodded to Stefan and moved over enough to permit him to join the closed circle.

The odds still appeared to be in Aryseeth's favor. Now it was four against eight. Adrienna held her breath when she realized that four of the new combatants did not carry swords or daggers to the fray. They held whips in one hand and a length of chain in the other.

Hugh and William smiled before dropping their swords. They moved a step out of the circle. Immediately Guy and Stefan repositioned themselves so they were back-to-back.

William spread his legs and squatted, making a smaller target of his overlarge frame. Hugh turned his body sideways toward the now approaching men.

Before she knew what he was planning, he left the ground, stretched out a leg and planted the sole of his foot across one man's throat. She heard the sickening crush of bone before he even hit the ground.

Hugh spun around and landed nearly in the same spot he'd started at.

When one of Aryseeth's men drew back his whip, William tensed. As the long leather thong sailed toward him, William grinned until his teeth gleamed in the sunlight, reached up and tore the length from the air. Before the man could release the weapon he was jerked into William's arms.

Adrienna swallowed as another bone-crushing snap reached her ears.

Guy and Stefan had an easy advantage over the men

attacking them with swords and pikes. They were much quicker than their attackers and she couldn't help but notice that the two of them worked together as one fluid force.

There seemed to be no "you protect my back and I'll protect yours." Instead it was as if they blended into one man with four arms. She had no other way to explain it.

During the fray, one of the attackers bumped into William and fell against Hugh. Hugh grasped the man's head between his hands and with a quick twist broke that man's neck.

While William had regrettably suffered several bites of the lash, and Hugh appeared to be bleeding profusely from quite a few dagger wounds, the attackers had fared worse. They were down to two men.

Surely Aryseeth would now see the wisdom in calling a halt to this massacre of his own men. Instead, he whistled a third time.

Adrienna could not contain her gasp as almost twenty riders galloped down from the hill in front of her.

William and Hugh grabbed their weapons and rejoined Guy and Stefan in the circle. Hugh looked across the field at her and held her gaze for a moment. Adrienna bit her lip to keep from crying. She would not go back on her vow of silence. Nor would she forget the blade hidden between her breasts.

Dear Lord, she did not want it to end this way.

Aryseeth's breath was hot on the back of her head. "Did you truly think I would let them live? Did you believe that you would be free?"

She closed her eyes and ignored him. But Sarah stiffened and Elizabeth squeezed her hand so tightly Adrienna wondered if her fingers would be broken.

Of course Aryseeth couldn't let the women's reaction go unnoticed. He moved closer to Sarah, whispering, "I have never bloodied one as fair as you before. Will you cry for mercy when I spread your legs?"

Adrienna gripped Sarah's hand tighter, willing her to remain silent.

But when Sarah did not respond, Aryseeth shoved her to the ground and stood over her. "Perhaps I should do it now, here, with your nearly dead husband watching. Let your screams be the last thing he hears."

Sarah closed her eyes and remained motionless.

Adrienna looked up at the field and prayed that William would do nothing to get them all killed. He held himself rigid and if it were possible his glare of hatred would have killed Aryseeth where he stood. Hugh's mouth moved. He was saying something to William. Adrienna could only guess that her husband was trying to keep his friend steady.

Aryseeth stepped back. "Get up."

Sarah rose, took her place and grasped Adrienna's hand with her own trembling one.

"Let us not be hasty. I wish you not to miss what is to come."

Unable to look away, Adrienna stared in horror as the mounted men began to bear down on Hugh and his friends.

Her chest constricted painfully. Her breath caught in

her throat. And just when she thought she could stand no more, Elizabeth released her hand and pointed at the hill. "Look. Dear God, look."

A force of at least fifty men crested the hill. At the head of the line a red pennant fluttered in the breeze. As the flag bearer turned down the path that would bring them down to the valley, the rampant lion came into view.

Adrienna fell to her knees. She didn't know how the men had come to be there and at the moment it did not matter. She was more than willing to accept the miracle of King Henry's assistance.

Sarah turned to Aryseeth and asked, "Are you ready to call an end to it now?"

Aryseeth raised his hand as if to slap her, but thought twice when William growled before stalking across the field toward them.

The man lowered his hand and cried, "Halt."

William stopped in his tracks.

Hugh and Guy joined William and approached the women.

Stefan made a move to head toward the tents. He'd taken no more than two steps when one of Aryseeth's men caught him off guard from behind and killed him.

Adrienna fell forward onto her hands and remained kneeling on the ground until the earth stopped spinning.

Elizabeth once again collapsed. Immediately going to her aid, Guy explained, "She is with child again."

Hugh helped Adrienna to her feet and pulled her into his arms. "Are you ready to watch the sunset from the cave?"

Tears coursed unchecked down her face as she smiled up at him. "Yes."

He looked up as King Henry entered the clearing. "I may be a moment or two."

"It matters not. But I am not leaving your side."

Hugh hugged her tightly. "I would not ask you to."

King Henry stopped before them and rested his forearm on his leg. "Am I needed here?"

Hugh dipped his head in greeting before pointing his thumb over his shoulder toward Aryseeth. "It would be of great help if you would rid your land of the likes of him."

"I can do that." Henry waved a few of his men forward, ordering, "See to it that Lord Aryseeth and his men have safe escort across the channel. Inform my wife that these men are to go to…France. Let Louis deal with them."

"Thank you, my liege." Hugh wondered aloud, "How did you know we needed your assistance?"

Henry glanced toward Guy. "The Earl of Hartford had enough sense to send me a missive when his wife turned up missing. Then I heard a rumor that my guest had moved his entourage north when they were supposed to be headed south. Since your wife's sire lives in the area and your own lands are not far from here, it did not take much thought to put the occurrences together." He stared directly at Hugh. "Using sense instead of might is something you possibly should consider on occasion."

Hugh had no choice but to nod. "I will try."

Henry rolled his eyes to the sky. "Of course you won't. In the meantime, am I free to leave now?"

Adrienna sighed with relief at the king's obvious good humor. She placed her hand on Hugh's chest and answered for him. "Yes, my lord, I will see to it that the earl stays out of trouble until he sees the value of using sense."

"I wish you luck with that, Lady Wynnedom." Henry flicked the reins to his horse and nodded at Sarah. "My Lady Remy, I am surprised to see you here."

Sarah flushed and touched William's arm. "I am with my husband, milord."

"Husband?" Henry's eyebrows rose in apparent disbelief.

William stiffened. "Aye, milord. Husband."

"Interesting position for one of my wife's...informants."

Adrienna inhaled softly. Hugh shook his head. They'd guessed that Sarah's position was far from palace whore. But they never would have guessed she worked as the queen's spy.

From the look on William's face she would have some explaining to do very soon.

The king moved on. "Hartford, I have news of your daughter."

Hugh hoped for Guy's sake that the news would be good. But for right now his attention was focused solely on Adrienna.

"Are you going to take all night?" Hugh chided Adrienna as she inspected his wounds for the third time since they'd arrived at the cave.

"No." She applied another layer of salve to the one

on his back. "You would not be happy should this become infected."

"Perhaps not, but I would be much happier if you would cease your worrying."

"I can't help but worry, it's what I seem to do best."

He turned around and tugged her onto his lap. After pulling her chemise over her head, he nuzzled her breast. "No, there is something else you do quite well."

"Hugh."

He looked out at the curtain of water. "The sun is getting ready to set."

"Mmm, so I see."

"I thought we had plans for the evening. Did you not mention something about seeing the reds and oranges on my flesh as I made love to you?"

Adrienna faced him on her knees and straddled his outstretched legs. "I could have said that. Maybe. It is possible."

The hardness of his erection pressed against her. Adrienna smiled. Using his shoulders for support she lifted her hips and slid slowly down the length of him. "You were saying?"

Hugh moaned. "Nothing."

She tightened her legs, rose and slid down again. "Nothing?"

He pulled her legs out from under her, held her tightly against his chest and leaned forward. "Hang on."

Adrienna locked her ankles behind his back and her arms around his neck.

He leaned forward on his hands and stretched out his

legs behind him. Finally, lying atop her, he took her head between his hands and brushed his lips across hers. "This is better, is it not?"

Adrienna looked up at him and watched the play of the setting sun's reds and oranges flicker across his face. It marked him with the heat of desire flaming in her heart. "Oh, much better, my love. Much, much better."

* * * * *

Look for Elizabeth's and Guy's,
Sarah's and William's stories.
Coming soon.

Dante Raintree stood with his arms crossed as he watched the woman on the monitor. The image was in black and white to better show details; color distracted the brain. He focused on her hands, watching every move she made, but what struck him most was how uncommonly *still* she was. She didn't fidget or play with her chips, or look around at the other players. She peeked once at her down card, then didn't touch it again, signaling for another hit by tapping a fingernail on the table. Just because she didn't seem to be paying attention to the other players, though, didn't mean she was as unaware as she seemed.

"What's her name?" Dante asked.

"Lorna Clay," replied his chief of security, Al Rayburn.

"At first I thought she was counting, but she doesn't pay enough attention."

"She's paying attention, all right," Dante murmured. "You just don't see her doing it." A card counter had to remember every card played. Supposedly counting cards was impossible with the number of decks used by the casinos, but there were those rare individuals who could calculate the odds even with multiple decks.

"I thought that, too," said Al. "But look at this piece of tape coming up. Someone she knows comes up to her and speaks, she looks around and starts chatting, completely misses the play of the people to her left—and doesn't look around even when the deal comes back to her, just taps that finger. And damn if she didn't win. Again."

Dante watched the tape, rewound it, watched it again. Then he watched it a third time. There had to be something he was missing, because he couldn't pick out a single giveaway.

"If she's cheating," Al said with something like respect, "she's the best I've ever seen."

"What does your gut say?"

Al scratched the side of his jaw, considering. Finally, he said, "If she isn't cheating, she's the luckiest person walking. She wins. Week in, week out, she wins. Never a huge amount, but I ran the numbers and she's into us for about five grand a week. Hell, boss, on her way out of the casino she'll stop by a slot machine, feed a dollar in and walk away with at least fifty. It's never the same machine, either. I've had her watched, I've had her followed, I've even looked for the same faces in the casino every time she's in here, and I can't find a common denominator."

"Is she here now?"

"She came in about half an hour ago. She's playing blackjack, as usual."

"Bring her to my office," Dante said, making a swift decision. "Don't make a scene."

"Got it," said Al, turning on his heel and leaving the security center.

Dante left, too, going up to his office. His face was calm. Normally he would leave it to Al to deal with a cheater, but he was curious. How was she doing it? There were a lot of bad cheaters, a few good ones, and every so often one would come along who was the stuff of which legends were made: the cheater who didn't get caught, even when people were alert and the camera was on him—or, in this case, her.

It was possible to simply be lucky, as most people understood luck. Chance could turn a habitual loser into a big-time winner. Casinos, in fact, thrived on that hope. But luck itself wasn't habitual, and he knew that what passed for luck was often something else: cheating. And there was the other kind of luck, the kind he himself possessed, but it depended not on chance but on who and what he was. He knew it was an innate power and not Dame Fortune's erratic smile. Since power like his was rare, the odds made it likely the woman he'd been watching was merely a very clever cheat.

Her skill could provide her with a very good living, he thought, doing some swift calculations in his head. Five grand a week equaled $260,000 a year, and that was just from his casino. She probably hit them all, careful to keep the numbers relatively low so she stayed under the radar.

He wondered how long she'd been taking him, how long she'd been winning a little here, a little there, before Al noticed.

The curtains were open on the wall-to-wall window

in his office, giving the impression, when one first opened the door, of stepping out onto a covered balcony. The glazed window faced west, so he could catch the sunsets. The sun was low now, the sky painted in purple and gold. At his home in the mountains, most of the windows faced east, affording him views of the sunrise. Something in him needed both the greeting and the goodbye of the sun. He'd always been drawn to sunlight, maybe because fire was his element to call, to control.

He checked his internal time: four minutes until sundown. Without checking the sunrise tables every day, he knew exactly when the sun would slide behind the mountains. He didn't own an alarm clock. He didn't need one. He was so acutely attuned to the sun's position that he had only to check within himself to know the time. As for waking at a particular time, he was one of those people who could tell himself to wake at a certain time, and he did. That talent had nothing to do with being Raintree, so he didn't have to hide it; a lot of perfectly ordinary people had the same ability.

He had other talents and abilities, however, that did require careful shielding. The long days of summer instilled in him an almost sexual high, when he could feel contained power buzzing just beneath his skin. He had to be doubly careful not to cause candles to leap into flame just by his presence, or to start wildfires with a glance in the dry-as-tinder brush. He loved Reno; he didn't want to burn it down. He just felt so damn *alive* with all the sunshine pouring down that he wanted to let the energy pour through him instead of holding it inside.

This must be how his brother Gideon felt while pulling lightning, all that hot power searing through his muscles, his veins. They had this in common, the connection with raw power. All the members of the far-flung Raintree clan had some power, some heightened ability, but only members of the royal family could channel and control the earth's natural energies.

Dante wasn't just of the royal family, he was the Dranir, the leader of the entire clan. "Dranir" was synonymous with king, but the position he held wasn't ceremonial, it was one of sheer power. He was the oldest son of the previous Dranir, but he would have been passed over for the position if he hadn't also inherited the power to hold it.

Behind him came Al's distinctive knock on the door. The outer office was empty, Dante's secretary having gone home hours before. "Come in," he called, not turning from his view of the sunset.

The door opened, and Al said, "Mr. Raintree, this is Lorna Clay."

Dante turned and looked at the woman, all his senses on alert. The first thing he noticed was the vibrant color of her hair, a rich, dark red that encompassed a multitude of shades from copper to burgundy. The warm amber light danced along the iridescent strands, and he felt a hard tug of sheer lust in his gut. Looking at her hair was almost like looking at fire, and he had the same reaction.

The second thing he noticed was that she was spitting mad.

nocturne™

IT'S TIME TO DISCOVER
THE RAINTREE TRILOGY...

There have always been those among us
who are more than human...

Don't miss the dramatic first book by
New York Times bestselling author

LINDA
HOWARD

RAINTREE:
Inferno

On sale May.

Raintree: Haunted by Linda Winstead Jones
Available June.

Raintree: Sanctuary by Beverly Barton
Available July.

SNLHIBC

REQUEST YOUR FREE BOOKS!

Harlequin® Historical
Historical Romantic Adventure!
TM

2 FREE NOVELS PLUS 2 FREE GIFTS!

COMING NEXT MONTH FROM

HARLEQUIN® HISTORICAL

HHCNM0407